The CAMPAIGN

D1188861

TRACEY RICHARDSON

Bella
BOOKS

2012

Bella Books, Inc.
P.O. Box 10543
Tallahassee, FL 32302

Printed in the United States of America on acid-free paper
First published 2012

Editor: Nene Adams
Cover Designer: Linda Callaghan

ISBN 13: 978-1-59493-282-3

Other Bella Books by Tracey Richardson

The Wedding Party
Blind Bet
No Rules of Engagement
Side Order of Love
The Candidate

Acknowledgments

I can hardly believe four years have gone by since my novel *The Candidate* introduced the gorgeous senator from Michigan, Jane Kincaid, and her romantic sidekick, Secret Service agent Alex Warner. They've been a very good four years in many ways. I think a lot of people around the world decided what they wanted and didn't want in their politicians. People began to hope again, and that's a good thing, particularly in such economic and politically unstable times. I believe there are a lot of good people out there, good people working hard to make this world a better place, and so I tell myself that Jane Kincaid is not just a product of my imagination, but that she lives and breathes in many public people today. And yes, someday the U.S. will have a woman president and hopefully she will be a lot like Jane. I would like to thank all those readers and fans who urged me to do a sequel to *The Candidate*. I resisted for a long time, but the four-year interval and the 2012 election inspired me to give a little more air time to Jane and Alex. Thank you to Cris S., who reads my manuscripts and gives me honest and accurate feedback and always believes in my abilities. Thank you Bella Books and the tremendous Bella team, and thank you readers for giving me a reason to keep doing this. My friends and family deserve my gratitude for their support and encouragement. Brenda, thanks for your awesome web page work, and Karen for your terrific video-making skills. To my hockey team, you women rock! Finally, thanks most of all to my partner, Sandra, for all her support and for letting me be me.

About the Author

Tracey Richardson is also the author of *The Candidate*, *Side Order of Love*, *No Rules of Engagement*, *Blind Bet* and *The Wedding Party*. She was a Lambda Literary award finalist for *No Rules of Engagement* and has been a finalist several times over for Golden Crown Literary Society awards. Tracey's *Side Order of Love* also won first place in contemporary romance in the Rainbow Romance Writers awards for excellence. Tracey works as a daily newspaper journalist and lives in the Great Lakes region of central Ontario, Canada with her partner and dogs. She also teaches fiction writing. Visit Tracey on Facebook and at www.traceyrichardson.net.

CHAPTER ONE

There was something about the name, enough to make Jane Kincaid pause to scan her overcrowded memory. *Julia Landen.* Familiar and yet not, like driving along a road with recognizable twists and turns, but set in a completely different and unfamiliar landscape. She stared at the name on the page, rested her finger on it, hoping she might suddenly remember this Julia Landen and in what capacity she knew her.

"What?" Corey Kincaid, Jane's sister and senior political advisor, looked up with concern from the sheaf of papers in her lap.

"It's nothing." *Probably*, Jane thought.

Corey frowned deeply. "Is there something on the itinerary you don't like? Because if there is, I need to know right away if I have any hope in hell of changing it."

They were going over Jane's itinerary for a three-day visit to California that would unofficially kick off the bid for re-election. In many ways, it seemed like just last year she was facing the long grind of asking voters for their support, laying out her vision for the future, and speaking until her voice was raw and her body practically worn to a skeleton. Four years had passed in a blur of meetings, speeches and trips. Make that boring meetings, redundant speeches, and trips that had lost their newness and exotic sheen a long time ago.

Now, however, things were about to get fun again because she could put aside the business of governing as vice president and begin focusing on one of her biggest joys in politics—campaigning.

She and President Dennis Collins, unchallenged within the party, could skip the gauntlet of Democratic primaries and go directly to the public to amass funds and support. Once the Republicans finished pummeling each other during the nomination process, the Collins-Kincaid campaign could really step it up and unleash an all-out warfare for another term. The grind would begin slowly, finally climaxing in the few months between the nomination convention and Election Day in November.

Returning to Corey's question about the itinerary, Jane laughed. "Yeah, two things. This whole fund-raising whoring I have to do, plus all the sweet talking and cajoling with the WPC." She did not enjoy begging for money or sucking up, two essentials of her position at times. On this trip, she would be required to do both.

Her smile mischievous, Corey relaxed and said, "At least it's not whoring *at* the WPC. On second thought, that might be kind of fun, don't you think?"

"Okay, that is so not funny!" Jane protested. Well, it was a little bit funny, she admitted to herself. The Women's Political Caucus, which she chaired, consisted of women politicians from across all party lines around the country. The organization had its share of members who seemed to shed their inhibitions as well as their heterosexuality after a few drinks. It wasn't unusual for a few of them to flirt openly with her. The most overt and persistent offender was California's governor, Amy Roberts, who'd made it clear on several occasions that she would welcome a little one-on-one mentoring with the country's openly gay vice president. The fact that Jane was happily partnered didn't seem to register with the governor. Or Amy Roberts simply didn't give a shit, which was more likely.

Corey tried to smother another giggle but gave up. "I'll bet Governor Roberts would be only too happy to contribute to the campaign if you did a little whoring with her."

"In her dreams!"

"For what it's worth, she's nuts to hit on you, considering that your girlfriend carries a gun."

"I'm beginning to think Amy has a death wish." Jane sighed. "Frankly, if we didn't need California, I'd tell her to kiss my butt… and my gun-toting girlfriend's too."

Jane had initiated the national nonpartisan caucus to encourage women politicians to seek higher office, and to mentor and support one another. As politics remained mostly a man's domain, the committee was her way of giving back a little, of trying to pull her sisters along with her, but hooking up for a night was certainly not part of the mission statement. Amy Roberts's come-ons were an unwanted distraction she absolutely abhorred.

"Might as well throw my butt in there too while you're at it," Corey said.

"Hey," Jane said slyly. "I think it'd be a great idea if *you* went out to dinner with the governor and convinced her to support us. After all, you're a member of my senior staff. I trust you to stand in for me *any* time."

Corey's face instantly drained of color. "Don't even joke about it!"

"What? I'm sure she'd find my little sister extremely attractive. In fact, I'd even bet money on it." Pushing Corey's buttons just like when they were kids, Jane waggled her eyebrows, which had the intended effect of infuriating her sister further.

"Remember, I set your campaign schedule, and if you're mean to me, I'll schedule you for an appearance with that smarmy, lecherous old Sam White next time we're in Seattle."

Corey would be evil enough to do it too, Jane decided, because unlike the kid sister seven years her junior who didn't dare fight back, the adult Corey was fully capable of it now.

Jane's skin crawled at the mention of Sam White, Seattle's mayor. Months ago on a trip to the city to officially open a new factory, she and Corey had laughed all the way home over the mayor's embarrassing and inappropriate antics. With stale booze on his breath and his double chin jiggling, he'd repeatedly asked her to join him on his sailboat for a drink. He'd proven harmless but completely revolting, especially when he constantly tried to brush up against her.

"You've got to help me out," she recalled pleading to one of her Secret Service agents. "Because if he comes near me again, I think I might have to hurt him."

After the unpleasant incident, by her request old Sam White was kept at least a dozen feet away from her.

She shivered. "All right, truce."

"Deal." Corey winked. "That means keeping me out of the line of fire whenever Amy's in the same room. Yuck!"

"Oh, Corey," Jane teased, shaking her head. "Imagine if she only knew you were a virginal baby dyke. My God, she'd be salivating buckets over you."

"Jane!" Corey recoiled against the dark blue sofa, her sheaf of papers falling across her feet like autumn leaves. She looked absolutely horrified, and for a moment Jane felt a sliver of guilt.

"Oh, relax, my little lamb. I'm not going to serve you up for slaughter. I promise to protect you from all the big bad predatory lesbians out there. And if I can't, Alex will."

Corey had come out to her two months ago. Or at least, she'd stepped a toe out of the closet, delivering the rather stunning news that she was *curious* about women, and while she wasn't particularly looking to date a woman, she wouldn't say no if the opportunity arose. Jane had always assumed her sister was straight, since she'd always had boyfriends. They hadn't been close growing up, and were only beginning to grow close now that Corey was on her staff. That Corey had confided in her was another step forward in their relationship.

She'd tried not asking too many questions or talking too much about it because she wanted to give Corey the space to figure it all out. Today, however, was the first time she'd ever teased Corey about her sexuality, and it felt good. Secretly, she worried about her baby sister. She didn't want Corey getting hurt or going through a conga line of women until she found the right one. Jane had been lucky. Her first woman lover, Alex, turned out to be the love of her life.

"Can we get back on topic?" Corey asked, quickly gathering her papers and her composure.

"Sorry. I'm feeling a little punchy just thinking about this trip."

"It's only a quickie. It'll fly by. Besides, March is almost upon us. Time to start getting your face out there and start drumming up support *and* money, no matter how much whoring and arm twisting it takes."

"Yes, I know. The reality of the campaign. I feel like an old war horse this time instead of a bucking young stallion, full of noble ideals."

Corey grinned at her. "You're still a stud, and a noble one at that. It'll get more fun once we know whose ass we're going to kick in November. And we *are* going to kick ass."

"Yes, I know, and I look forward to it. I just feel so out of practice…so, I don't know, out to pasture."

She had spent much of the last three years out of the limelight and in a supporting role to President Collins. The sharpness of her competitive spirit had dulled considerably in her secondary role. She only hoped she could summon it at will, that campaigning would come as easily to her again as riding a bike.

"I miss the primaries," Jane lamented. "Four years ago, those were what I enjoyed most about the campaign. It gets your blood going like nothing else…out there in front of all those people, giving those fiery speeches, seeing the country, talking to people, listening to them, your hands blistered and swollen from shaking so many hands, people pulling at you, wanting a piece of you. It's crazy, but a good kind of crazy."

Campaigning was a high like no other. Campaigning was *real*. Campaigning was getting down in the trenches as opposed to sitting in some glass tower, directing, presiding and signing endless papers. She couldn't wait to get back to it.

"I'm sorry I missed all the fun," Corey said. "But it'll get crazy again."

Yes, Jane thought, it will. She'd been younger and more politically naïve then—a forty-three-year-old junior senator from Michigan who'd made it a two-horse race with Democratic frontrunner Dennis Collins.

Her grassroots campaign had been a hit with voters because she talked to people like they were important, as though their lives and their problems mattered to her, and she convinced them that they could work together to make the country a better place. She gave them hope. Because of that, her popularity skyrocketed. Practically overnight, she achieved rock star status. Collins, who had barely edged her out to take the party's nomination, had little choice but to enlist her as his running mate.

Jane knew she'd need to rekindle that brand of fire that fueled her personally and powered her campaign. Her incendiary appeal was the main reason she was on the ticket again. That fire would keep her there.

"I wish you'd been around for it too," Jane said softly. Corey had been in England at the time, teaching at the London School of Economics. She'd only returned stateside a year ago. After much begging and cajoling, she had agreed to join Jane's staff. Corey's business acumen and organizational skills, as well as her family loyalty, were all assets. Corey was the person Jane trusted more than anyone else in this town, besides Alex of course.

"But what's important is that you're around this time," she added.

Corey returned to her papers. "So tomorrow night is the big fund-raising gala in Hollywood. That part's going to be fun at least, rubbing shoulders with the stars."

Jane rolled her eyes. In her experience, Hollywood types were no different than the business executives and lower-tier politicians who wanted to brag to their friends later that they'd hung out with the Veep, and either given her some useful advice, or pressed their personal issues and concerns with her. They all just wanted to be seen with someone as important as Jane Kincaid. Not only seen with her, but seen as having some sort of influence.

"Then the day after is lunch with the WPC in Sacramento, followed by a four o'clock speech to the state assembly on education. Then dinner with—" Corey grinned evilly. "Governor Roberts.

The third day, you do a sit-down with the *L.A. Times* editorial board, then lunch with Mr. Moneybags, Forrest Mitchell."

"Thank God we're heading back to Washington right after that." Jane glanced down at her briefing package. "And that we're not bringing the entire circus with us. It'll be almost quiet."

Only a handful of journalists, Secret Service agents, her press secretary, her personal assistant, and Corey were slated to take the trip with her. Alex was coming along too, thank goodness. Since moving from protection work to a desk job with the Secret Service three years ago, Alex had accompanied her on many of her working trips, which made them seem almost like a vacation. They'd often steal away for a nice dinner or a walk on a beach. They chatted in bed late into the night, allowing her to decompress, took long baths together, and lingered over room service breakfast if there were no pressing engagements. Yes, Alex's presence made the demands of the job much easier to swallow. She'd have never gotten through the campaign four years ago without her, and she wouldn't this time, either.

Jane stared again at the list of journalists accompanying them to California. She knew all of them except for this Landen woman and yet...*damn*. The name meant *something*. Had she given her an interview during the last campaign? Or maybe during her Senate years? *Shit*. Had Landen been a lobbyist at one time? Had they met on a more personal level? Then realization struck like a runaway train. Julia Landen was the name of Alex's ex-girlfriend, she felt certain, but this couldn't possibly be the same person. What were the odds of *that*?

She cleared her throat, ignoring her pounding heart. "There's a new reporter on this detail, Julia Landen. Who is she, do you know?"

"Nope. Do you want me to find out?"

"Yes, please." She didn't feel like explaining, nor did she want to alarm Corey. "If she's going to be tagging along, I'd like to know a little about her and welcome her to the team."

***

Alex Warner listened for her lover's arrival. She'd been given a heads-up from one of the uniforms at the White House that the motorcade was on its way home.

Home was One Observatory Circle, the vice president's official D.C. residence. Such a very long way from the trailer park she'd called home as a kid in North Carolina. Alex sometimes thought she should pinch herself, see if it was real, but she had never been afraid to dream. Had never been afraid of the obstacles in the way of those dreams, either. The dreamless and the weak might be intimidated by the world she moved in, perhaps feel unworthy, but not her.

While she would consider anyplace with Jane home, the vice president's mansion consisted of way more space than they would ever need. The Victorian mansion, built in 1894, comprised 9,100 square feet of living space spread out over three stories plus a basement. Living in it was like living in a museum. It was downright lonely here sometimes, almost ghostly when Jane was out of town.

Jane had laughed when Alex had told her she was sure a ghost roamed the spacious third-floor attic that had once been servants' quarters. A few times, she had heard coins dropping on the floor above their heads at night, but not Jane, who slept like the dead. Jane didn't believe in ghosts and had told her that worrying about the living was more than enough.

Alex glanced at the ornate black walnut mantel clock over the fireplace. Only six o'clock, earlier than usual for Jane to be calling it a day, but with the trip to California tomorrow morning, she'd need her rest tonight.

At the first rumblings of two Chevy Suburbans in the drive, Alex lit the candles in the silver antique candelabras on the dining room table. She was uncorking the wine when Jane stepped through the front reception hall, cheerily calling out to her.

"Coming," Alex replied, confirming the fire leaped and crackled in the fireplace before she went to Jane and enveloped her in a warm, extended hug. "You're home early, sweetheart. I was counting on it."

"Hmmm, that sounds rather cryptic."

Alex pulled away but not before giving Jane a teasing kiss. "I haven't a clue what you're talking about."

"The fact that you're home a bit early yourself, and that you were counting on me being early as well? Sounds like you've got something up your sleeve." Jane's eyes narrowed. "Hey, wait a minute. You'd better not be buttering me up to tell me you're pulling out of the trip with me tomorrow."

Alex laughed, amused by how close Jane had come to guessing the truth. "Don't worry, I'm coming to California."

Following the divine smells to the dining room, Jane gasped in pleasure at the candles, the roaring fire and the china place settings for two. Stainless steel lids covered the serving dishes.

"Oh, honey, this looks marvelous," she said. "Don't tell me you sent the staff home too?"

It was rare for them to have a quiet, romantic dinner in a house all to themselves, so it came as no surprise that Jane was onto her plan. "Damn, I'm getting too predictable."

"Oh, no, you're not," Jane said, leaning over the table to give Alex a sizzling kiss, nipping playfully at her bottom lip. "I hope you left dessert up to me."

"Darling, you *are* dessert."

"Oh my God, you read my mind!"

Alex sucked in her breath as Jane's dark brown eyes sparkled lasciviously. Jane's beauty still paralyzed her, the spark between them as incendiary as ever. She wouldn't have guessed that four years after falling in love, she would still melt under Jane's gaze, still grow weak-kneed from her touch. Life and the maelstrom of politics got in the way of many things, but had not dimmed the love between them.

"Maybe," Jane teased, "we could skip right to dessert."

"Oh, no, you don't. Didn't your mother ever teach you that eating dessert first was bad for you?"

"Yes, but mother didn't know what she was missing!"

Alex laughed before turning serious. She would not let Jane skip dinner, no matter what might be waiting at the end. Privately, she worried about the coming campaign and all the bone-wearying demands placed on Jane.

She gentled her voice. "With the campaign starting, my love, you need your strength, and that means not skipping meals, and no cheating on your sleep either."

"Aw, crap. Do you always have to be so pragmatic?"

"Yes, as a matter of fact. Now feast your eyes on this!" With a flourish, Alex removed the steamer lids, revealing fragrant beef burgundy with garlic and rosemary roasted potatoes, and a mélange of roasted vegetables. There was no way Jane would consider skipping this meal.

"Oh, Stella overdid herself this time," Jane said in excitement. "This looks wonderful!"

Alex poured the wine while Jane doled out the food.

As they ate ravenously, Alex decided it was a good time to tell Jane her news. "Honey, I'm coming to California with you, but I'm not going to join you on Air Force Two," she said. "And don't worry, I'll be there in time for the Hollywood gala later on, okay?"

"Damn," Jane said with a playful wink. "I was counting on us joining the Mile High Club again."

Alex thought of the handful of times they'd made love in Jane's quarters on Air Force Two. The demands on Jane's time and frequent interruptions by staff had made it nearly impossible, but they'd managed an occasional quickie. "You're almost convincing me to change my plans."

"Seriously, is something wrong?" Jane asked.

"No, everything's fine. I have a meeting with my chief right after lunch."

Jane raised her eyebrows in alarm. "What's up?"

"I want to take a sabbatical of sorts until after the election."

For three years, Alex had been working for the technical development and planning division of the Secret Service's Office of Protective Research. Her job entailed examining the protection branch's long-term goals and objectives, and planning for disasters. The office was a think tank of sorts. While the work was interesting, she wanted to be at Jane's side during the grueling campaign. Only a leave of absence would allow her to do that. She and Jane had discussed the idea in generalities, but she hadn't committed to it until now. She'd wanted to be sure her leave wouldn't damage her career opportunities down the road. She would be looking for exactly those assurances from her boss tomorrow.

"Really?" Jane grew animated. "You'll travel with me? Campaign with me?"

"Absolutely. You know I want to be by your side through the whole thing. Besides, I won't see you for the next nine months if I don't."

While spending time with Jane was important to her, it was not the only motivation for joining her on the campaign trail. Jane's safety, security and well-being were too important to leave up to others. No one could protect her as well as she could. While protecting Jane would not be an official role for her because of their relationship, she would be armed and by her side, ready to act in her capacity as a member of the United States Secret Service if she absolutely needed to.

"Oh, sweetheart, I'm so pleased. Relieved, actually." Jane clinked wineglasses with her in a celebratory toast. "I was hoping you would do this, but I didn't want to ask. Are you sure you're okay with it?"

"More than okay. You're more important to me than anything else in this world."

"Still, it's an awfully big sacrifice. You're sure about this?"

Alex knew Jane often worried that their world revolved too much around her and her political aspirations—that Alex was the one making all the sacrifices. Jane tried to compensate sometimes, tried to make her feel that she was the center of the world as much as possible, but it was a tightrope act.

Alex needed to feel that what she did was important too, but in the grand scheme of things, Jane's work was and always would be more important. Jane was first in succession to the leader of the free world and might be president herself one day. Jane was trying to make the country—and the world—a better place. She couldn't begin to compete with that, nor did she want to. She wanted Jane to succeed. Facilitating that success was part of being Jane's partner.

"I love you, Madam Vice President," she said. "As long as you don't get sick of me, I look forward to being gum on your shoe for the next several months as you traipse around this ol' country of ours." She felt her smile disintegrate as she thought of the mundane, exhausting aspects of campaigning. "Even if it means holding a few babies and shaking about a million hands."

Jane's smile broadened. "Have I ever told you how much I admire the selfless dedication of the United States Secret Service? And specifically of Agent Alex Warner?"

"No, but you can show your *wife* Alex Warner later."

Jane gave her a seductive leer. "Oh, you can count on that."

Over crème brulee, she and Jane chatted about the campaign, the mood of the country, the prospects of the Republican candidates, and their ticket's chances for re-election. Jane seemed upbeat and confident, but over coffee, the conversation faded ominously.

"Alex, there's something I need to tell you before we go to California."

Alex's stomach clenched. She had a feeling Jane was about to drop a bomb, like the time she'd revealed she was going on a risky five-day tour of the military bases in Iraq two years ago. Sitting back in her chair, she opened herself to the fear, disappointment or worry that Jane's words were surely about to unleash. Whatever happened, she could take it. She would have to. "Okay."

Jane looked at her for a long moment with steel-eyed frankness, the same look Alex had seen her use with aides and staffers when she was about to impart something unpleasant, or direct them to do something unpleasant. Jane's expression was implacable and uncompromising, but her eyes softened slightly as if to lessen the blow.

"There's a reporter from the *Miami Herald* who's just joined the White House press corps. She's going to cover the campaign," Jane said, blinking once. "It's your ex, Julia."

Struck dumb, Alex didn't breathe for a moment. Not much shocked her anymore. After years as a state trooper in Michigan, and then an agent with the Secret Service, she expected the unexpected. She'd been trained to absorb information quickly, to not react emotionally.

Calmly, she replied, "Okay. That's a surprise."

Jane waited. When Alex said nothing more, she added, "Julia's coming on the California trip."

Alex's thoughts raced, but she remained silent. Why the hell was Julia in Washington? she wondered. Julia had to know that she and Jane were an item. Hell, everybody in the free world knew that. Why would she show her face here now? To cause trouble? To remind her of the pain she'd caused all those years ago? To embarrass Jane? The deeper her thoughts took root, the angrier she became. Whatever Julia's motives, this sudden, unwanted presence in Washington could mean nothing but unpleasantness.

Quietly, Alex said, "Can't you make a call?" She didn't want to reveal her anger or her fear. "Get her thrown out of the press pool?"

Jane's lips twisted into a tiny ironic smile. "On what grounds? Because she's the bitch who hurt my girlfriend a decade ago? I'm sure my political foes would love me to do that. Catfight at the White House. Can you see the headlines?"

Alex drummed her fingers impatiently on the table. Of course, Jane was right. Manipulating the press would look bad. "Do you want me to have a word with her?"

"What, like bully her into quitting or something? Oh, sweetheart, I appreciate your chivalry, but—"

"Fuck!" Alex exploded, pounding the table once, hard, her smashing fist ending her resolve to stay calm. "What the fuck does Julia think she's doing? This is our fucking life, and now she wants back into it as a member of the press? This isn't a game. There's a fucking election coming. We don't need this bullshit."

"Well, let's hope she doesn't think it's a game. I'm sure she's a professional. She won't do anything to jeopardize her career or the campaign. I have to give her the benefit of the doubt that she won't do anything stupid."

"Well, I don't have to give her anything."

"No, I suppose you don't. But I don't want you doing anything stupid either, Alex."

Alex sighed loudly in acknowledgment. Again, Jane was right. They would stay calm and let Julia make the first move. Hell, maybe she was getting all wound up for nothing.

A headache threatened. Alex rubbed her temples. Julia wasn't just an ex. She was her *only* ex, really, if she didn't count the minor flirtations and part-time girlfriends she'd had in high school. She and Julia had met early on in college and fallen in love. She'd followed Julia to her home state of Michigan when Julia was offered a policing job. Not long afterward, Alex was hired by the force too.

Alex had thrived as a cop. She'd loved it, while Julia craved something more cerebral, something different. Unfortunately, Julia had decided to remake her life—without Alex—with about as much warning as a tornado. But however heartless and cruel her ex-lover's actions had been, Julia wasn't stupid. Committing career suicide by trying to damage her and Jane wasn't something she'd expect of her. Besides, their failed relationship had been *years* ago.

"So," Alex finally said, still exasperated, "how are you going to deal with her in California? And after that?"

Pausing, Jane shrugged. "I'll have no choice except to treat her like any other member of the press, but I'm not happy about it. I'll be civil toward her, nothing more. She hurt you, Alex. Badly. I can't pretend I don't despise her for that."

"Well, she's not on my Christmas card list, either. Christ, I didn't even know she was a newspaper reporter now." She'd had no contact with Julia since that day she had come home from working a night shift more than ten years ago to find the house they'd bought together cleaned out. There'd been a terse note, nothing more. Devastated, she spent the next two weeks in a drunken stupor, calling in sick to work, ignoring phone calls from concerned friends, closing herself off to the world.

A couple of years later, when Julia extended an olive branch through a distant, mutual friend, she considered it too little, too late. In her mind, Julia didn't exist anymore. She refused to revisit their past or forgive her, so she coped the best way possible by forgetting Julia Landen's existence. Until now, she hadn't thought about her in years.

Alex pressed her hand into Jane's. "It'll be okay, sweetheart. Julia can't cause us any trouble, even if she wanted to."

"No. We've not hidden anything from anyone. And as a couple, we're solid."

"Yes." Alex thought of an old song from the seventies. "Solid as a rock, my love."

CHAPTER TWO

As much as Julia Landen had heard about Air Force One and its vice presidential twin, Air Force Two, nothing had prepared her for the real thing. Sitting in the massive leather seat, sipping her complimentary glass of white wine, she marveled at the plush surroundings. Nothing had been spared in terms of comfort. The carpet was thick and richly textured, the TV screens high-definition, and real paintings hung on the walls. The heavy glassware was engraved with the presidential seal, one of the constant symbolic reminders of the plane's importance.

Julia considered herself lucky to be one of four journalists making the trip to California with Jane Kincaid. Lucky to even be where she was, considering that she had worked her way up from an inauspicious start with a gay and lesbian newspaper in Miami seven years ago. For what was not much more than coffee money, she wrote book reviews, interviewed gay and lesbian newsmakers in the area, relentlessly followed the murder of a homeless gay teenager until the case was solved, which had finally gotten her noticed by other newspapers. She was hired by the *Jacksonville Daily Record*, and then a year later by the *Miami Herald*. Each new job meant more money, better assignments. But this! This was the pinnacle of her journalism career by far.

Three weeks ago, she had been completely blown away when she was offered the prestigious White House beat. She hadn't quite understood why she was chosen, and no one at the paper had given her a straight answer. She suspected she'd been given the assignment because she was from the same state as Jane Kincaid, or because she was one of the few unmarried reporters on staff able to pick up and move to Washington at a moment's notice. That part certainly hadn't been hard. She had a couple of close friends in Florida, but no love interest.

In any case, she'd jumped at the chance. Now here she was, flying across the country on Air Force Two. She smiled at her good fortune and looked out the window at the sun-drenched skiff of white clouds floating below the airplane's massive baby blue wing. If things went well in Washington, who knew? Maybe a plum job with the *New York Times*. She'd love to be a roving columnist for the country's biggest newspaper, going wherever she wanted, tackling whatever issues interested her, and enjoying total freedom, almost as though she were her own boss.

"Hey, Julia," said Will Carter, Jane's very handsome and very obviously gay—at least obvious to her—press secretary. He'd introduced himself earlier that morning. Now he crouched on his haunches in the aisle beside her seat. "Enjoying the flight so far?"

"How could I not. It's the best ride there is."

He smiled his agreement. "You're the nine-hundred-and-eighty-second guest to fly on Air Force Two in this administration."

"Seriously?"

He laughed. "I've got a thing for numbers."

"Obviously." Julia liked Will Carter and his easy manner.

"By the way, the boss wants to see you."

Her smile dissolved, as did her cheerful mood. Feeling like she'd been summoned to the principal's office, she grabbed her briefcase and followed Will to the back of the plane. She hadn't met Jane yet, hadn't even seen her get on the plane. The vice president and her Secret Service agents had entered from the rear, while reporters, guests and staff used the front entrance.

The thought occurred to her that Alex might be here as well. She hoped that wasn't the case. She wasn't sure if she was up to seeing the two of them together yet and experiencing the awkwardness with her ex that was sure to come eventually.

Nervous sweat filmed the inside of her collar while she waited outside Jane's private suite. Will—no, Carter, he had told her to call him—departed with a look that said *good luck*. Now she was *really* nervous. Not only was Jane figuratively, if not literally, the second most powerful person in the country, she was also Alex's girlfriend. Alex's partner. How many people in the world could say their ex was sleeping with the vice president of the United States? *Jesus!*

Jane opened the door herself, beckoning Julia in with a tight but not unfriendly smile. She was beautiful, of course. That came as no surprise. Tall and slender—the photos and television images hadn't lied—Jane's dark, shoulder-length, wavy hair looked like it belonged to a shampoo model. Alex would have been a fool *not* to fall for her, Julia decided.

Jane's tone was neutral. "Ms. Landen, I'd like you meet my sister and chief political advisor, Corey Kincaid."

A younger, slightly shorter version of Jane, Corey politely if a bit warily shook Julia's hand.

So far, the reception had been distinctly chilly, Julia thought. She hoped it'd be a quick meeting.

"Please," Jane continued. "Have a seat. Would you like something to drink?"

"No, thank you." Glancing around, Julia saw a small sitting room with four bolted down leather seats facing each other and a small circular table in the middle. Sitting down did nothing to alleviate her tension.

"So I guess you've figured out I'm Jane Kincaid." Jane's smile was more attractive, confident and relaxed this time. Her teeth were white and perfect, of course.

Was there anything *not* perfect about this woman? "Yes, I figured that out through my powers of deduction," Julia answered, returning the smile to lighten her words. She could not help feeling inferior about her own looks, even though she'd heard regularly enough throughout her life that she was good looking, that her honey-blond hair and blue-gray eyes were qualities others admired and envied. But she was no Jane Kincaid, exuding that aura of hard-core power and quiet, confident leadership. She wondered if men made the same kind of analytical survey of one another's attributes, and decided they likely did not, that they operated more on instinct.

"I wanted to meet you and personally welcome you to the press pool," Jane said smoothly.

"Which," her sister cut in, "precedes the interrogation and torture session, of course."

Julia wanted to laugh but didn't dare, grateful to Corey Kincaid for trying to break the ice a little. "Kid gloves before the clubbing?"

"Exactly." Corey smiled devilishly.

Julia decided she liked her right away.

"You won't need to worry about any of that," Jane said with a straight face, "as long as you give us good press."

Julia's nervousness prevented her from deciding whether or not it was a joke, but surely it was. "I'll try my best."

"That's all anyone can do." Jane said, facing her and leaning forward in her seat a fraction of an inch. To Julia, the almost imperceptible movement signaled the small talk was over. "Look, Julia...if I may call you that?"

"Of course."

"I know you were with Alex for a period of your lives. That you were partners and loved one another a long time ago. She's told me a lot about you."

Julia's insides tightened. Jane undoubtedly knew what she'd done to Alex. *Yes, poor Alex, who didn't deserve what I did to her.* She had been a complete shit, the way she'd left her. But it was too long ago to feel anything other than a distant, diluted kind of guilt, like the kind of guilt she felt now for having lied to her mother about why she broke curfew on prom night. Not because her car broke down like she'd said, but because she was giving her boyfriend Bradley Jakes—her first and last boyfriend, as a matter of fact—a blow job under the football bleachers.

But Jane was right to bring up Alex, she realized. They'd shared a history, and because of that history, they were all linked. "Yes, we did. And we both moved on."

Jane's dark eyes danced a little with what were surely her own private thoughts and feelings about Alex. For a tiny instant, a flame of jealousy flared inside Julia. She would never again share with Alex all the things Jane now shared with her. Probably never had, if she were honest with herself. Nevertheless, the realization hurt a little. Alex had not only moved on, but obviously moved up. *High* up. There was simply no competing with Jane Kincaid. Alex had upgraded from a Fiat to a Ferrari. She couldn't help but feel a twinge of inadequacy.

"Is there some reason," Jane said carefully but directly, "other than career opportunity, that you took this assignment?"

"No, ma'am. It was a career opportunity of a lifetime for me, and I intend to take full advantage of that opportunity."

"So you have plans beyond the *Miami Herald*?"

"If things turn out well, sure."

Jane began tapping an expensive looking silver pen on her knee, her gaze straying. When her eyes returned to Julia, they were dark and opaque, like black onyx. Probably the same look she gives her adversaries, Julia thought.

"As long as you don't climb over me or Alex to get there," Jane said. "Are we clear?"

Rattled, Julia swallowed under that granite gaze. She'd heard Jane was funny, warm, nice and smart as a whip. But this tough side of Jane, launching right into her concerns without preamble, surprised and intimidated her a little. She nodded, deciding Jane would not respect her if she was not direct in return.

"I'm not here to cause any trouble, if that's what you're thinking. I was the one who walked out on Alex. I have absolutely no reason to wish her ill. She's a good woman, and it's water under the bridge as far as I'm concerned. I hope she feels the same."

Corey shared a private look with her sister, and then said to Julia, "Don't expect any special treatment or favors because of your past relationship with Alex, all right?"

"Of course not. Whatever I do, I want it to be on my own merit."

Jane and Corey stood in unison, signaling an end to the meeting. They shook her hand again. At the door, Jane turned to her. "Have the others in the press pool initiated you yet?"

"What?"

"You know, played a joke on you or done something deplorable to initiate you."

Crap, is she kidding? She must be! "Um, no. At least, I don't think so."

Corey shot her a wink. She seemed to be enjoying this far too much. "Oh, trust me, you'll know it when they do."

***

Corey Kincaid loved to watch her sister work a crowd. As usual, this crowd adored Jane and seemed quite willing to fall over backward and do cartwheels for her. Jane didn't have to win them over, yet she took the time to greet each person—almost all of them celebrities in the film and music industries—like old and intimate friends. She shook hands eagerly, kissed hundreds of cheeks under the grand ballroom's chandeliers, laughed like the joke she'd been told was amusing and original, whispered unimportant confidences, and touched people's arms or shoulders affectionately. Her subjects basked in her attention, charmed and probably feeling lucky to be in her company, to be her *friend*.

It was a gift, and one Jane had either inherited or learned at a young age from their father, a long-time and much adored governor of Michigan. Corey didn't have those same gifts, the combination of charm on one side, killer instinct and political astuteness on the other. Oh, she knew what it was like to stand in front of an audience. She'd been a professor of business for many years in London, but teaching was different. You didn't have to charm and impress your students with just the right word or touch. In the end, they only wanted your knowledge.

"She's really something, your sister," said a voice beside her.

Corey turned to the middle-aged actor, better known for being the son of an ultrafamous actor than for his own skills. His father had been one of the film legends of the fifties and sixties. "Yes, she is," she answered.

The actor introduced himself, though of course Corey already knew who he was. She knew most of these people on sight alone. Sighing deeply, he shook his head, a strong whiff of alcohol on his breath. "It's tough sometimes being in the shadow of someone so *great*, isn't it?"

Corey smiled. What else could she do? She'd gotten used to living in her father's shadow when she was young, and he *was* great. Now Jane, and she was great too, her greatness on a much grander scale than their father's. Jane used her outgoing personality and supreme curiosity about the world to take her to political heights their father had never known, perhaps never even seriously desired.

Her shadow had grown large and imposing in a very short time. Four years ago, when she campaigned for the presidency, Corey had been overseas building her own career, trying to build a life with Jason, staying far away from her sister and her overnight rock star status. She'd wanted her own life then, her own identity. Nearly a year ago, her relationship with Jason over for good, her teaching career gone stagnant, she had been easily swayed by Jane's pleas to return stateside and join her staff. She'd traveled to the opposite end of the spectrum, firmly in Jane's shadow, ensconced in her career, and she was happy. She had no regrets.

"I guess," she said after a moment, "it's up to us to make our own light, hmm?"

The man thought about that, but thinking seemed to be hard work under the gauze of alcohol. His smile was sloppy and slightly predatory. "I like that. I must remember that line."

Corey excused herself to drift around the room, thinking how surreal it seemed, hanging out with rock stars and film idols. Barbra was here. Sally Field, Queen Latifah, George, Brad and Angelina, Jodie, Beyoncé and Jay-Z. Though she'd never considered herself the starstruck type, she had to admit the reception was pretty damned cool.

Moments later at the buffet table, Corey asked Alex, "Do you ever get tired of this?"

Alex smiled wearily, dutifully filling a plate for herself and one for Jane. "Kinda, yes. I mean, I always knew they were just regular people who happen to work at something that makes them famous, but when you get to know some of them...wow."

"I can imagine. You get to see all their warts?"

"Oh, yeah. Like who drinks too much, who does drugs, who's angling for work, who's looking for a blow job from someone more famous than they are. Look hard enough, and you can even spot the married ones cruising the room." Leaning close, she whispered, "And William over there? Won the Oscar for best actor two years ago? Dumb as a post."

Corey giggled. "How come I never hear this kind of dirt from Jane?"

"She's too nice, that's why."

"Too much the politician, you mean." Corey knew Jane was very careful about what she said about others, as though gossip was a virus that might infect her.

"Okay, how about too much of a *nice* politician."

Corey liked Alex. A no bullshit woman, but kind too. Quick and smart, always levelheaded, a good match for Jane because she kept up with her and was fiercely loyal. Corey knew Alex would sacrifice anything for Jane, yet her self-respect was absolute.

"You okay about Julia Landen joining the press corps?" Corey asked. She'd been wondering how Alex had taken the news.

Alex shrugged, balancing the two plates. "Not like I have a choice in the matter."

"But you're okay?"

"I guess. Why not? It was a long time ago."

That was true, but that didn't mean it didn't still hurt, Corey thought. Jason was a while ago too, but she still felt the dull edge of pain, blurred around the edges now but it was still there. "Jane and I gave Julia the gears today. I don't think she'll be giving us any trouble."

Alex laughed, clearly amused. "Leaned on her like a couple of mobster hitmen, did you? That I'd like to see."

"Okay, maybe not quite like that, but I don't think she has a secret agenda up her sleeve as far as I can see."

"Good thing or you'll kick her ass, right?" Alex said, still clearly amused. "Sorry, better run. Jane needs to eat before the speeches start."

Corey watched Alex bring Jane's plate to her. Jane interrupted her conversation with a couple of potentially big donors to thank Alex and give her a kiss on the cheek. She liked how they were together—strong, affectionate, loving, never seeming to take each other for granted.

Four years ago, she'd been shocked by the news that Jane was in a relationship with a woman; she'd not seen that coming. But she quickly got accustomed to the idea, particularly after observing them together, and she couldn't be happier for her sister. She only wished she could find that same brand of happiness with someone. Yes, even if that someone was a woman.

The middle-aged actor who'd spoken to her before, the smell of booze sickeningly thicker on his breath now, sidled up to her again.

"Doing anything later, sweet thing?" he asked.

Corey tried hard not to laugh. Or to throw up. "Ah, yeah. Sleeping."

"Want some company?"

Losing the battle, Corey erupted into scathing laughter. Not *your* company, she wanted to say, but she knew her laughter would get the message across. Red-faced, he got the drift and staggered away. God, did he think she was that desperate?

Now she understood what Alex meant about seeing these people with all their warts. Good thing the press hadn't been allowed in. The reporters were outside, allowed to scrum with Jane and the celebrities in the lobby of the hotel as they entered, but that was all. Secret Service and hotel security prevented them from getting any closer.

She wondered if Julia could be trusted, if she was the kind of reporter who would burn you if you revealed something in confidence. She supposed she would find out sooner or later.

CHAPTER THREE

Across the dinner table, Jane furtively studied Alex, who was nearly falling asleep in her soup, and felt sorry for her. Alex had put in a full workday in D.C. before flying out in time to make last night's Hollywood gala. The jetlag had finally caught up to her. Poor darling, she thought. She was lucky to never have had much of a problem with jetlag herself.

She'd told Alex many times that she didn't need to accompany her to every boring meeting and speech when they were on the road, but Alex often insisted that she'd rather be with Jane than killing time alone in a strange city. This dinner meeting with Governor Amy Roberts, her nerdy, boring *beard* of a husband Ronald, and her equally uninteresting assistant Melanie, was about as tedious as it got. She'd ditch the governor right now if she could. The constant gushing over her education speech earlier at the State Capitol was embarrassing. A decent speech, she had been happy with it, but it certainly wasn't *the speech of the year*, as Amy kept calling it.

The speech had been rife with real-life anecdotes about the ghetto-ization of education, poor kids who weren't getting the same public education as their middle-class counterparts, and how this kept them out of the good colleges and limited their opportunities. In typical Jane Kincaid fashion, she'd harvested inspiration out of bleak hopelessness, finally urging the assemblymen and women to put more money into education in poorer neighborhoods, an investment that would pay off for generations, she had told them, an investment in the future, like building important infrastructures.

The speech went over well, but not as stunningly as Amy described. The woman was a supreme ass-kisser, ridiculously so, though not the worst she had endured in politics.

Jane noticed Corey's subtle eye rolling, and gave her sister a knowing smile. Corey had less patience for political B.S., but more time and experience would broaden that skill. Hours spent in meetings, on airplanes, and negotiating the finer points of a bill developed patience to a high art.

"Well," Amy announced a little too anxiously. "What do you say we discuss a little private business in my library, Madam Vice President?"

"Of course," Jane replied without enthusiasm.

Quietly, she pulled Alex aside, suggesting she return to the hotel for some rest. Two Secret Service agents and their driver would remain behind, she pointed out, and Corey would stay with her, intuitively knowing she would want a timely interruption if the private session with the governor became too agonizing.

Alex attempted to rebuff Jane's suggestion, but not too strenuously. With her leave from work granted, they'd have lots of time to be together, and one thing they'd both learned from the last campaign was the importance of taking rest when the opportunity arose. Alex agreed without further argument and kissed Jane goodbye. They'd see each other in bed later, and the thought gave Jane a little leap in the pit of her stomach.

In the library, a cozy fire crackled in the fireplace, and the lighting was dim and intimate. A tray containing a heavy crystal decanter of light amber alcohol and matching snifters sat nearby. The scene was almost romantic, a thought that darkened Jane's mood considerably. This was *not* where she wanted to be, and she did not wish to give Amy the idea that they were friends. Jane decided to cut to business right away.

"About my education speech today, Amy, I wasn't bullshitting. It's not just rhetoric. Your state, L.A. in particular, has seen a large spatial reorganization of poverty over the last three decades. Poverty is no longer confined to inner-city neighborhoods. It's spread like a patchwork to the suburbs. There are pockets of poverty all over the state, and they are growing."

"We have a huge immigrant population, as you know," Amy said defensively. "They aren't confined to one or two neighborhoods anymore."

Jane held up her hand. "Of course, and they move to wherever they can get the cheapest housing. But they're mired economically. Most cannot get out of their predicament of crappy jobs, if they can even get one of those. Increasing economic mobility for second- and third-generation immigrants usually only happens through education. It's the best way, and that's why your state needs to increase its education spending, improve schools in those neighborhoods, and give those people a better foothold."

In the dim light, Amy's face purpled. Governors didn't like federal pols telling them what to do, but education and health care were Jane's pet projects. Collins claimed economic matters and foreign policy for himself, leaving Jane to handle what he contemptuously called the country's fucked-up domestic agenda. That was fine with her, because she cared about making a better society. She felt strongly that the country could not be a true world leader without cleaning up its own messes.

Besides, Collins wasn't exactly burning down the house with his economic and foreign policies. He was fucking up both of them quite nicely, as a matter of fact. If she succeeded him in four years, she'd be able to start fresh on those screwed-up portfolios, being sure to distance herself from him and coming up with her own economic and foreign solutions.

"Of course, I've never shirked the education agenda," Amy said without much conviction. "I agree wholeheartedly with you, but you do know my state is flat broke."

"I know times are tough, Governor. They're tough everywhere, but I think your state can be a real model for this, for using education to pull people out of poverty," Jane said. "You could make it your own brand, shepherd it along."

Amy brightened. "We could work closely together on it, Madam Vice President. Share the glory, so to speak."

Jane knew better than to become too ensnared in state affairs. Too much downside, not enough up, but since she trumpeted the merits of education wherever she went, Amy had a point. If California improved its schools and their programs, and redistributed education dollars more fairly, she could bask in some of its success as long as she was careful not to be perceived as meddling.

"I leave it in your capable hands, but I would love regular updates and I'd be happy to speak again in Sacramento anytime."

Amy reached for the decanter on the small circular table between them. "Care to try some of our homegrown brandy? Germain-Robin. Very much like cognac, some say even better than the stuff that comes from France. I think you'll find it pleasing."

Amy had thought of everything, including setting out her drink of choice, but that wasn't surprising, Jane decided, more annoyed than flattered. Amy was thorough in her ass-kissing.

"Thank you," Jane said, accepting a snifter. The brandy smelled divine and tasted even better—smooth, clean, expensive. Might help her suffer through the meeting a little better. "So, the campaign. The president and I are expecting your full support. Do we have it?"

Amy smiled enigmatically, sipping brandy gingerly. She clearly enjoyed her thirty seconds of power, but that was all she'd be allowed. The governor needn't fool herself that she was some kind of kingmaker. Jane and Collins had won California last time around and they would win it again this time, with or without Amy Roberts. It'd be a lot simpler if Amy was on board right from the start.

"We're always pleased and proud that the great state of

California plays an important role in choosing the country's president," Amy boasted. "It's not something I take lightly at all."

"Nor do the president and I. We need your state. We want you on board, Amy. You're a Democrat. Any wavering by a Democratic governor is not acceptable to us. We need to come strong out of the gate. The president and I are going to do great things over the next four years, really create a legacy. You're either with us or you aren't. Do we have your endorsement, or do you plan to have your people work a little harder to get those federal dollars we like to hand out?"

Playing hardball hadn't always come easily to Jane, who'd decided in college to go into medicine, not politics. She eventually developed a taste for politics, including a talent for its nastier side. Over a dozen years ago, she began earning her political stripes after a stint with Doctors Without Borders, and then formed a national group of fellow doctors who wanted to make a difference in society. She lobbied their agenda with multi-nationals, the U.S. Senate and Congress, state assemblies, the American Medical Association and pharmaceutical companies. Afterward, she ran for the senate in her home state of Michigan and won handily. Her father's reputation in politics helped pave the way for her, but mostly she earned her win through sheer hard work, determination and smarts, like everything else she attempted.

"I'm a good Democrat," Amy declared. "But if I may speak honestly, it's *you* I'm interested in."

Oh, God, Jane thought. *This again.* Amy had made advances before, nothing too overt that could come back to haunt her, but this was too much, even for her.

There was no doubt Amy was a closet lesbian, or perhaps bisexual. In any case, for whatever reason, Amy liked coming on to her, and didn't seem to understand that she wasn't the least bit interested. Amy's lack of respect for her and her relationship with Alex was inexcusable, intolerable and pissed her off no end.

"This isn't about me," Jane said icily.

"Oh, yes it is." Amy smiled, a glint in her eyes. "In four years, Collins will be history. Then it'll finally be your turn, which is how it should have been all along."

"Look, I'm not interested in four years from now. We're talking about *this* election and this election only. The Collins-Kincaid ticket needs and expects your support."

"And if the rumor is true?"

Jane's throat tightened. She loosened it with another sip of brandy. "What rumor?"

Amy's chin rose in victory, the little power trip apparently galvanizing her. "The rumor that Collins is going to dump you in favor of someone…*straighter*. Someone more acceptable to the right."

Jane had heard that rumor since the minute she was sworn in as vice president. Collins's dislike for her wasn't much of a secret since he'd felt forced into putting her on the ticket in '08. He'd needed her then and needed her now because she brought something to the ticket that he never could—emotion. If Collins was the distant and stern father figure, she was the approachable, slightly rebellious daughter/sister/friend who connected with voters. The personal dynamics between her and Collins were none of Amy's concern, however.

"The president and I are a team," she said, "a united team. We're going to be a team for the next four years. Any other notion is just vindictive gossip meant to divide our supporters and distract the voters."

"That may be so, but if the president should dump you, he will no longer have my support."

The declaration of support for her, and her alone, from someone as powerful as a governor reminded Jane that others might chip away at the ticket, trying to divide her and Collins. Any public fissure between them, a public choosing of one over the other, would be disastrous.

"Don't be ridiculous, Amy," she said. "It's Collins and Kincaid right to the finish, and I won't entertain or tolerate discussions of any other scenario. Your support for us both must be firm and unconditional."

"Of course, Madam Vice President. Publicly, that is. What I said tonight is between us. You have to know that I'm not the only one who would pull support from Collins and give it to you. If there was some kind of reason to, that is. To a lot of people, you're the winner on that ticket, not Collins."

Jane shook her head. "I don't want to hear it, Amy. No one's getting dumped from the ticket and there's going to be no coup d'etat."

"Whatever you say, Madam Vice President."

"Good. That's settled then." Jane had a funny feeling the matter was not settled at all, but she set her drink down and stood abruptly. "Thanks for dinner and the drink, and for your support, of course."

Amy got up, placing her hand softly on Jane's arm. "I'd love to do this again next time you're in town. In fact, you should think about joining me for a weekend at my place on the beach some time. A little one-on-one brainstorming about the campaign perhaps, hmm?"

Not on your life, Jane thought. "I'm going to be awfully busy the next few months, but thank you anyway."

"Of course, but if you ever need to get away…"

I need to get away all right, like right now. "Good luck with your education bill," Jane said. "I'll be watching its progress."

"Thank you Madam Vice President." Amy's smile was sickly sweet, like the frosting on a thousand-calorie donut. "I'll be watching your progress too."

I'll bet you will.

***

Alex had her second wind by the time she entered the hotel lobby. Could have been the coffee she had at dinner, or the shit she'd had to swallow watching that horny governor make goo-goo eyes at Jane over dinner. Well, Jane could more than handle herself, but Alex had little appetite for the necessary evils of political schmoozing and sucking up, which hadn't bugged her nearly as much when she was a protection agent on other details.

She had always been able to stand in the background, remaining cool, relaxed and indifferent, like a jungle cat ready to spring into action. She could easily tune out the things she didn't care about or that had no bearing on her job. Hell, she could write a book about all the things she wasn't officially supposed to know. But watching Amy Roberts come onto the love of her life had nearly made her throw her self-discipline out the nearest window and leap over the table.

She glanced at her watch. It would be at least another hour or more before Jane returned. Too keyed up to go to bed, she considered calling Carter and asking him to join her for a drink, but she remembered he'd gone ahead to Los Angeles to prep for Jane's visit tomorrow. She headed toward the hotel bar anyway, content to enjoy a solitary drink.

A glass of merlot in front of her, she idly watched the Los Angeles Kings game on the TV over the bar and tried to ignore the persistent tingling in her spine. She had the sixth sense that most cops and special agents possessed—her Spidey sense, she liked to call it, although it was really instinct finely honed by years of law enforcement. Right now she felt someone watching her. Intently.

Her overt attention on the hockey game, she let her instinct take root until she felt confident she was not in any danger. Judging the moment, she quickly spun around to catch the eyes of a woman staring at her. Eyes she hadn't seen in a decade.

Well, well, she thought unhappily. *We had to stumble across one another sooner or later.*

Julia sat alone in a booth, an empty wineglass in front of her. She'd tried to avert her eyes when Alex caught her staring, but now she gazed back, looking as resigned to their meeting as was Alex herself. A tilt of her chin signaled an invitation.

Grimly, Alex joined her ex-lover. Some sort of dialogue was inevitable, she supposed, even if it was short and not so much on the sweet side, because they would be seeing a lot of each other on the campaign trail. *Might as well get this over with.*

"Looks like you need a refill," Alex said tonelessly, thudding down hard on the chair as though depositing a heavy load.

"You're right." Julia signaled to a passing waiter.

Alex added a refill to the order. She needed it. "I know I'm expected to play nice," she said to Julia, "but not until I know what the hell you're doing here."

"I'm working, as you well know. I work for the *Miami Herald* and they assigned me to cover the Collins-Kincaid campaign. They've put me on the White House detail."

"Just like that. Out of the blue."

"Yes, basically." Julia's tone sounded innocent enough. "They approached me about it, and it would have been career suicide to turn the assignment down."

Alex burned with questions. Doubts too. She was determined to get to the bottom of things. When the waiter returned with their drinks, she quickly polished off the remains of her first glass before taking the second.

"So," she began, her voice as brittle as a stick ready to snap. "Why are you really here, Julia?"

"I told you, Alex. To cover the campaign. I'm on the White House detail until further notice."

"Are you trying to fuck with us?"

Julia gave her the tiniest smirk. "The cop in you is always thinking the worst, huh?"

"You were a cop once too. And now you're a journalist. So don't act like I hold the title on cynicism. I asked you a question."

Julia absently stroked the stem of her wineglass. Alex's gaze unwillingly traveled to those slender, graceful fingers. Julia always did have the most beautiful hands, too nice for police work. In hindsight, it shouldn't have come as such a surprise that Julia wasn't cut out to be a cop, that she wanted to do something different with her life. It was the way she'd gone about it that had nearly destroyed Alex.

Julia sipped her white wine deliberately before answering, "Do you think after all these years I'd try to fuck with you now? If I were so inclined, that is. Which I am not."

"You fucked with me before. When you left me."

"Please. I know I hurt you, but I wasn't trying to fuck you over."

"Look, people can be unpredictable. You know that. How do I know you aren't holding some grudge about the fact that I'm with Jane Kincaid and I'm ecstatically happy?"

Julia set her glass down so hard, Alex expected it to shatter. "Why on earth would you think I have some kind of grudge? I was the one who left *you* without warning. I was the one who threw it all away, not you. I would never resent you for moving on. *You* should be the one with the grudge."

"Yes, but still…I'm the one—and Jane—with everything to lose."

"Oh, please. Get over yourself."

Alex considered the suggestion as she sipped her wine. She did sound a little self-centered, but from where she sat, she had to figure everyone was gunning for Jane. And if they were gunning for Jane, they were gunning for her. And vice versa.

"You can't fault me for calling your motives into question," she said at last. "Politics is one giant shark tank. There are people out there who will do *anything* to destroy Jane's career, her life, and by extension, mine too."

"I think I hurt you enough," Julia said quietly. "I have no intention of hurting you any further. Or hurting Jane Kincaid, whom I don't even know and have no ill feelings toward."

"It's all water under the old bridge for you, huh?" She had suffered deeply from Julia's abandonment, sliding into a depression that lasted months. She'd quit her job and moved away, but she'd never outrun the feelings of rejection, of being victim to Julia's thoughtless and harsh treatment. Guilt, confusion and anger had haunted her for years.

"After ten years, I should hope so," Julia answered evenly. "For you too."

"Easy for you to say." Alex couldn't keep the bitterness from her words. "You weren't the one who came home to an empty house one night after work with nothing but a shitty note that explained absolutely *zero*. You weren't the one with all the pieces to pick up."

Julia's eyes widened perceptibly. She seemed shocked by the rawness of Alex's pain, by the glass-like sharpness in her voice.

Well, too bad, Julia. You need to take responsibility for what you did. You need to see what it did to me, that it nearly destroyed me.

"Alex, I am so sorry for what I did to you. I wasn't happy, you had to know that. And if I hadn't left abruptly, you would have just followed me to Florida."

"Obviously you didn't want me to follow you. You didn't want me in your life. Fine. But it was cruel the way you went about it, after all the years we'd been together. Christ, we met as college freshmen. We grew up together. I'd have done anything for you, don't you understand that?"

"Yes, and that's exactly why I had to leave the way I did."

"Because you didn't love me enough, isn't that what you mean?" *Goddamn*. She hated this conversation, hated rehashing all this ancient history, exposing a pain that shouldn't be so damned strong after all these years. Talking about it made her feel inferior, adolescent, needy. Just the sight of Julia took her back to a time she didn't want to relive.

"No, it wasn't that." Julia hesitated, her eyes clouding with emotion. "You followed me the first time to Michigan. You took that job with the state police because of me. Don't you see? I didn't want you doing that again. I didn't want to be responsible anymore for your career path, for your *life*, for your happiness. I needed to look after myself. I needed to find my own happiness and worth without having to worry about yours."

Great, so she'd been nothing but a *responsibility* for Julia, a weight she'd had to drag along. She let the new revelation burn a raging trail through her gut until it flared out, spent. "And so, did you find this worth and happiness you were searching for?"

Julia looked away, lost in her thoughts. "Yes and no. I started over again. Took a journalism program at college for a couple of years, got a job at the bottom and worked my way up. And yes, I love what I do. I love being a newspaper reporter." She looked at Alex, tears welling in her eyes but not spilling over. "I never fell in love again, though. I've never come close to what you and I had together."

Well, that part was at least satisfying in a totally bitchy way, Alex decided. "I wish you hadn't waited ten years to say you're sorry."

"Me too. It was wrong of me not to apologize sooner and give you an explanation, and it was wrong of me to hurt you the way I did. But the truth is, we weren't strong enough as a couple to start over." Julia took a long drink of wine, seeming to struggle with what she wanted to say next. "I'm sorry, Alex, but I didn't love you enough to start over with you."

Alex winced. That hurt, but at least she was finally hearing the truth. "Okay, you were doing good until you added that last part."

"I know. I'm sorry. But hey, it worked out okay in the long run, right? We're both doing jobs we love. Hell, you hit the jackpot."

"You mean Jane?"

"Yes, Jane. You love her, don't you?"

"Very much. She's the love of my life, the one I was waiting for." *Pow! Take that, Julia.*

"I deserved that."

"Look, I don't want to fight, okay?"

"Me either. Friends?"

Drinking the rest of her wine quickly, Alex stood to go. It wasn't her choice to have Julia in Washington and on the campaign trail, but she sure as hell had a choice in how she felt about it. "Let's not go that far yet."

It was going to take more than a few contrite words and crocodile tears to convince her that Julia's motives were completely innocent.

CHAPTER FOUR

Corey had experienced her share of outlandishly extravagant mansions in her life, but nothing like this. Even by Bel Air standards, Forrest Mitchell's home stood out. The three-story Tudor structure resembled a palace with vines sprawling across the dark stone work, massive leaded glass windows, and several wings, even a couple of turrets. The winding circular drive led past an elaborate marble fountain, moving on to sculpted green topiaries standing sentry at the front entrance. The place had to be worth tens of millions of dollars.

Of course, Mitchell himself didn't greet her, Jane, Carter, Alex and their small gaggle of Secret Service agents. A butler, apparently drawn straight from an old British movie, complete with accent, courtly manners and a three-piece suit, led them into the mansion.

Inside, the home was no less ostentatious. Corey admired the ceilings—which pretty much reached into heaven—Italian marble floors, wood paneled walls and crystal chandeliers that looked like they might shatter at the slightest provocation. She shared a brief look of awe with Jane. Everyone in their party seemed impressed, which was exactly Mitchell's intention, she felt sure. He could have met them on neutral ground, but no, he wanted them to *see* how much money he was worth. Money was power, and Mitchell had a boatload of it.

He greeted Jane and her entourage deferentially, but his manner was all for show, Corey knew. His fake smile and the defiant angle of his chin told her he was no more impressed by having the vice president of the United States in his home than if she were the gardener.

"Finally," Mitchell said, settling his beady eyes on Jane. "I can't believe it's taken all this time to meet face-to-face. It's lovely to see you. Please, everyone, follow me to the library. Will, nice to see you, as always." He pointedly ignored Corey and Alex, even after Jane made introductions.

There were floor-to-ceiling bookshelves in the library, high-backed leather chairs and an antique desk about the size of a small warship. Jane was the first to take a seat.

"I have your assurance, Forrest, that our meeting is entirely off the record?" Jane asked.

"No one will know a word of it." His smile stretched his face until it looked like it might crack under the deep tan and layers of makeup. A George Hamilton clone.

"It'll be our little secret."

Corey hoped he meant what he said. Mitchell was undoubtedly the wealthiest, most powerful and influential gay man in the country, although few knew it. He acted like an anonymous dictator hiding in his castle behind his henchmen, a mysterious background presence pulling all the strings. She had learned recently that Forrest Mitchell headed up a loose, mostly secret affiliation of gay men and lesbians in powerful positions across the country. The group fought the good fight mostly, but they had a means-justifies-the-end mercenary code of conduct. Mitchell was not beyond bribing or blackmailing a judge or a politician, or forcing a celebrity out of the closet. His money made him Jane's friend, but his radical agenda and unethical machinations could be a potential grenade to the Collins-Kincaid campaign. The campaign needed his money all right, but not his dirty brand of politics and his dubious deeds, which was exactly why this little meeting had been kept off Jane's official itinerary.

"Good," Jane answered with a firm smile. "I'm counting on it."

A beautiful boy, probably no more than eighteen, Corey guessed, poured the drinks: sparkling water for the visitors and bourbon in a thick crystal tumbler for Mitchell that dwarfed his delicate, bejeweled hands. The boy left the room after a regal bow to everyone.

"We could sit here all day and talk about the weather," Mitchell said, crossing his legs daintily and sipping his drink. "Or about the Lakers, the price of oil, or any number of things. But let's skip all that nonsense, shall we?" Like a pin pricking a balloon, his pretensions had clearly evaporated.

"Good plan, Forrest. We have a plane to catch in an hour," Jane said.

He laughed, a high-pitched, nasal sound resembling some kind of strange, exotic bird. "That's a good one, Madam Vice President. Though I have a funny feeling they'll hold the plane for you. If you ask them nicely, that is."

"I'm sure they would." Jane leaned closer as if letting him in on a secret. "The thing is, though, since this meeting is off the record, the press will start getting awfully antsy if I'm late getting back to the airport. They tend to ask questions when that happens. I'm sure you know how persistent they can be."

"Yes, I suppose they do get a bit crusty if you make them late for happy hour or whatever the hell they're in a rush to get back to Washington for. Okay, then, how about this: how much do you want from me?"

Corey choked on her Perrier, but Jane didn't blink an eye. She remained as cool as the glass in her hand.

"Oh, Forrest, we're not going to be as pedestrian as that, are we?" Jane asked. "You're not a bank, after all, and I'm not a little old lady with a blank withdrawal slip in my hand."

Mitchell laughed again, but more appreciatively this time. It was obvious he was testing Jane, and Jane was having none of it.

"You're right," he conceded. "Numbers are for bean counters and desperate people. Jesus, what does the inside of a bank even look like these days?"

Carter cleared his throat. "It looks a lot like your home, actually: ornate, pretentious, a little intimidating."

Mitchell leveled his laser-sharp gaze on Carter. "Well, that is the whole point, don't you think, William? The display of wealth is really the display of power. And power *is*, as you know, what makes this ol' world go 'round."

Corey had never heard anyone refer to Carter as *William*. He cringed at it too, like he was a kid being called out by the teacher. Clearly he didn't care for Forrest Mitchell. Carter frowned deeply. "We don't really want to begin a discussion about power, do we? It's beneath us."

Mitchell screwed up his tiny mouth. "You're right, William. No point in wasting time speaking of the obvious, so..." He turned his full attention to Jane. "I am a big supporter of yours, as you know."

"You mean of me and the president," Jane replied coolly.

Corey knew Jane wouldn't be drawn into a game of supporters aligning with either her or Collins, as though the campaign were some kind of contest between each other and not a joint endeavor. She'd probably lose at that kind of game in the long run anyway, because Collins had a lot of moderates as supporters, including some Republicans.

On the other hand, it wasn't exactly a secret that Collins viewed Jane's sexuality as a liability. If he could dump her from the ticket and still win, he'd do it in a flash. If Collins thought his wealthiest supporter—Mitchell—was only donating to the campaign because of Jane, it might help solidify her place on the ticket, Corey concluded.

"Ah, well, I suppose if you want to put it like that, then yes. But I have to be completely honest with you," Mitchell said. "You and I are on the same team, Madam Vice President. President Collins is not. In fact, he's not even in our league."

Jane had to know full well what Mitchell was referring to but she quirked her eyebrows at him questioningly.

Mitchell's face clenched with emotion. "Collins will never lift a *finger* to advance gay rights. Surely that is painfully obvious to you by now."

Jane tried to defend the meager advancements made during the Collins-Kincaid first term, but Mitchell dismissed her attempts. He reminded her in words enigmatic enough to preserve his mysterious political achievements that the repeal of Don't Ask Don't Tell was more *his* victory than the administration's or of any lobby group.

"What I'm saying here," he continued, "is that Collins is the big obstacle. He doesn't want to scare away the moderates and the few conservatives in his pocket. I understand that. But surely if you were top dog, you would be much more, how should I say it—*sympathetic*—to the cause. It goes without saying I'm all for that."

So that was it, Corey thought. If Jane somehow vaulted to the top of the ticket, or if she ran for president four years from now, Mitchell's financial support was hers for the asking, but there was a price. In return, he would expect her to take decisive action on gay rights with respect to federal matters such as immigration and tax laws. He would expect her to make gay rights one of her top priorities.

"Mr. Mitchell," Jane replied evenly, "I appreciate your support, but I can assure you the ticket remains as it is and it will be a second Collins-Kincaid term. Beyond that, well, let me say that I like to keep *all* of my options open. For the record, my view of the job of president is one that is more of conciliation, of forging cooperation and brokering deals that are good and fair for everyone, rather than letting one specific but contentious issue drive the agenda. One-issue politicians don't tend to have long careers, nor do they tend to accomplish much in office."

"Spoken like a true politician." Mitchell's smile was full of condemnation. "We can be more honest with each other, no?"

Jane smiled benignly. "I thought I was."

Mitchell's laughter contained no mirth. "All right, let me make things a little clearer. I'll support you and Collins with a generous donation. But if you *really* want my support—*all* of my support—you and I could go far. We could accomplish great things together, but only if you have the b—, I mean, the *stomach* for it. And I do understand your penchant to be cautious about certain contentious issues." Mitchell set his heavy crystal tumbler down and stood, signaling the meeting was over. "But I'm not a very patient man."

"I'll thank you in advance for your support of President Collins and myself." Jane rose to shake his hand. "Thank you for meeting us. It was a pleasure."

"Likewise. You'll find a check in your campaign treasury by tomorrow. Looks like you'll make your plane after all, Madam Vice President."

Cocky bastard, Corey thought as she and the rest of the group piled into a sleek limo for the ride to LAX and Air Force Two. A glass partition gave her, Jane, Alex, and Carter privacy from the Secret Service agents in the front seat.

Jane anxiously drummed her fingers on her knee. "Can you believe Mitchell was ready to broker some sort of deal with me? Made it sound like he'd personally bankroll me if I went rogue."

Carter looked like he'd just swallowed something very unpleasant. "Sounds great if you're looking for a puppet master."

"Well, luckily I'm not."

"People like him are never satisfied anyway," Carter continued. "Not unless there was a gay revolution with him as the masked superhero. I swear that's how he fancies himself."

"Is that his ultimate goal?" Alex asked. "A revolution?"

Carter shrugged. "He's got all the power and money he could ever want. He's heir to the biggest chain of department stores in the country and a crapload of successful wineries and distilleries. His influence knows no bounds—politicians, judges, business execs, news organizations. He usually finds a way to get what he wants."

"Is he dirty?" Corey asked, anticipating the answer.

"He's ruthless," Carter said. "He doesn't get his own hands dirty, but yes, his victories are usually speckled with the brown stuff."

"A good reason to keep our distance," Jane said.

Alex nodded at Carter. "You seem to know a lot about Mitchell. Does he really have his own gay mafia?"

Glancing around the limo, Corey considered the fact that Jane seemed to have her own little gay mafia, though she herself wasn't officially considered part of Jane's *gay* inner circle. *Yet*. Her newfound lesbian curiosity remained a well-guarded secret, but that would need to change if her curiosity actually culminated in sex one of these days. Jane would not tolerate secrets from any of them that might bite her later, especially during an election year.

"Yes," Carter answered, "but it's more like his own little band of revolutionaries that he's in control of, except they like to stay out of the light. What they do is all very underhanded and very much behind the scenes."

"It's all for a noble cause though, isn't it?" Corey asked.

Jane shook her head. "Noble or not, it's the way Mitchell goes about his business that I don't like. I'd rather see changes effected from the inside, working within the system, not from outside with things like blackmail, bribery, or whatever other tactics he uses. In my opinion, he's totally discreditable. I mean, how can he consider something a victory if he attains it in such a despicable way?"

Alex closed her hand affectionately over Jane's. "Darling, I've told you many times, you're too ethical for this business."

"Mitchell must not think so. He thinks if he can throw enough money at me, entice me to the top of the ticket, then I'll be happy to do his bidding."

"Because you're gay?" Corey didn't know if being gay automatically gave entrance to an exclusive club, although she suspected it did—a club with secret handshakes, codes and that elusive thing called gaydar.

She was a stranger in a foreign land, a lesbian virgin when it came to inside knowledge. She wondered if she might be initiated into the new world once she actually had sex with another woman. Like a dream suddenly going from black and white to Technicolor. Like Dorothy traveling to the land of Oz. She almost laughed out loud at the analogy. Well, sex of any kind right now would be wonderful. She'd lost track of how long it had been since she last had sex, but guessed it'd been over a year. She was at the point of nearly climbing the walls in frustration.

"Probably," Jane replied. "Damn it, he implies that I don't do enough to advance the gay agenda, that I turn my back on my own people because I don't have the balls for it. His insinuations piss me off."

"Bullshit," Carter said angrily. "Just living your life as you are speaks volumes. You're the vice president of the United States who also happens to be gay. You treat it like it's no big deal, which is how it should be, because pretty soon the voters start thinking it's no big deal too. You've done a good job of not defining yourself as the *gay* vice president, but simply the vice president, and a damned good one. Don't let Mitchell make you think you have to be the poster girl for the entire gay community. Do that and it'll be your downfall."

Corey knew Jane walked a careful line. She lived her personal life without lies or shame without flaunting her sexuality too much either. That she was in a strong, committed relationship helped. Alex was quiet, happiest in the background while Jane took the spotlight, but she was a firm fixture in Jane's life, and neither made an apology for it.

Alex was treated no differently than if she were Jane's male life partner. If she and Jane could legally marry in D.C., they would. Jane was publicly clear on that score, while making the fine distinction of saying they were in no hurry for their legal union. Privately, of course, Jane thought it a travesty that they couldn't marry in D.C. or her home state of Michigan, Corey knew, but her sister was patient and confident the gains would be steady and incremental. Base hits for now, followed by the occasional double or triple, Jane liked to say.

"Whoever called politics a game sure wasn't kidding," Jane quipped. Rubbing her eyes, she closed them and leaned into Alex. "That bastard is *not* going to own me."

"No one owns you," Alex soothed. "Except maybe me."

Jane didn't hear her. She was out like a light, napping the few remaining minutes to the airport.

The crowd on the tarmac was much larger than expected. At least a thousand people shouted and waved, some carrying the brand-new Collins-Kincaid signs with their stark blue, red and white colors. It had been Corey's suggestion—Democratic blue with enough red and white to suggest that Jane and Collins were America's team. The waving signs made her proud to see her design dotting the horizon of exuberant faces.

Jane plunged into the crowd, the agents scrambling to keep up with her, but Alex stayed at her elbow. If Alex was surprised that nearly as many hands reached for her as for Jane, her expression didn't show it. She greeted people gamely, though not as enthusiastically as Jane, who seemed to draw strength and energy from the surging bodies. She pressed hands, accepted the occasional bouquet, shared words, accepted thanks and autographed a few placards. Her smile was amplified, her exhaustion seeming to lift like a fog burned off by the warming sun. Crowds invigorated Jane, not the endless backroom wheeling and dealing, the networking, the fundraising, the strategizing and ceaseless bullshit. In the middle of a crowd, Jane was in her element.

Jane turned to Corey, giving her a wink that said, *this is why I love my job*. Whenever Jane had that look about her and that infectious energy, Corey was ready to follow her to the ends of the earth.

CHAPTER FIVE

Three weeks in Washington, and Julia still found it difficult to work up solid contacts in the White House and on Capitol Hill. It was a tough town to crack. Her new reporter buddy in the White House press corps, Dane Williams from the *Chicago Tribune*, tried to reassure her, telling her it took months, even years to build up a rapport with reputable sources, but she wasn't that patient. She didn't know how long her assignment here would last, possibly only until the election was over. She would never get a bigger shot at furthering her career.

She wasn't looking for instant fame, notoriety or a six-figure contract. She wanted to do a good job, build up her résumé, and then go for the kind of job she really wanted, such as a roving columnist or reporter for a big newspaper with a national reputation. She could travel as much as she wanted and write about whatever and whomever she wanted, have an expense account without limits, and flexible deadlines and timetables. After that, maybe she'd even write a book or two.

Her impatience led her to the Hay-Adams Hotel: old, gentrified, storied, and just across from the White House on the other side of Lafayette Square. The basement bar, called Off the Record, was an unofficial hangout for staffers from the White House and the Hill, as well as journalists and sometimes foreign dignitaries. The bar was famous for classic martinis and even more classic clients, Julia had heard. Dane had helpfully suggested she spend a couple of evenings a week at the bar if she wanted to get to know influential people in a relaxed setting. She wasn't sure her wallet or her liver could stand that kind of pace, but sharing a few drinks might lubricate some of the barflies into sharing things they probably shouldn't. That was her short-term hope, anyway. In the long term, she might be able to work up contacts for stories, people she could go to for quotes or confirmations.

Julia arrived after eight o'clock. She would have preferred spending the evening reading the latest Elizabeth Sims mystery in bed with a glass of wine on her nightstand and Ralph, her silver tabby, curled up at her feet. But what the hell. She spent most nights that way, and all it got her was a shorter pile of books to read and warm feet from Ralph. Just one drink, she told herself, and if no Deep Throat materialized, she'd call it a night.

The bar had an exclusive clubby feel to it. The high ceiling was covered in pressed tin, the walls in dark wood panels. There were blood-red leather banquettes, a gleaming semicircular bar, and plenty of small private alcoves for hushed conversations.

She imagined that many secret deals had been cut here over the years, perhaps over fragrant cigar smoke and dry martinis in the Roosevelt and Kennedy years, stale cigarettes and sour whisky in the Nixon era.

Taking a seat at the bar, Julia smiled at the bartender, an elderly man with an Irish accent and cigarette-stained teeth. She ordered a cosmopolitan. Feeling hungry because she'd skipped dinner, she gratefully pawed at the silver dishes of peanuts, wasabi peas and smoked almonds.

"That's why I come here. For the nuts." A tall man with bristly silver hair and scrutinizing brown eyes materialized beside her. He sat down like it was his personal stool and scooped a handful of almonds into his mouth.

Note to self, skip the almonds from now on.

"How you doing, Fred?" The stranger nodded at the bartender. He spoke in a slight southern drawl, perhaps a North Carolinian accent like Alex's. He smirked disapprovingly at Julia's cosmopolitan when Fred set the cocktail before her. In a voice he probably deepened for her benefit, he ordered a martini—shaken and with plenty of olives.

Jerk, Julia thought, and then remembered the reason she was here. She sat up straighter, angling herself slightly toward him. "By the way, I'm Julia."

"I know. Landen, right? *Miami Herald?*"

Julia's mouth slackened in surprise. "Yes. Do I know you?"

"Don't look so surprised. It's my business to know anyone hanging around the White House these days, especially anyone with their nose so far up the rumps of Collins and Kincaid. You're covering their campaign."

Julia took a swallow of her drink, supremely insulted by his remark and unnerved that this stranger knew so much about her. "I'm sorry, but who are you?"

His smile was predatory and intimidating, as though he enjoyed toying with her, or perhaps enjoyed trying to make a fool of her. "Jake Ainsworth. I work for your enemy."

"My enemy?" *I don't have any of those, do I?*

Ainsworth shook his head, presumably at her ignorance. She wanted to smack the arrogance off his face. "I'm the assistant campaign manager for Colby Harrison."

Colby Harrison was the frontrunner in the race for the Republican nomination for president. He was conservative with a capital "C." If his momentum kept going, he would be Collins's opponent this fall.

"Colby Harrison is hardly my enemy, Mr. Ainsworth," she said. "I'm a newspaper reporter reporting—*objectively*—on the Democratic re-election campaign."

He laughed like she'd just told him the funniest joke in the world. "You're not going to pretend to be one of *those*, are you?"

"One of what?" she snapped, getting more impatient and pissed off by the second, although she was well aware Ainsworth was goading her.

"One of those journalists who *pretends* what they're doing is noble. You know, all for the public good and just presenting the facts. That kind of B.S."

"So you're saying you think I'm a cheerleader for the incumbent administration? I'd love for you to give me some specific examples because you're wrong. Dead wrong, mister." *Go ahead, make my day, asshole. All of my stories have been objective and fair.*

As she waited for his smart-ass retort, she caught a glimpse of Corey Kincaid sliding into a booth with Jane's chief of staff, Stephanie Cameron. The booths were so private that she could no longer see them once they'd taken their seats. She wondered if Corey had seen her sitting here with Mr. Personality.

"You know something?" Ainsworth said, his eyes losing their hostility and morphing into something creepy that she didn't want to analyze too closely. "You're really hot when you're upset."

Hot? Did he really say hot? "I'm not upset. And I'm not hot," she huffed. "What I am is mystified by where you get your ideas."

"You see, your lips get fuller and redder when you're upset, and your eyes get darker, and your chest—"

"Okay, hold it right there, buddy. My chest is off limits, thank you very much." If she were still a cop, she'd arrest him. For what, she wasn't exactly sure, but she'd find some reason...theft of nuts or something.

He laughed mockingly and took a swallow of his martini. "Damn, you're striking one of your greatest assets off the list."

Now she really wanted to smack him. Or put the heel of her boot up his ass. Instead, she stood, clutching her drink in her hand without a clue what to do next.

"You're not going to throw that at me, are you?"

"Are you daring me?"

"Julia, hi." A breathless Corey suddenly appeared at her elbow. Julia hadn't thought Corey was the knight-in-shining armor type. In fact, she'd not given much thought to her at all since the California trip.

"Sorry, I didn't realize you were here until now," Corey continued.

"I got the time mixed up and thought we were meeting at nine. I have a table for us."

"Well, well." Ainsworth turned to Corey. "How goes everything in the world of that gorgeous but misguided vice president of ours?"

"Just fine, Jake. Just fine. Better than fine, actually."

"Good, because she only has a few more months in the job. Guess that means you do as well." He sighed heavily. "Too bad the place isn't going to have the same glamour when Harrison is inaugurated. Got to hand it to you Democrats, you always beat us in the looks department."

Corey rolled her eyes but said nothing more.

"Goodbye, Julia," Ainsworth called after her as she and Corey walked away. "You were more fun than I expected."

"Jesus," Julia said after sliding into the booth. "What a creep!"

"Yes. Supremely annoying and a pompous ass, but harmless as far as I know," Corey said. "He gets his jollies out of being insulting."

"Well, thanks for riding in on your white horse and rescuing me. You even had me fooled for a minute about having an appointment with you." She had not yet met Corey and Steph so informally, and was not even on a first-name basis with either of them.

Steph glanced at Corey, her admiration clear. "You won't find anyone better at thinking or acting on her feet."

"Except my big sister. She's the master."

"Well, big sister has had more practice than you, my dear. Listen." Steph turned her attention to Julia. "It's not you Julia, but I have to get out of here. Early meetings tomorrow, and I've got some prep work to do at home tonight. Let's talk another time." She slipped out of the booth and threw a twenty on the table. "Buy yourself another cosmo on me, okay? My way of apologizing for running out."

Julia smiled at her. She didn't know Stephanie Cameron very well, but she liked her bluntness. She liked all of Jane's staff and if that made some people think she was a cheerleader, well, so be it. At least dealing with intelligent, cheerful people on a daily basis made her job a hell of a lot more pleasant.

"Thank you, I'd be happy to buy another drink on you. Then Mr. Ainsworth might finally have some evidence that I'm biased."

Both women laughed, and Corey said, "Well, if that's the secret to good press, I'll buy you as many drinks as you want!"

Steph said her goodbyes and left, deliberately avoiding the path near Ainsworth.

"Thanks," Julia said, still a little breathless from her run-in with Ainsworth. "But you'd have to do considerably better than a few drinks."

Something in Corey's eyes flared briefly, as though a flirtatious comeback might be on its way. Julia hoped so, though she hadn't heard anything about Corey being gay, and hadn't even considered the possibility until now. She stared into Corey's attractive brown eyes and at the intelligent and pleasant face that looked so much like her better known sister's, hoping for some sort of signal. She found Corey's beauty far less intimidating than Jane's. Not because she was less pretty, but because she was much less powerful.

"You drive a hard bargain," Corey finally answered, turning serious. "I hope Ainsworth wasn't trying to pry any information out of you."

"No, he wasn't. Actually I'm not sure what the point of the conversation was, other than to trash talk me and the administration, and getting me totally worked up."

"He's good at that, but he's one of those people always angling for something."

"I was hoping to do a little angling of my own," Julia confessed. "I was told this was a good place to work up sources."

"It does seem to be the place a lot of staffers go to unwind after a long day, and you certainly aren't the first reporter here hoping to hear something useful. To be honest, we're all hopeful of that. Whether you're a reporter or a staffer, you're always working, searching for something or someone that will help you do your job better. Opportunity building, I call it." Corey sipped her white wine and ordered them both another drink from a passing waiter. "This city is a snake pit, and none of the snakes ever sleep. You either keep up or you're prey."

"Wow. That sounds a little scary."

Corey's wink lightened her words. "If you're a hunk of raw

meat, it is. Speaking of meat, Ainsworth looked like he wanted to devour you."

"Yeah, well, a goat would stand a better chance with me."

Corey raised her eyebrows in amusement, but said nothing until their drinks arrived. Apparently emboldened, she asked, "Is your past relationship with Alex common knowledge?"

"God, no. I'm very private. Four years ago, when your sister was running for president, there were a couple of gossipy stories in the papers about Alex that mentioned me, but only my first name. Journalists and the paparazzi were never able to fully identify me. Sheesh, even Ralph doesn't know about my well-kept past."

"Ralph?"

"My tabby."

Smiling, Corey shook her head. "Where did you ever come up with the name Ralph?"

"My grandparents were big fans of that old television show *The Honeymooners*. You know, Ralph Kramden?"

"Is your cat chubby and boorish like Ralph Kramden?"

"No. He's sweet, lovable and a big wuss."

"Well, I'm sure your past is safe with Ralph. But if others in this town knew about you and Alex, plenty of them would use it as leverage, either to get something out of you, or to try to embarrass Jane and Alex."

"Look, Corey...can I call you Corey?"

"Of course, but only if the first names go both ways."

The softness of Corey's voice eased some of Julia's exasperation. Why was everyone so paranoid about her working in such close proximity to Jane and Alex? What were they afraid of? Did they think she'd give a tell-all interview to the tabloids about her past with Alex? That she'd do something embarrassing like, God forbid, talk about her sex life with Alex? Or worse, that she still wanted Alex and was here to get her back?

She felt her face warming but indignantly said, "I am not here to cause any problems for Alex or Jane. I didn't even go looking for this assignment, okay? I'm just trying to do my job. The past is the past. I have no intention of revisiting it and stirring anything up."

Corey's expression softened further. "That's not what I mean.

I believe you, Julia. What I'm trying to say is that if certain people figured out about you and Alex—the paparazzi, Jane's opponents and critics—they'd hunt you down and make your life hell. Perhaps even discredit you in your job. Discredit Alex too. Anything that discredits Alex discredits Jane by extension. It's a bit of a powder keg. That's all I'm saying."

"Well, if anyone wants to track down my past with Alex, I won't make it easy for them."

"Will you give me a heads-up if that ever happens?"

If Corey was trying to manipulate her, Julia picked up no such vibes. Inexplicably and perhaps even prematurely, she trusted Corey. If Corey intended to sweetly lure her into a trap, well, so be it. She had to trust *somebody* in this town if she was going to get anywhere. Since Alex wasn't really talking to her and Jane was almost completely inaccessible, it might as well be Corey.

"Yes, I'll let you know if that ever happens." Now she wanted something in return. "Can I ask you a question?"

"Sure."

Julia didn't know how to tiptoe into the subject, so she didn't. "Is Alex happy?"

"Yes, she is. Why?"

"I want her to be, and I'm glad she is. It's…I know I'm not her favorite person in the world. I don't know how to make up for what I did to her."

"Do you think you need to?"

Julia mulled that over. No, she didn't *need* to, she decided. Their breakup happened a long time ago, she'd already apologized, yet Alex clearly remained hurt.

"It was a long time ago," she replied, "but I don't want her to hate me. I'm not the person I was then—unhappy in my job, unhappy with everything about my life, and not knowing what to do about it except to chuck it all and start over again. I'm not proud of the way I handled things. I would do it a lot differently now."

Corey eyed her suspiciously. "Are you still carrying a torch for Alex?"

That was an easy one to answer. There had been a time when Julia might have gone back to Alex if Alex had shown any interest, but Alex hadn't, so she had moved on.

"No, not at all. I had some regrets after I left her. Times when I thought I might have made the biggest mistake of my life, but I knew that after taking such a drastic step with Alex, there was no going back. I've made my peace with myself over the past. I'm not sure Alex has, though."

"I guess some people hold onto pain longer than others." Corey averted her eyes.

Julia had seen the pain in her eyes when she spoke. Corey had been hurt by someone too. It wasn't really fair that Corey knew all about her past and that they were having a one-sided conversation, but it was part of the game. Julia knew full well that Corey was judging how well she could trust her, how much integrity she had.

"I'd really like it if Alex and I could at least be friendly as long as I'm in Washington, but if not, I understand." Julia sipped her drink. "What about your sister? Do you think she hates me?"

"No. Jane doesn't hate anyone. Well, almost no one. She's careful, a little on the cynical side, but there's nothing hateful or vindictive about my sister. She's the most fair-minded person I know. She will give you the benefit of the doubt."

Julia felt relieved. If Jane made things difficult for her, her career would suffer a serious setback. "It seems so lonely to me here."

"The town or the work environment?"

"Both, I guess."

"You're right, it is." There were still traces of sorrow in Corey's eyes. "Everyone in this town is so, I don't know, on guard all the time. It's like everyone is so busy trying to protect their turf, or busy climbing over top of someone else to get what they want. Then there's the ungodly hours and travel. There's little time to forge friendships." She took a long sip of wine. "Or anything else."

"Great. Sounds like my long dry spell isn't going to be quenched anytime soon."

Corey raised her eyebrows before lifting her glass in a salute. "Well, at least we can quench our thirst for wine, if nothing else."

Julia convivially clinked glasses with Corey. Two amigas in the desert of love, she thought. She would love to know if the gay vibes coming from Corey were just her imagination. She'd probably never know, because Alex certainly wouldn't enlighten her, and she could never come right out and ask Corey. She was a professional, so was Corey. Definitely *not* a good idea to even entertain thoughts about Corey's sexuality and availability. Oh, well, she was here to work, not date.

Her second drink finished, Julia wasn't far from tipsy. Time to leave, although a Deep Throat had eluded her. At least Corey had been a welcome surprise—they'd made a good connection. Her instinct told her she could trust Corey. She stood to shake her hand, glad for the warmth she received in return.

"I'd like us to be straight with each other on the job," Corey said. "It's give and take with the press, and I'll do my part."

Julia smiled at the word *straight*. She'd rather be gay with Corey… *but hey, a girl can't always get what she wants*. "That sounds very good to me. I'll see you around?"

"You bet." Corey gave her a sly smile. "Say, those other White House reporters ever give you a hazing yet?"

Crap. She'd forgotten about that. "No. Why?"

Corey began to giggle lightly. "I was only kidding about that stuff, but if you need any protection from them, let me know, and I can throw some kind of scoop your way that will have them licking their chops in envy."

Julia laughed at the thought of being the envy of anyone in this town. "I love your idea. Thank you."

CHAPTER SIX

Jane loved the West Wing's Cabinet Room. She loved the combination of functional and beautiful in its working fireplace, antique paintings on the walls, tall leather antique chairs, and a gleaming oval table that seated two dozen.

Like a knife set to a sharpening stone, her awareness heightened whenever she entered the Cabinet Room. She felt as though she might somehow glean insight from being in the very place where such important national decisions had been made over the decades—war strategies, the Cuban missile crisis, Nixon's resignation, budget deliberations. Like an old oak tree with rings of wisdom and age beneath its bark, this was the place, even more so than the Oval Office, where the White House's battle scars could be found.

For the meeting on campaign strategy, Jane's staff was dwarfed by the president's. She'd brought along her chief of staff Steph Cameron, press secretary Will Carter, Corey—now her official campaign manager—and a recording secretary to take careful notes. Collins had pulled in all of his generals as well as a few of his foot soldiers, some of whom were relegated to the extra chairs along the wall. His chief and deputy chief of staff, his campaign management team, and his top strategists and speechwriters looked solemn and uninspired.

Throw some black crepe around the room and it might look like we're planning a funeral, Jane thought. *There should be energy and optimism in this room, not such bleakness.* Outlook seemed to be the main difference between her staff and Collins's, and it worried her. On this ticket, they needed energy, enthusiasm, vigor, and if they didn't have them now, they surely wouldn't gain them once things got tough throughout the course of the campaign.

"I want the attack ads against Harrison started right away," Collins announced as his opening salvo. "For the love of God, please tell me again why we've waited this long."

A young campaign aide—Jane couldn't remember his name—cleared his throat nervously. "I believe we were waiting for this month's Super Tuesday so we could be sure Harrison was the clear frontrunner."

Collins, who always looked perfectly groomed and regal, slashed his hand through the air like an impatient film director. "We knew weeks ago he was the frontrunner. Nothing's changed. Christ, it's the middle of March. There's no damn way anyone's going to catch him now. Let's put the crosshairs on his balls. Now!"

The young aide shook his head in defiance. Poor little lamb, Jane thought. *Brave, though.*

"We didn't want to go after him too early and give his campaign credibility," the aide said. "You authorized—"

"I don't need a history lesson from you, boy, on what's gone on around this table the last few weeks. Jesus Christ, are you even allowed to drive by yourself yet?" Collins grumbled disparagingly about Ivy League nancy boys.

Chastened, the young aide shut his mouth. Jane knew none

of the president's other paid staff had the guts to stand up to him when he was stubborn and moody like this, which happened a lot of the time, in fact. In public, he was the voice of reason, the calm and judicious father figure. Privately, Dennis Collins could be crude, temperamental, insensitive and a first-class bully. He didn't scare her, however.

"Mr. President," she interjected. "It was wise not to go after Harrison too early. In my opinion, it remains wise to continue to back off for a while longer."

The look from Collins could have stripped the dye from her low-heeled black shoes. "Why in *hell*, Madam Vice President, should we allow that shitbag to keep trashing us? Are you suggesting we keep taking it up the ass from him and not utter a word of protest?"

Jane sighed to herself and tried not to roll her eyes. Collins could never resist a homophobic remark in her presence. If he intended to raise a reaction from her, he wouldn't succeed. "If we take him too seriously too soon—publicly at least—it gives him credibility. And if we hit him hard now, what are we left with later?"

"I'll tell you what we're left with later. Handing him his ass in the election."

"That's a given," Jane answered smoothly. "If we attack Harrison too severely right now, we come across as worried, as though we can't defend our own platform and have to go on the offensive. Secondly, we risk voters thinking of us as bullies or meanies. He's a capital 'R' Republican at the extreme opposite to us in every possible way. He'll slip up. When he does, we'll be there to jump all over it."

A quiet murmur rose and fell around the room.

Collins chewed on an unlit cigar before he spoke. "Well, do you dimwits agree with her or what?"

"She does have some good points," his campaign manager, Danny Steele, grudgingly admitted without looking at Jane. "Perhaps it would be prudent to lay off Harrison awhile longer, maybe even until he's the official nominee."

"Wait in the weeds till then, is that what you're saying, Steele?"

"Yes and no, Mr. President. We should still attack his record and his party, just not *him*."

Collins chewed some more. When his blue eyes swung back to Jane, they were like dark ice. "All right then. We'll play it like this. We'll continue to attack Harrison's record and his ridiculous promises. I'm going to stay clean on this. Keep the official ads that bear my name looking like kindergarten artwork for now. Jane, I want you to start sharpening your claws."

"Sir?" she asked in surprise.

Collins removed the tattered, mushy cigar from his mouth and squeezed it between his fingers. "See, you're going to be my little attack dog. You're the one who attracts the crowds, who gives everybody a hard-on. I don't want you playing nice with Harrison. *You* attack him from now on because you can get away with it. Everyone will still love you."

She nodded benignly at the smug smile and malicious words, unwilling to express how she felt about his order. "Anything you say, Mr. President."

"Glad to hear it. In fact, I want you at that big fundraiser with me in New York City at the end of the month. I'll speak at the luncheon. You can speak at the Central Park concert afterward. Everyone'll be smoking dope and drinking at the concert anyway, so it's as good a place as any for you to start flinging some shit at Harrison. Hell, you could probably sell them a bag of steaming dog shit and tell them it was roasted chestnuts, and they'd believe *you*. Anyway, that's where I want you to start going after Harrison. And at any other opportunity that presents itself."

Jane was well aware that her popularity, especially among young people, and the poor and disenfranchised, sorely annoyed Collins. She scored extremely high on integrity and trust polls, higher than any national politician in years. People trusted her, and it wasn't an act, or Collins would have gladly copied her. Instead, he remained cool, distant and unemotional. She supposed his new tactic of making her the attack dog was a way to make her seem less angelic and more like a bitch. Well, if he wanted her to be the bitch and him the good guy, let him try. She'd make him regret his decision.

***

Alex set the thick binder down on the nightstand when she heard Jane enter downstairs. Another late day at the office, she thought, and it was only going to get worse as the campaign ramped up. Setting her reading glasses down—an unfortunate consequence of turning forty—she tiptoed out of the bedroom, padding down the stairs in her boxers and T-shirt to find Jane rummaging through the refrigerator. She couldn't resist a surprise attack on that round, unsuspecting ass. She pinched it, causing Jane to leap and smack her head on the fridge door.

"Ouch! Did they teach you how to move like a butterfly and sting like a bee in Secret Service school?" Jane asked. "No, wait, that was Muhammad Ali, wasn't it?"

"They didn't teach me how to box, but they did teach me how to be very observant. So if you're going to stick that cute ass out like that, what's a girl to do?"

"Hmm, how about warning me first?"

"And take all the fun out of it? I don't think so!"

Jane finally settled on a small container of strawberry yogurt.

Alex handed her a spoon. "Long day, huh?" she asked the obvious.

"Long day sitting on my ass arguing with Collins and his stuffed shirts about campaign strategy. Jesus, you have to say something three different ways and practically scream at them before they even begin to listen, and even then it's only with one ear." Jane spooned yogurt into her mouth at a furious pace. "Four more years of beating my head against the wall. God, there'll be nothing left of me."

"Oh, sweetie." Alex wrapped her lover in a tight embrace, squashing the empty yogurt container between them.

Jane was a real threat to Dennis Collins. She was smarter, more politically astute, much more likeable, and had a vivacious personality that absolutely dwarfed his. Collins was straight and a man—the two tangibles that had put him in the Oval Office over Jane, but times were changing, and quickly. A woman—and a lesbian—as president was no longer a fantasy or a utopian dream. Jane was the next great hope for America. Collins undoubtedly knew it too. He would do whatever he could to keep Jane in her place, to contain her ambition, and to remind the electorate that this was *his* time. *He* was the president, and history would damn well wait. Of course, if she did manage to succeed him one day, he would claim some of her success as his own, as though he had been the architect of it all along.

Yes, thought Alex, she had learned a few things about politics over the last four years. "I'm going to run you a bubble bath and you can tell me all about it."

"Yes and then no."

"Huh?"

"Yes to the bubble bath, no to talking more about it."

"All right, no talk of work tonight."

Jane smiled against her neck. "You're half right."

"I am? I thought I was always right."

Jane's low throaty laughter tickled her skin. "Well, you *are* right more than anyone I know, but I was going to suggest no more talking at all tonight. About anything."

"Hmm, I like that idea. As long as the talking gets replaced by some sort of action."

"Ah, you read my mind exactly! A little action is exactly what I need after a day like today."

"In that case, I'm happy to sacrifice for my country."

"Now, how did I know you were going to say that?"

"Because you know I'm a loyal, hard-working American who will do anything for my country's vice president, including getting down on my knees."

Jane growled happily and kissed her vigorously. "Now you're talking, baby."

Moments later, Alex and Jane reclined at either end of the large soaker tub, mostly silent save for discussion of a few minor household matters. She knew it wasn't unusual for Jane to want peace and quiet after a particularly stressful day of work. Jane would talk more about it eventually—they talked about everything. Jane included her in all aspects of her work. She confided in her, respected her opinion and advice, and drew strength and energy from sharing.

Alex might not be a political animal like Jane, but she knew what was important, knew instinctively what Jane needed and what was good for her, and knew Jane valued her input.

Alex began massaging the soles of Jane's feet resting in her soapy lap, enjoying the low moans of pleasure each stroke elicited. She would never have foreseen such a secondary role for herself in a partnership, the role of a supportive wife standing stoically in the background, compromising her own ambitions, revolving her world so subordinately to someone else's. She had never pictured her life this way, yet she *had* pictured herself thoroughly in love, ensconced and invested in her mate's life, working together in a fully committed partnership. She was meant to be half of a whole, even if that whole was something greater than she ever dreamed. Jane's ambitions had easily become her ambitions, and Jane's life so much a part of her own that the seam between them had grown invisible.

This was exactly how her life was meant to be, Alex thought, the sum of her relationship much greater than its parts. It had never been that way with Julia, and it wasn't just because they were practically kids when they first got together. She'd loved Julia. They'd had great sexual chemistry. But seeing Julia now reminded her that their love had been a mere facsimile, never meant to survive the storms, and never meant to become an entity of its own like her relationship with Jane. She and Julia were two people who'd hitched their worlds together for a brief time, tributaries that flowed into a large stream before meandering off again in different directions.

"You look deep in thought, my love," Jane commented.

Alex jerked her attention back to the present. "Not really. But I admit I'll be glad for both of us when this election is over."

Jane squeezed her eyes shut for a moment. "I have a funny feeling about it in the pit of my stomach."

"You do?" Jane had a great instinct for expecting the unexpected, almost like a sixth sense. "Good or bad?"

"Not sure yet. Good, I think."

Alex thought of the thick binder on her nightstand, known as *The Album* in Secret Service parlance. It contained profiles of anyone deemed a threat to Jane and Collins, especially those who might be in the vicinity of New York City during the scheduled campaign visit in two weeks. Same as the agents on the protective detail, she would memorize the book. Every time she scanned crowds, those photos would be in the forefront of her mind. She never forgot that Jane's safety was *always* at risk, but at least she felt she had a role in protecting her.

She wondered what it was like for the other candidates' spouses, to be fearful for their loved one's safety, and to have not a shred of control over it, to constantly be on the outside. She wasn't foolish enough to think that every possible threat against Jane would always be discovered and thwarted, but at least she was in the thick of it with her eyes wide open and a weapon at her side. She would do everything in her power to keep Jane safe, and her power was significant.

Jane's eyes opened, and she stroked Alex's forearm tenderly. "Ever wonder what our life will be like when all this craziness is over?"

"You mean when it's just us?" Alex began to chuckle. "I'm not sure that's ever going to happen, but it's a nice thought."

"Yes, a nice little fantasy. We probably wouldn't know what to do with ourselves anyway without the constant interruptions, the high stress situations, the traveling, the meetings and the decisions that need to be made every waking minute."

"Oh, trust me, I can think of at least one thing."

That got Jane's attention. Her smile turned needy and hopeful. "Care to tell me about it?"

"Life's too short for words," Alex said with a grin. "I think what's needed is a little demonstration."

"Honey, you read my mind perfectly." Jane sprang from the tub and reached for her towel. "Because what I could really use after a day like today is a good fu—" She batted her eyelashes playfully. "I mean, a little lovin'."

Alex laughed as she followed her naked wife to the bedroom. She found it sexy as hell when Jane spoke explicitly. Such a rarity, rather unbecoming of a vice president of the United States, and it turned her on. "Hmm, a little lovin' is a given. But I was thinking more along the lines of your first thought."

Jane's eyes danced with promise and anticipation. "You won't get any arguments from me."

Stretched out on the bed, the warmth of her body mingling with Jane's as they lay side by side, Alex burned with arousal. So often work or travel interfered with their intimate time. She was torn now between wanting to make slow love to Jane or giving it to her fast and hard. Jane made up her mind for her.

"Oh, Alex, please, not slow," she whispered urgently, running her nails provocatively along Alex's bicep. "I need you on top of me. Let me feel you inside me."

Alex rolled on top of Jane, kissing her mouth. She slid her hand down Jane's soft, tight belly and lower still, to the tenderness of her inner thighs. Jane was already wet, a wet trail leading Alex home.

"I love you, baby," Alex mumbled as her fingers found Jane's softness, so hot and wet. She closed her eyes, concentrating on the textures at the end of her fingers, Jane's urgency in the palm of her hand.

"Alex," Jane breathed. "Sweetheart, I need you inside me. Please."

Oh, yes. She wanted that too.

Holding Jane tightly, her mouth between Jane's breasts, she entered her sharply and suddenly. Jane gasped in pleasure at the penetration, closing around Alex's finger, a warm and wet clenching that set Alex's clit throbbing wildly.

She moved inside Jane and slipped in a second finger, pushing her own aroused clit against Jane's thigh. She began riding the bucking coaster of Jane's desire to higher and higher peaks and plateaus. Fast and hard, tightly and in perfect sync, she plunged toward Jane's climax.

Alex's mouth found Jane's nipple. Jane's sharp cry signaled the onslaught of orgasm, and Alex held her until the spasms stilled.

"Oh, God, I needed that," Jane said between breaths.

"That, my dear, was only the first course."

Jane laughed drowsily. "I'll be wrecked by the time we get to dessert."

"All right. We can skip dessert as long as I can get two more orgasms out of you tonight."

"Ha! I'm good but I'm not that good. Especially after a long day."

Alex moved alongside Jane, enclosing her in her arms. "I'm only teasing, my love. I'd like nothing better than for you to fall asleep in my arms."

"Mmm, that would be heavenly. But there's something I need to do first."

"Nope. Whatever needs doing, I'll do it."

"Oh, no, you don't. You are not depriving me of that!"

"What?"

Jane rolled on top of Alex. "This!" Her eyes sparkling with renewed energy, she slid down Alex's body.

Oh, Jesus, Alex thought at the first touch of Jane's mouth on her. *Oh, Jesus, yes! Don't stop baby, don't stop don't stop!* She knew she would be fast, too fast, because it'd been over a week since her last orgasm. Her body craved Jane's touch. Now that she had it, she could not get enough. Like a thirsty field ravenous for rain, she greedily sucked in all the pleasure as if fearing another drought would follow. She tried to slow her body down, to sink into the rapture driving her mad, but it was no use. With Jane's mouth locked firmly onto her, her hips rose, and she bucked hard once, twice, and gushed into Jane's mouth.

She wondered then, as Jane moved back into her arms, whether she would ever get enough of this woman.

CHAPTER SEVEN

Corey had known exactly what Jane was up to, even if the plan hadn't been verbalized.

She'd helped Jane write the speech, and also helped defend it against a very skeptical and disapproving Stephanie Cameron. Steph almost always urged the cautious approach. Jane often complied, but not this time.

Jane wore a knowing smirk when she said to Corey, "If Collins wants to unleash me on Harrison, that's exactly what he'll get. You know how attack dogs can be."

"Wild? Unpredictable? Hard to call off?" Corey laughed, and then set to work with Jane on the speech that was about to blow the lid off the gay rights debate, which Collins had so far successfully managed to ignore.

He didn't want gay rights as a chink in his armor. If he had to carry that albatross around his neck, he might as well hand the election to the Republicans, he'd said on more than one occasion. Liberal equaled weak, he repeated like a mantra to anyone who listened. Jane was different. With her, what people saw was what they got. No pretensions.

Jane's smile dissolved as she looked over the speech again. "It's the right thing to do. Right Corey?"

"Yes, it is." Corey understood that Jane needed a little bolstering before stepping on this landmine. She was happy to give it to her.

"Gay rights is one of the few areas we can distinguish ourselves from the Republicans."

"Yes. That and gun control."

Jane rolled her eyes. "True, but it's better to be seen *giving* rights than taking them away. I'm afraid gun control is going to have to wait. My only problem with this," she said, pointing at the computer screen, "is that it plays exactly into Forrest Mitchell's plans. The last thing I want is for him to think he's pulling my strings."

Corey nodded. Jane wasn't the kind of candidate who liked to be indebted to anyone, but that was sometimes easier said than done. Advancing a political agenda took a lot of negotiation, a lot of give and take. Jane was certainly familiar with that.

"Look," she soothed, "just because you're going to break your boss's balls over gay rights—"

"No, I'm busting Colby Harrison's balls over gay rights," Jane corrected, throwing Corey a sly wink.

"Right. Harrison. Anyway, Mitchell doesn't hold the license on advancing gay rights." *The arrogant son of a bitch.* "On the other hand, it might give Collins a little scare if he thinks you're in some kind of partnership with Mitchell."

Jane was silent a moment before she declared, "Hell, I'm used to walking a fine line. It's what I do. Push things enough to move forward without going off the track." She closed the laptop, smiling widely. "Let's give Harrison the ass kicking he deserves. As for the president, he can consider this a little wake-up call. He wants an attack dog, that's what he's getting."

Now in Central Park, Corey chuckled to herself. Jane was a sleeping dog the president should have let lie.

The spring evening air felt cool and sharp. The crowd, estimated at forty thousand, seemed in a happy, buoyant but relaxed mood, as if sluggishly emerging from winter. Collins's luncheon speech at The Plaza had been anti-climactic, conservative words for a conservative audience, but these were Jane's people: young, hip, energetic, liberal in their values, eager to listen to a politician who seemed to respect them. Corey thought the gathering had the undercurrent of a pep rally.

Jane's fifteen-minute speech was scheduled as the intermission act. Faith Hill and Mary J. Blige had each given thirty-minute performances. Springsteen would follow Jane's speech.

Corey sat on a lawn chair at the side of the stage, near a couple of Secret Service agents and beside Will Carter. She knew Alex roamed around somewhere, watching the crowd for weirdoes. Always working to keep Jane safe, even when she wasn't on duty, Alex never got to sit, watch her partner and enjoy the moment.

While Corey appreciated such loyalty and dedication to her sister, she sometimes worried that Alex didn't have enough of her own life. Had it been *her*, she'd want her own life, but then, she had no clue about that kind of devotion between couples. She couldn't define where the individual Jane or Alex ended and the other began. She'd certainly never felt that way with Jason. No, with him life had been a constant exercise of fitting a square peg into a round hole.

She glanced at Carter, his profile handsome in the twilight, his notepad and pen ready to take notes of the crowd's reaction to Jane's speech. Carter didn't have a life either, as far as she could tell. In fact, none of them did. They were all soldiers on a mission, called to serve and sacrifice, and forced to put their own lives on the back burner.

She didn't see how most varieties of love—save for the kind of love Alex and Jane shared—could bloom in this desert. Most days she felt okay sacrificing her personal life because it was all for a higher purpose. Other times, like now, she wished she was sitting in the crowd, maybe on a blanket, huddled close with someone she cared about, enjoying the music and the energy. Someone once said, "you don't miss what you've never had," but she knew that wasn't true.

She caught a glimpse of Julia seated in a roped off area for the press. They'd recently passed each other in hallways and parking lots, and the airport once, but they hadn't talked since their impromptu meeting at the Hay-Adams two weeks ago. Too bad, Corey thought. It'd be nice to have a friend in town, someone to talk to other than one of her colleagues, but one who still understood politics and the demands of her job.

On the surface, she had to admit to herself that the optics of hanging out with Alex's ex would not look good. On the other hand, the relationship was so far in the past, a friendship with Julia could hardly qualify as any kind of lesbian drama or silly love triangle. Not that she planned to become intimate friends with Julia, or anything deeper. She had little time or energy to date anyone right now, but if just about every facet of her life were different, well, Julia wouldn't be a bad choice. She seemed bright, naturally interested in politics, and her work was above average. *Oh, hell, Corey, who are you kidding? She's gorgeous with those blue-gray eyes and that killer body. Jesus.*

She couldn't help but notice the lovely breasts hidden beneath the tight blouses and sweaters Julia liked to wear. She'd have to be blind or hopelessly straight not to notice those luscious breasts, so round and full. She imagined they would be firm yet soft to the touch, a little more than a handful. *Christ, does this mean I'm a breast woman?* The thought had never occurred to her. Hell, she couldn't even remember looking at a woman's breasts before, at least not like *that*, but not only was she looking now, she was practically salivating, wanting to touch them suddenly, wanting to squeeze them gently like Charmin. That's it, she thought with mild alarm. *Working in politics has finally made me lose my mind!*

"Carter," she whispered worriedly.

"Yeah?"

"Is it normal to be hypersexual when you first realize you're gay?"

Carter eyed her seriously before cracking a slow grin.

She'd admitted to him on the California trip that she was sexually intrigued by women. He'd teased her about it, compared her to being a life-long minivan driver who suddenly decided to go for the hot sports car. He, Alex and Jane were the only people who knew she was interested in sports cars.

"Oh, yeah, definitely," he answered. "I call it making up for lost time."

"Crap, that's what I was afraid of," Corey said, staring again at Julia. Julia's chest, more accurately. "Since when is there time during an election for *that* kind of thing anyway?" The only people she figured were having any sex were Jane and Alex, and that was only because they were together twenty-four-seven.

Carter's eyes followed her gaze. "Oh, there's always time to do a little sports car driving, election year or not. Especially when the car is as hot as *that* one! That's a top-down kinda model, don't you think?"

Corey flushed. "What the hell are you talking about?"

"Come on, you've been watching her all evening. Watching a certain part of her anatomy all evening is what I meant."

"Have not," she answered hotly.

"Have too. Besides, it works out perfectly. I've already asked Julia to join us at that gay nightclub tonight after we're done here."

"You *what?*"

"She's practically part of the family anyway."

"Yes, and that's the problem. Does Alex know about your little invitation?"

"Alex and Jane aren't coming. They decided their presence would cause too much of a distraction."

Corey nodded. Loss of anonymity was the unfortunate part of being famous and popular. The campaign staff would have to throw a private party one of these days so that Alex and Jane could cut loose and have some fun. She made a mental note to plan one.

"Look, inviting Julia along wasn't part of the deal," she said, falling into a pout.

"What have you got against it? You seem to be getting along with her fine, and besides, it's all part of my master plan to woo the press."

"You're so full of crap," she said under her breath. "Okay, look, I don't have anything against it, I just...I don't know. I don't know her and I don't want her to think—"

"That you're lusting after her?"

His annoying little brother act made her want to slap him. "I don't know what the hell I was thinking when I came out to you, and no, I am not lusting after Julia Landen." Okay, she was, but only a little, and only because she was sex-starved and insanely curious about bedding a woman.

"Oh, come on, you know I want only the best for you, Corey."

"Thanks for your help," she grumbled, not truly annoyed.

To Corey's relief, the emcee's introduction of Jane ended their conversation.

The crowd erupted, chanting Jane's name and holding lit lighters and cell phones in the air. The raucous welcome continued for several minutes before Jane could speak. She thanked them, gave them a dazzling smile, and complimented the City of New York by saying it was her favorite city in the world to visit. She wasn't bullshitting, Corey knew. She really did love to visit New York, but had no intention of living here.

Jane launched into her theme of the inclusiveness and diversity of New York City, its historical importance, its bedrock of American democracy. She talked about how the city had become home to so many immigrants over the centuries, home to people looking for a better life.

"We're still looking for a better life," she said. "And I'm not talking about a bigger house, or a new car, or a second big screen television. I'm talking about a better life where each and every one of us can hold our heads up with pride, with respect, with dignity. Where each and every one of us is valued for who we are, for what we can do for each other, and for what we can do for our country. I'm talking about a better life where the laws of this land are applied *equally* to everyone." She waited for the applause to abate. "I'm talking about a better life where each of us *matters*, not only to our friends and our families, our neighborhoods and communities, our workplaces, but where each of us matters to our civic leaders and lawmakers. Where each of us has a voice."

"Yes!" the crowd cheered.

"I don't think that's too much to ask. Do you?"

"No!" the crowd cried.

Jane smiled at them regretfully, shaking her head. "You see, there's at least one group of us who will *never* matter to Colby

Harrison. There's one group of us Colby Harrison would rather see deprived of the rights we *do* have. If you are gay in this country, Mr. Harrison would really you just—*poof!*—disappeared. Got cured. Left the country. Something, *anything* other than demand equal rights and respect. Anything other than to stand up and demand that you matter to *him* and to your country! That you deserve the same things as your neighbor, your co-worker, your pastor."

The crowd erupted into roars. Jane tried to quiet them. "*Equal* rights, ladies and gentlemen, not special rights. Equal rights for every citizen. Equal application of the law with respect to income tax, home ownership, immigration, adoption. And yes, marriage, as this great state understands. I'm talking about equal rights for *every* American! Isn't that what we've fought wars for all these centuries? Isn't that what we've sacrificed for? Striven for? *Died* for?"

"Yes!" the crowd chanted, many fists stabbing the air.

"Mr. Colby Harrison isn't in favor of equal rights for all. Mr. Colby Harrison wants to take us back decades, turn back the clock to the good old days when women, immigrants, the disabled, African Americans, were left behind. Left behind and told that the equal rights they demanded were simply not meant for them."

Corey winced. She knew that introducing racism, even without using the word, was like throwing a sirloin to a pack of hungry dogs. The media were going to be all over this speech, and Harrison would go into full attack mode. But that's how Jane wanted it, she reminded herself. Jane was fully braced to battle both Harrison and Collins over the fallout from making gay rights the opening salvo of the campaign.

"We're not going to wait anymore. We're not going to wait because our time is now!" Jane went on to call gay rights the civil rights battle of this decade, perhaps even the century. "It is my fight, and as Americans, it is the fight of all of us. It is the final frontier of human rights in this country. It is a matter of when, not if. It is the *right* side of history, and if you are not on the right side of history, Mr. Harrison, then you are *wrong!*"

The crowd shouted, cheered and surged forward. People practically stampeded the stage.

"Hold on," Jane cautioned as calmly as if she had been discussing something as innocuous as poetry. "Hold onto that fighting spirit, because we will need it down the road. We will need to be vigilant. And we will need to make it known, in no uncertain terms, that we will support the fight, and we will lead the fight for equal rights across this country, and we will *demand* victory. Anything less is simply unacceptable."

She ended it with a JFK quote—she liked to quote the Kennedys, not because they were Democratic royalty, but because their own father, in the embryonic stage of his political career, had been close personal friends with John and Robert Kennedy. "As John F. Kennedy once said, my friends, 'the new frontier is here, whether we seek it or not.'"

"Jesus," Carter said over the noise of the crowd. "I think we've just moved to the vanguard of gay rights."

He looked as worried as Corey felt. Gay rights was an important issue to Jane—to all of them—but this moment could very well define the election for her and Dennis Collins, and it could box them into a corner. On the other hand, it might be a stroke of brilliance.

"This will separate us from the Republicans in one hell of a hurry, that's for sure," Corey said, sharing a nervous look with Carter.

"I need a drink," Carter said, rubbing his temples.

"Me too. When this speech hits the news tomorrow, it's going to be nuts."

"Come on. Let's go."

There would be no further official comment on the speech tonight from Jane or any of her staff, Corey had been told. The speech would stand alone, but that didn't stop Carter's BlackBerry from sounding like a Geiger counter at a nuclear plant as they settled into a VIP booth on the upper floor of the huge gay dance club. Her BlackBerry did the same frenzied beeping. For a while, the two of them silently thumbed the miniature keyboards like automatons, oblivious to the pounding dance music and writhing bodies on the floor below them.

"Don't you two look like the life of the party!"

Corey glanced up. Julia stood over them, shaking her head admonishingly and looking youthful in the multicolored strobe lights that turned her hair various shades of pink, blue and lavender.

Glancing at her watch, Corey felt guilty. Had they really wasted an hour already? She slid her phone into her purse. There was really no more work to be done until tomorrow's seven a.m. breakfast meeting when Collins's staff would undoubtedly spend the entire time berating them for Jane's inflammatory speech. *It'll be worth the ringside seats to watch the fireworks*, she thought in amusement.

Carter invited Julia to sit down, "We were waiting for *you* to get this party started."

"I might have been able to get my story filed sooner if you'd given me a heads-up about the speech," Julia complained, but she was smiling.

Carter grinned cockily. "Pretty spectacular, huh?"

"It's clear you're pegging Harrison as your opponent. Does this mean the gloves are officially off now?"

"Oh, no, you don't," Carter said. "You aren't getting anything out of me. We'll be having a press conference tomorrow. TBA."

Julia looked cute with her pretend pout. "No special favors?"

"None." Carter signaled the waitress for a round. "What'll you have?" he asked Julia.

"Cosmopolitan, please."

Corey remembered Julia's pink drink from the Hay-Adams and decided to order the same. Carter made it three. He wasn't afraid to be seen drinking girlie drinks, she thought fondly. In fact, he enjoyed the reactions his choices sometimes prompted.

"If I can't get anything from *him*," Julia said to Corey with a sly smile, "maybe I should work on you."

Corey's face warmed. She prayed the blush wasn't noticeable. Please don't say anything, she silently begged Carter. *Too late.*

"Oh, I think that'd be a great idea. Corey would love to be worked on. Wouldn't you, Cor?"

She shot him as cutting a look as she could muster. "Sorry, but I think I'm embattled enough to be beyond bribery or sweet talking."

Julia's forehead wrinkled in concentration. Corey had a flash of how she might have looked as a child concentrating on a puzzle. All Julia needed to do was stick out her tongue to complete the picture. *Very cute.*

"I'm sure there is something I could come up with if I just thought about it hard enough," Julia replied.

Corey detected no innuendo in her tone, which she found almost disappointing.

"Maybe you could talk her into a dance later," Carter suggested. Corey winced. There was absolutely nothing innocent about *him*.

Corey ignored him, taking her drink from the tray offered by the waitress. She checked out her surroundings for what seemed like the first time, surprised that it really didn't seem much different than a straight nightclub except for the fact there were more guys dancing, they were dancing with each other, and the guys could actually dance.

Julia's eyes flicked across the crowded floor. "I wonder if this is anything like Studio 54 in its heyday."

"From what I've heard, I doubt it's as outrageous," Carter supplied. "But it would be cool if you could go back in time and have just one night there, wouldn't it? God! Sex right out in plain view, all the coke you could handle, guys in drag, Donna Summer instead of Lady Gaga, a giant disco ball about the size of the moon over the dance floor." Judging by the stupid look on his face, he seemed to be experiencing some kind of nirvana.

Corey shook her head. "No thanks. Sounds like a nightmare to me. A piano bar is more my style, I guess."

Carter laughed at her. "Oh, yeah, I forgot you're a virgin in places like this. It's not too much for you, is it?"

"No," she answered too quickly.

Julia's expression was indecipherable. "Wow, this is your first gay club experience?"

Corey swallowed dryly. "When it comes to gay things, I'm afraid there's a lot of firsts ahead of me." Oh, God, she thought. *Why did I just say that*? But Julia only smiled charitably. Or maybe it was pity. *Please, anything but that.*

"Well." Carter stood like he was calling a press conference to order. "That's it for me. We're going to have to be on our game bright and early tomorrow morning."

"What, you're not even going to dance?" Corey panicked. He was leaving her alone with Julia. On purpose. Christ, what was she supposed to do? How was she supposed to act?

"Sorry, sweetcakes. I'm not as young as I used to be."

He left before she could give him shit or at least threaten his life. *Bastard.*

"Do you have to leave too?" Julia asked quietly, a note of disappointment in her voice.

"I probably should, but I feel like I just got here," Corey replied.

"Good, because you can't come to a place like this without at least one dance."

Did that mean Julia was asking her to dance? The idea alternately scared and thrilled her. She had a whole pile of reasons why she should follow Carter out the door and hop in his cab with him, and Julia Landen was reason number one. She swallowed the rest of her drink, deciding to be brave if Julia asked her. When she looked up, Julia stood in front of her, crooking a finger in her direction.

"Seriously?" Corey asked. "You obviously haven't seen me dance before."

"Come on." Julia grabbed her hand, held it tightly, and led her down the winding staircase to the dance floor.

Rihanna's "Rude Boy" was so loud, the beat pounded inside Corey's chest like a second heart. On the crowded floor, they had to squeeze between a six-foot-five drag queen and a short lesbian with spiky gray hair who made up in energy what she lacked in height.

"Oh, yeah," Julia cried, spinning in a full circle. "I haven't danced in ages! This feels awesome!"

Corey tried to keep up with Julia's steps, but she faltered. She didn't have the athletic grace to be a natural dancer, and she was too inexperienced to comfortably wing it.

Crap, she thought, this doesn't bode well for my first sexual experience with a woman if I can't even dance decently! Or maybe it meant she wasn't really gay, because it seemed like every gay person in the world knew how to dance, or at least the ones who braved the clubs. *Shit. I shouldn't have come*, she told herself morosely. *I don't fit in here.*

"You're doing awesome," Julia shouted at her, somehow reading her mind. She reached for Corey's hand and spun her around.

Miraculously, Corey didn't trip or fall flat on her face. "Thanks, but you're being too kind."

"Nonsense." Julia took both her hands this time, placing them gently around her waist. Her flat, tight waist, Corey noted with pleasure. "Close your eyes and feel the way I move, and then try to move to the same rhythm."

Oh, God, is this some kind of torture test? A lesbian litmus test? Would someone jump out and tell her she was being punked? All right, calm down, she told herself as she tried to ignore the sweat rolling down her sides. *Feel the music and the way she moves, just like she told you.*

She found obedience difficult because the sway of Julia's hips reminded her of regions of her own body that hadn't been visited in a while. Regions she wanted—*needed*—to be visited by a woman. Not any woman, but a woman she clicked with, a woman who was gorgeous, smart, warm and funny too. A woman she could be herself with. A woman like Julia.

"Are you feeling it?" Julia asked her.

Oh, yeah, she felt it all right. She felt turned on, actually, her body heating up like a Roman candle, and she was too young for hot flashes. "Um, yeah," she answered stupidly. "I'm feeling...a lot, as a matter of fact!"

Julia smiled, moved even closer, and slid Corey's hands a little further down her hips, moving sexily, almost sashaying, giving her the full effect of those hips sensuously swaying.

Corey licked dry lips, feeling her own hips respond to the rhythm Julia set. They were dancing close, moving together to the music. It was almost like sex. In fact, they weren't the only people out here practically having fully clothed sex.

She prayed there were no cell phone cameras trained on her right now. Oh, hell, even if there were, this moment was worth it. She'd never a touched a woman this intimately before, had never been held this closely before by a woman, nor moved together with a woman like it was a publicly acceptable form of foreplay. An image of Alex floated in her mind, images of Alex and Julia moving like this, doing things to each other. *Shit*! She did not want to think about Julia and Alex in that context, because it felt sort of creepy or somehow incestuous.

"I'm sorry," Corey said. She pulled away, the unwelcome visions like a splash of cold water on her libido.

"A little overkill for your first time?"

"Something like that."

"Come on." Julia led her off the floor and back toward their table. "Let's get you another drink so you can cool off."

Thankfully, Julia didn't ask her a million questions about how she was feeling, or about why this was her first visit to a gay club, or even if she felt she was really gay or just experimenting. She didn't need an interrogation right now.

"Sometimes," Julia said over their second drink, "you have to take a step back before you can go forward."

True, Corey thought, but only sometimes. Jane never seemed to lose ground every time she gained it. Jane dove into whatever she did, fully committed, fully determined, and always came up a winner. Not her, though. She had to struggle to find the things that mattered to her, like wasting a couple of extra years in college before concentrating on business studies, eventually earning her PhD and teaching in London at the London School of Economics. Even her relationship with Jason, her lover for five years, always had some degree of difficulty.

Teaching colleagues at first, it took a year of dancing around their mutual attraction before they began dating. There were constant issues—his ex-wife, his fourteen-year-old daughter, their twelve year age difference, their dueling careers. Nothing was ever simple for her. Maybe it was the same for Julia.

"Do you think," Corey said, "what you said is true in general, or just true for you?"

"It's definitely true for me," Julia replied. "If there's a speed bump or a sudden detour in the road, I seem to find it, but I always tell myself that as long as I *am* moving forward, it's okay. Sometimes taking the scenic route is better anyway."

Corey laughed. "Better as in eating no-fat yogurt versus ice cream?"

"Or a virgin drink versus the real thing?" Julia smiled mischievously. "All right, point taken. It's not *always* better, or maybe it's only better in a certain way. Sometimes life just is what it is. I've learned to roll with it when I need to, but I'm still learning how to stop wasting time over regrets…over things I can't change."

Corey wondered if Julia meant Alex. "True, but if we're stuck too much in the ruts of the past, how can we possibly move forward?"

"Okay, is that a trivia test? Are you going to tell me who said that?"

"I think I made it up."

"Hmm, we're quite the philosophers after a couple of drinks, aren't we?"

Corey laughed. "I think I'll take philosophizing over dancing."

"Why? You were doing well on the dance floor. Experience is the trick, that's all."

"People say experience makes up for a lot of deficiencies, but they only say stuff like that when they're trying to make you feel better."

Julia winked at her, slowly and provocatively. This time there was, no mistaking the innuendo. "I happen to believe experience *is* the best teacher."

They were definitely in flirting territory now, and with it came a new round of heat to Corey's cheeks and a flutter in her chest. Something felt so right, so familiar, sitting here with Julia talking, flirting and acting like the rest of the world had fallen away from them.

"Oh, there's a song I haven't heard in a couple of years," Julia said, tilting her head toward the ceiling. "What do you say we give this one a whirl?"

A slow song. Corey guessed she must have looked extremely doubtful because Julia went out of her way to defend the idea, saying, "It doesn't take any special skill, you just need to hold onto me and I'll lead. I promise."

"With reassurance like that, how can I say no?" Be brave, she told herself. *You can do this.*

She and Julia melted into the other couples on the dance floor, quickly nestling together like they'd done this before. It was true, she only had to relax and let Julia take over.

Julia held her close, expertly moving her around the floor in slow, sure steps. Corey marveled at how well they fit, but more than that, she marveled at how this woman who looked like a magazine model, not a reporter, could hold her, move with her, listen to her, and look at her the way she did. Maybe, for once, something in her life didn't have to be complicated. Maybe it could be as easy as moving across this floor together, molded perfectly together as one.

Corey looked at Julia, surprised to find her mouth a mere inch away, and her eyes, those blue-gray eyes, brimming with undisguised attraction. Her fears and doubts slipped away, and suddenly the idea of kissing another woman felt exactly right. When they began to kiss, she fell into it without any reservations, deciding to simply allow herself to *feel* for a change. Julia's lips, soft and pliant against her own, shot a bolt of heat straight through her center. The kiss obliterated all sense of time, their surroundings, everything. It was magical, and everything she'd ever hoped or dreamed it would be. She didn't want it to end, but when it did, she felt the absence of Julia's lips immediately. The starkness was like a sudden gust of icy wind on a warm day.

"Thank you," Julia murmured into her ear. "I've wanted to do that since the first time I met you on Air Force Two."

"You did?" Corey asked in surprise.

"Uh-huh," Julia said, smiling against her cheek.

Okay, so there it was, out in the open. Julia was attracted to her. Now what? Corey wondered. What did the lesbian manual have to say about *that*? Were they supposed to go out on an official date now? Have sex? Panic bubbled up inside her. She had absolutely no idea what she was supposed to do with this... this kiss, this attraction. She knew too many logical reasons why she should forget about it, except she knew she could not forget. Ever. Keep it simple, she told herself. No complications. No regrets.

"It's okay," Julia whispered. "It's only a kiss."

Only a kiss to *her* maybe, but to Corey, the door to a whole new, frightening world had just been flung wide open. She knew with certainty her life would never be the same again.

CHAPTER EIGHT

Of course it wasn't just a kiss, not to Julia. She didn't go around kissing women at the drop of a hat, although her little display on the dance floor last night might have signaled the exact opposite. For her, the kiss with Corey had been a scorching epiphany, a reminder that she was a red-blooded lesbian with carnal desires. Desires for someone she was very attracted to and wanted to get to know better. She had not expected things to develop so quickly between them—to go from an unplanned drink together at the Hay-Adams and passing each other at work to kissing at the club.

There was no mistaking that Corey had been into that kiss too. With every fiber of her body, it felt like, but minutes later she'd grown distant and uptight about it, tried to cover it with idle conversation and a couple of jokes, but Julia knew Corey was confused, maybe even embarrassed. Most likely it was very out of character for Corey to kiss a friendly acquaintance like that, and now as Julia tossed and turned in bed, she wished they'd arranged to have breakfast this morning so she could explain that it wasn't exactly habit for her either to act on her attraction so quickly and so demonstrably.

She thought back to the awkward cab ride they'd shared to The Plaza, how they'd talked safely about Jane's speech, which was sure to send the campaign into a new and tempestuous stage. Corey seemed noncommittal about the whole thing. Julia understood. As an outsider and a reporter, there was no way Corey would give her the inside scoop.

"You ever get the sense sometimes," she had said to Corey in the cab, "I don't know, like something's coming?" And something *was* coming, either in her personal life or maybe in this campaign, but she felt as though a shadow loomed large. A threatening shadow, or something harmless but definitely overwhelming. She couldn't be sure which it was.

Staring at her reflection in the cab's window, Corey had waited a moment before she replied, "Something's always coming. There's always another wave in the ocean. They keep on coming."

Julia thought about the remark while she waited for sleep to come. She could handle waves, as long as they didn't become a tsunami.

Her biggest wave had come when she'd abruptly pulled up stakes with Alex, quit her job with the state police, and started over in journalism school. She'd survived, but she certainly didn't want to implode her life again so dramatically. She was thrilled with her career choice, and had even learned to be content being alone, though it'd be nice to share time with someone occasionally. And a bed. Sex one of these decades would be nice, she thought with a smile.

Considering Corey as a potential sex partner, enticing as it was, gave her pause. Corey was definitely inexperienced with women. Was she wise trying to pursue anything with Corey, who was straight, or bi-curious, or at the very least, a novice dyke?

Corey being Alex's sister-in-law raised another big red flag—a red flag about the size of a Broadway stage curtain.

Yes, leaving it at a kiss was exactly the right thing to do, she decided. *Wasn't it?* Yet she could not forget Corey. She could not forget the way their bodies had felt together on the dance floor, nor could she forget the sizzling kiss that still made her breathless and her knees weak. She could not forget that she was attracted to Corey in all the ways that mattered.

Sleep finally came, and with it, a dream of making out with Corey in the back row of the White House movie theater, while Jane and Alex sat two rows ahead. The dream woke her with a start, creeping her out a little. She had no intention of ever double-dating with Alex and Jane, or of making out with Corey in their presence. Eww, she thought, and tried to get back to sleep.

In the morning, she made the shower cold to drive lascivious thoughts of Corey from her mind as well as the images of last night's dream. She didn't want to begin to analyze what it meant to have Jane and Alex practically in her and Corey's laps while they made out.

Julia scurried to the morning's press event, pulling her notebook and tape recorder from her bag. There was a definite buzz of anticipation among the reporters, a signal that Jane Kincaid's press conference would start any minute.

The venue, Grand Central Terminal, was impressive. She had never visited the iconic institution before. Actually, she'd only ever been to New York City once in her life—a high school trip—and her class had never made it to the grand old train station. The building's craftsmanship was remarkable, she thought, glancing around at the high dome-shaped ceilings, leaded glass, marble floors, and brass handrails everywhere. A lectern had been set up in front of the spectacular brass, four-faced clock in the center of the lobby, right below the massive American flag hanging starkly from the ceiling.

"I still can't figure out why they're having the press conference here," Julia whispered to her *Chicago Tribune* counterpart, Dane Williams. "After last night's speech, it should be in Greenwich Village."

"Yeah, in front of the Stonewall Inn." Dane shook his head. "That would make more sense, but my guess is that she'll try to distance herself from the speech."

"Why would she want to do that?"

"Because Collins probably had a stroke over it. You think he wants this campaign to become embroiled in gay rights? Shit, he's hardly better than Colby Harrison when it comes to that kind of thing."

Julia hadn't personally met President Collins, though she'd attended a couple of his press conferences. He struck her as cold and aloof in a calculating way. Someone you might approach to clinch an important business deal, but not someone you'd want to sit and have a drink with and discuss last night's Capitals or Wizards game. He certainly didn't come across as gay friendly. He'd kept his distance in the repeal of the military's Don't Ask Don't Tell policy, choosing to leave the matter up to the Department of Defense, the courts, the Congress and Senate—anyone but himself. If Dane was right, Collins wouldn't want Jane wading into the lavender waters either.

Jane's entourage entered, flanked by some of Collins's heavyweights, his deputy press secretary and his top campaign advisor. *Yup, Dane was right.* They'd definitely gotten to Jane, she thought. Carter, who stepped up to the podium, looked grim and disheartened. The mood of the room felt like a blanket had been thrown over a fire.

"Welcome, ladies and gentlemen of the press," Carter said solemnly. "Thank you for coming. Vice President Kincaid will speak shortly to make an important announcement, but first, the ground rules. There'll be no interviews with the vice president today, no scrumming, and absolutely no questions. After the press conference, you're all invited to take the train with us back to Washington." He gave the gathering a scouring look to drive home his point. "And there'll be no face time with the vice president on the train either."

The murmuring among the reporters grew to a roar of indignation. "What do you mean, 'no questions'?" someone yelled. "Don't you know it's an election year? You can't shut us out now!"

More vociferous complaints, more whining. Julia was as unhappy as the rest. After such a fiery speech last night, she believed it was only fair to quiz Jane about it today. Colby Harrison had not responded to her speech, but his silence wouldn't last. Jane had undoubtedly gotten his attention, and gay rights would now become a contentious campaign issue. It burned Julia that Jane could make such provocative statements and then take no questions, but what else could the reporters do? If they wanted to keep the story alive today, they were at the whim of Jane, Collins and their staffers to make some kind of comment.

Julia caught a glimpse of Corey standing behind Jane. Corey didn't look very happy, and she was doing everything she could to avoid looking at Julia. Her heart sagged in disappointment. Maybe Corey was still spooked by that flaming kiss on the dance floor, perhaps to the point of permanently closing the door on the possibility of more of those kisses. Great, Julia thought. *What a banner fucking day this is going to be. No story to write on the biggest speech of the campaign, and now I've lost my only friend in this town.*

"Ladies and gentlemen," Carter announced, "the vice president of the United States."

Clutching a single piece of paper, Jane strode purposefully to the lectern. She looked a little tired, but not beaten or in any way remorseful. Julia caught a glint in Jane's eyes as she greeted the reporters, as if to signal that she was anxious to revisit last night's speech when the time was right, but not today.

They were gathered here, Jane told them, because of a very important announcement, one that would benefit the environment, the economy and travelers all over the country. Over the next several minutes, Jane unveiled the administration's plan to spend fifty billion dollars over the next six years on high-speed rail travel. Corridors along the West Coast, the East Coast, and the Midwest were the target areas. States would be encouraged to match the subsidies. Companies building high-speed trains would be given an immediate and significant tax break, she said.

"Progress," Jane noted, "doesn't come cheap. Neither does investing in the environment. Commitment to progress takes vision and dedication, but it's an investment in our future and in the future of generations to come."

With clogged highways, overburdened airports, and the continued rise in fuel prices, economic growth was suffering, Jane told them. High-speed rail travel would create jobs, foster economic growth and alleviate pollution, she promised.

"Smart," Dane Williams whispered.

"What?"

"Making this big announcement after last night's speech. Shifting the focus to the economy and the environment, and not giving Colby Harrison a chance to attack them on gay rights."

Julia shook her head. *Politics.* More fascinating to her than any other game on the planet. She was still a political neophyte, but she was learning quickly.

After Jane's announcement, the reporters continued to grumble about being denied the chance—the *right*, damn it—to lob questions at the vice president and her staff. Julia sympathized. Reporters hated being told what to do, or in this case, what they couldn't do, because it smacked too much of censorship and manipulation. If you were going to make a provocative speech, you had to have the guts to answer to it later. She was pretty sure that Jane would have been up for the challenge if only Collins's people hadn't gotten to her.

Carter told them to be ready to depart for Washington in twenty minutes, his tone making it clear he was in no mood to compromise. He looked no happier about the situation than she and the others felt.

Julia had not been on a train in so long, she'd almost forgotten what it was like. Not long after boarding, she found herself enjoying the rhythmic clanging and the slight swaying as Manhattan disappeared from view.

She remembered seeing television footage a long time ago of Bobby Kennedy's casket making this same rail trip from New York City to Washington, D.C. She remembered the images of Boy Scouts saluting, forlorn people holding *We Love You Bobby* signs, and other people weeping, their hats over their hearts.

She wasn't an ideologue or a political junkie by nature, but she'd started to enjoy the whirlwind of politics, the excitement, the drama, the unpredictability and the emotion. Much like her police career, and then journalism, each day on the campaign trail was different and brought a new set of challenges. She understood why people said politics got into the blood. It was addictive.

A tap on her shoulder signaled the arrival of Corey's executive secretary, an attractive woman in her fifties with thick silver hair and the bluest eyes Julia had ever seen.

The secretary spoke quietly with a deep southern accent. "Corey Kincaid was wondering if you'd mind joining her in the dining car."

The other reporters looked at Julia with envy as she got up and followed the woman, her thumping heart surely as loud as the grinding train wheels below. She didn't know if the invitation was an official request or something more personal, but she brought her work satchel just in case.

The secretary retreated with a smile as Julia joined Corey at a table. They had the dining car to themselves, as it was off-limits to the press without an official escort.

Julia smiled in an uncertain attempt to cover her nervousness. "Okay, you have to give me something good since you made a point of inviting me back here in front of everyone."

Corey chuckled, far more relaxed than she'd seemed earlier at Grand Central Terminal. "And if I don't?"

"Hmm…in that case, I'll have to make up something juicy."

"All right, how's this, then: Colby Harrison secretly has a gay lover."

Julia's mouth dropped open. "Oh, my God, seriously?"

Corey laughed, mischief flaring in her dark eyes. "No, or if he does, I don't know a thing about it."

Damn, Julia thought. She had to stop being so naïve and taking everything at face value. "I might have to get you for that."

"True, and I would deserve it," Corey said. "Sorry, I couldn't resist. Would you like a coffee, or a Coke or something?"

A waiter in a jacket as white as the tablecloth popped up, seemingly out of thin air.

"Sure, I'll have a coffee," Julia answered.

"Make that two," Corey told the waiter, and then nodded at Julia. "Late night last night, hmm?"

"Something like that." Julia remembered that as she and Corey had exited the cab together, she'd tried to think of a way she could get her back to her room. But Corey had been aloof in the cab, as though she couldn't get away fast enough. As uncomfortable as it was talking about last night, Corey was right to bring it up.

"About that," Corey said haltingly.

"I think I understand."

"I'm not sure that you do, Julia, but I think I need you to understand. It's why I asked you to join me here."

"Okay." *Please don't tell me you don't find me attractive, or that you'd had too much to drink, or...* All the possible excuses thundered through Julia's mind. She hated the kind of conversation where rejection was cloaked as something else. She knew the real message here: there was no possibility for them, which sucked because she really liked Corey.

The waiter reappeared, perfectly balancing a tray containing sugar, cream and two small ceramic cups. He set the tray down without so much as a single clink and disappeared as quietly.

"You know what?" Julia interjected, deciding to call a halt to the uncomfortable situation. Why put the words out there anyway when she already knew what they were? "I get it, okay? We were having a good time and we got a little carried away, that's all. We're both professionals, both trying to do our jobs here. Given the circumstances, there's no possibility of anything other than a friendly working relationship. I agree it's totally for the best." Pleased with herself, she took a quick sip of coffee, promptly burning her tongue. "Ouch! Damn."

Corey's smile erupted into a chuckle. "Sorry. That was quite the little speech you just gave."

If nothing else these last few years, Julia had learned to laugh at herself. Starting her life over at the age of thirty had taught her that handy little skill. She gave what she hoped was a self-deprecating smile. "It was, wasn't it?"

"Yes, it was, and totally not what I was going to say."

"It wasn't?"

"Nope, not even close."

"Okay," Julia replied. Perhaps her reporter's instinct was in serious decline because she didn't have a clue what Corey was thinking. First rule of journalism—*never assume anything*. She didn't know the second rule, but it was probably *keep your mouth shut and listen*.

"The thing is," Corey continued, nervously tapping her cup with a fingernail, "I like you, Julia. A lot. I don't really have many friends here. It's kind of an insular world I move in, but I really like hanging out with you."

Julia had been down this road before, attracted to someone who only wanted to be friends. It usually started out okay, but ultimately ended in heartbreak and a broken friendship.

"I like hanging out with you too," she said. "I don't really have friends in town either." She clutched her cup in both hands, fortifying herself. "But I'm attracted to you, Corey, and I don't want to just be your friend. I think it's only fair that you know exactly where I stand."

"Yes, and I want you to know where I stand too. I'm attracted to you as well, and…"

Damn it, why is there always a second part to that kind of declaration? "Yes?"

"Sorry," Corey whispered under her breath. "I mean…um, I want to ask you if you'd go with me to the White House Correspondents' dinner next week."

Julia's stomach flip-flopped. Was Corey asking her out? "You mean, as your date?"

"Yes, as my date." Corey's hand trembled a little, her nervousness adorable.

Well, well. After all the mixed signals, Corey was actually asking her out. *Go figure.* It felt a little like jumping into a murky pool where she couldn't see the bottom, but so had coming to Washington and taking a new assignment. She could feel her way through this situation, just like everything else she'd done.

"So that means you're okay about the kiss last night? Because it seemed like—"

"Yes. I'm okay about the kiss." Corey squarely held her gaze. "I admit I wasn't quite sure how to handle it at first. I'm sorry. I acted rather poorly."

"It's okay. You don't have to apologize."

"The thing is, it was all kind of new to me."

"Kissing a woman in public?" *Like I hadn't already figured that one out!*

Corey smiled. "Kissing a woman, period. It sort of threw me a little, I guess."

Julia grinned back, emboldened. "And I'm guessing you sort of liked it."

Sheepish but still smiling, Corey said, "Yes, which is why I'm asking you to go to the press dinner with me."

"In that case, yes."

Corey's smile widened, but failed to mask her concern. "Great. But Julia?"

"Yes?"

"Can we take things slow?"

Yes, slow was good. In theory, anyway. "Of course we can."

"Good," Corey answered, looking somewhat relieved.

Julia reached across the table and squeezed her hand lightly. "It will be fine. We'll make it fine, okay?"

"I'd like that."

"Me too. And now I think you'd better give me some kind of scoop so that my colleagues think I'm actually working."

Corey laughed, and thought for a moment. "All right, how's this? The lineup for the correspondents' dinner won't be announced for a couple more days, but I can tell you that Ellen is going to emcee."

"What? How did Collins ever go for a lesbian comedienne?"

"He didn't. He left all the arrangements up to Jane." Corey winked. "He's going to freak when he finds out, especially after Jane's Central Park speech."

Jane certainly had balls, Julia thought, beginning to admire her moxie. Under different circumstances, she'd like to get to know the vice president better, but that wasn't likely to happen. Julia's history with Alex would forever ensure some distance and a healthy amount of tension between them. At least Corey wasn't holding her past against her. For that, she was thankful.

"If I were the president," Julia joked, "I certainly wouldn't want to make enemies of the Kincaid sisters."

"I better not answer that or I might put my foot into it."

Corey could probably say a lot right now if she wanted, but Julia wouldn't press, careful not to take advantage. "I'd better get back," she said, wishing she could stay, drink more coffee, and share a few more laughs. It was so easy with Corey, so natural, but at the same time, she'd need to keep up the façade that they merely shared a professional relationship.

Maintaining the façade would be tougher for Corey, Julia realized as she made her way back to the press car. She didn't envy Corey breaking the news about their press dinner date to Jane and Alex. Hopefully Corey wouldn't cancel because she already looked forward to the date. She wanted to get to know Corey better. More than that, she wanted to kiss her again, only in private this time and for much longer. Like hours, perhaps. She fantasized about those kisses as the train wound its way south to D.C. By the time she disembarked, her mind was still in a pleasant fog. The ringing of her cell phone abruptly interrupted her thoughts.

"Is this Julia Landen?" The voice at the other end—a man's— was a deep monotone she couldn't identify.

"Yes. Who's this?"

"You don't need to know that. I have some important information for you. See that large blue recycling box about thirty yards to your right?"

Julia looked around sharply. The station was full of lunchtime crowds, trains arriving and departing, people walking steadily and purposefully past her, but she easily spotted the large blue box. Christ, someone had to be following her to know where she was, watching her right now. She scanned the crowds for men talking on their cell phones but there were too many to count, and she'd never be able to spot the people with tiny Bluetooth receivers clipped to their ears. *Shit.* She began to sweat, unsure what to do. Her racing heart propelled her to the blue box. She decided with more optimism than prudence that the situation wasn't dangerous. She was in public, surrounded by tons of people. She'd make sure she wasn't followed during the cab ride home.

"Okay," she said breathlessly into her phone. "I see it."

"There's an envelope for you underneath it. I trust you will do right by the American people." The line went dead. She pushed a button for the caller ID, but it came up unknown.

Okay, she told herself, *take a deep breath*. It was only a little information, an anonymous tip. Her imagination sparked as she thought of the old movie, *All the President's Men*. Perhaps this was her Deep Throat, her shot at something big, though it couldn't possibly be as dramatic as Watergate. Watergate tips didn't happen to people like her. On the other hand, maybe somebody was screwing with her, secretly filming her as she swallowed the joke hook, line and sinker. A practical joke by some of her colleagues, perhaps?

Julia bent down, tilted the box, and reached underneath to retrieve a plain brown envelope. Though tempted to rip it open right away, she clutched it to her chest, looked around one last time, and made for the nearest exit.

She'd know soon enough whether this was a joke, or something she should be worried about. She wasn't sure which to hope for.

CHAPTER NINE

The Oval Office never failed to impress Jane. The room's gravitas whispered in every footstep she took on the plush Democrat blue carpet, and stared out at her from tall oil portraits of Franklin Roosevelt and John F. Kennedy. She felt small in the sanctum of greatness.

President Collins liked to meet with her here instead of his working office next door. She guessed it was because he liked to wield the more ceremonial Oval Office as a symbol of his power and authority over her, to always remind her that he was top dog and she worked for him. He was right, but she preferred to think of herself as working for the American people first and the administration second. Collins could take his little show of authority and stick it up his butt, as far as she was concerned.

He sat ramrod straight behind his colonial-style desk, a cup of steaming coffee in front of him. He didn't offer her any, instead silently motioning for her to sit in one of the two chairs opposite him. They could sit on the sofas by the fireplace, which would be more casual, but no. He liked to keep things formal. *How ridiculous. Is the man that petty and insecure?* She would *never* do things this way if she were president. She would strive for an open door policy, to keep the mood light as often as she could, and treat people like people and not as objects.

"That was quite the maneuver you pulled in New York the other day," Collins said. "I'd forgotten how much of a wolf in sheep's clothing you can be." His frown became a scowl. "Especially when there's an election."

"Excuse me?"

"You pull it off very well. In fact, you might even want to try Hollywood some day."

He was really beginning to piss her off with this insulting nonsense, but she would not be goaded into a fight. Collins liked to poke people until their tempers flared. He liked to get the upper hand on their emotions and make them look foolish. Well, she wouldn't let him do that to her.

"I assume," she said coolly, "you're referring to my Central Park speech."

"You really stuck it to old Colby Harrison, didn't you?"

"You asked me to go after him every chance I could. That was as good a chance as any."

"Ah, yes. But you see, going after him on gay rights was also your way of sticking a thorn in my ass too."

"I'm sorry? I don't follow." She'd make him spell out his objections to her speech. She thought she'd done a brilliant job.

Collins sipped his coffee, his expression still somber. "What I'm saying, Jane, is not only are you trying to fuck him, but you're trying to fuck me too, pulling a stunt like that."

As tempting as it was sometimes, Jane never lowered herself to match his crudeness. She rarely swore, even less so around him. She didn't want anyone thinking she was his clone. She had more class in her pinkie finger than he possessed in his entire body.

"I'm not trying to screw anyone, Mr. President, other than

my lovely partner, Alex." Jane smiled inwardly. She loved reminding him she was a lesbian.

Collins made a face as though his coffee had gone toxic. Jane found it terribly rewarding. "You know exactly what I'm talking about," he thundered. "You had to go and attack Harrison on the *one* goddamned issue that you *know* could break my balls in this election."

"Mr. President, with all due respect—"

"No. I don't want to hear it. We already have the gay vote because of you, which means there is absolutely nothing to gain from this bullshit. We will lose the moderate voters and whatever Republican voters who might be vulnerable. You already know all of this, for Christ's sake! We've talked about staying quiet on gay issues in strategy session after strategy session until we're blue in the face."

Correction: Collins and his staff talked about it until they were blue in the face. Jane perfectly understood his reasons— his excuses—for burying gay issues. The problem was, she didn't agree with him. In her opinion, gay voters and sympathizers would quickly lose affinity for them if they took them for granted and never lifted a finger to advance gay rights. The fact that she herself was gay would only carry them so far. On the flip side, the moderate voters and conservative voters would not be fooled by avoidance tactics. While she didn't agree with the win-at-all-costs attitude of Forrest Mitchell and his cohorts, she thought it best to face gay issues head-on, to make gradual but steady advances. Shirking their responsibilities to pander to the right-wing bigots was a lose-lose situation.

She held the president's gaze. "I'm afraid we disagree on our basic philosophy with respect to gay rights. This is going to become an election issue whether we like it or not. It's better to be ahead of it than behind it."

He set his cup down hard enough to send coffee sloshing over the rim. "I don't care whether you agree with me or disagree, and I don't care about your predictions! Don't you get it?"

"Get what?" she asked, playing dumb.

Collins's face reddened, the vein in his neck throbbing. "I'm the goddamn president and you're not! I'm the one running this show. The people voted for *me*! And that means *I* decide our platform. I decide our policy. I set the agenda. And I don't want you being some freak show on the side!"

Collins had been blunt, crude and insulting before, but never like this. He was trying to diminish her value and her contributions to the administration and the ticket. He was trying to diminish *her*. Who the hell was he to call her a freak show? She was not going to sit here and silently accept his vitriol.

Seething inside, she kept her voice as neutral as possible. "We both know what I bring to this partnership. I am who I am, and I am not going to change for you or anyone else. I have been loyal to you and this administration. I will continue to be loyal, but do *not* ask me to stop speaking to and acting on my basic beliefs and values."

Collins stood abruptly. "If I could throw you off this ticket, I would," he spat, his anger nearly choking him.

But you can't, Jane thought with satisfaction as she stood too. She and Collins were equal in height, and his body language did not intimidate her in the least. "We both know that's not going to happen," she said. "We know what it's going to take to get re-elected. I will work hard to make sure that happens, but that's all I'm promising."

"If you make me look like a fool, you'll regret it."

"The only person I plan on making look like a fool is Colby Harrison."

Christ, Jane thought, how am I going to get through this election? *How am I going to get through another four years with this man?*

She'd hitched her wagon to Collins four years ago because he could win the presidency and she couldn't, at least not then. Serving as his vice president was the most powerful and highest profile way she could put her immediate fingerprint on public policy. She wanted to improve health care, education and the country in general. She wanted to help make things better for women, children and other minorities. Over the years, she'd learned how to play the game, even if it meant stomaching some unpleasant realities. She'd had to bide her time, playing party politics until it was *her* turn. She understood that, but knowing it and doing it sometimes proved excruciatingly difficult.

Standing face-to-face with Dennis Collins, the desk between them the only thing keeping them from slugging it out, Jane gritted her teeth and vowed to herself that she would do what she could to keep their growing animosity from the public eye. Privately, she'd pretty much had it with this guy. If *she* could dump *him* from the ticket, she would do it in the blink of an eye.

***

For two days, Corey hounded Jane to take a walk together in the Rose Garden.

Jane loved strolling through the Rose Garden and the South Lawn, but rarely had time to indulge. Last month, in perfect spring weather under the garden's fragrant cherry blossoms, she'd hosted an afternoon tea for a hundred honored volunteers. She'd not had the time to revisit the garden since.

Corey had not indicated the reason she wanted to walk outside with her, but Jane knew it must be important and it must be personal if her sister wanted to talk to her away from interlopers and eavesdroppers. Even when they were kids, she recalled, Corey liked to walk out her problems. When she'd been thirteen years old and fretting over some boy, she'd walked so far one evening that she had to call from a payphone for a ride home.

Jane finally relented after a lunch meeting with the Senate minority leader. She didn't have a lot of time—another meeting on the docket in about forty minutes—but she would give her sister as much of her time as she could. Corey liked to take it slow, aggravatingly slow sometimes, when it came to expressing her feelings.

As they strolled through the garden, Jane enjoyed the array of multicolored tulips in full bloom, the mass of grape hyacinths, and the flowering crabapples, their falling blossoms like perfumed snowflakes.

The garden would be a beautiful place for a wedding, Jane thought with a thrill. There'd been a wedding here for Richard Nixon's daughter decades ago. It would be perfect for her and Alex's wedding. Of course, as long as Dennis Collins was president, he'd never allow such a thing. The thought burned inside her chest. *That homophobic bastard*. What was he so afraid of? So threatened by? His fear only weakened him and made him vulnerable to attacks by their opponents. Yes, more than anything else, the president's fear about gay rights was going to hurt their re-election bid, but she could not get him to understand that. Her confrontation with him yesterday still rattled her.

"How about we sit here?" Corey asked, pointing to a white bench under a pergola woven with climbing rose bushes.

"Sure," Jane replied.

They sat down, thankfully protected from the sun, which was growing hotter as the day wore on. Jane couldn't remember a warmer April in D.C. The spring storms across the country were harsher than normal too.

"So," Corey said. "The White House Correspondents' dinner this weekend—"

"What? Don't tell me Ellen has pulled out?"

"No, no, nothing like that." Corey sighed quietly. "It's personal."

"All right. Is everything okay? Are *you* okay?" It occurred to Jane that she hadn't asked Corey lately how she was doing. They hadn't talked about anything personal since right after Christmas when Corey admitted that she was curious about women and might even be gay.

"Yes. Everything's okay and I'm fine."

Her sister's tone and her clenched hands made Jane think everything was not okay. "Why do I get the distinct feeling you're not telling me everything?"

"Probably because there is something I need to tell you, and I think it might not go over so well."

Jane laughed. She didn't mean to, and regretted it as soon as she saw Corey's worried frown. "I'm sorry, but whatever you need to tell me can't be as bad as what Jenkins told me a few minutes ago." Harvey Jenkins, the Senate minority leader, had broken the news to her that his party would do all it could to stall a bill giving tax relief to people who had to take time off work to care for terminally ill family members. He said it would cost businesses too much money. Yeah, she thought in disgust, more like cost the CEOs some of their outlandish bonuses.

Corey looked like the sky was about to cave in. "I'm not so sure about that."

All this drama queen stuff was so unlike Corey. If anything, she tended to understate things or keep things to herself. "Corey, what's going on?"

"The dinner. I want to bring a date."

"Great! Man or woman?"

"Woman."

Jane's heart danced. So her little sister was going to take her first tentative steps as a lesbian. She remembered coming out as a thrilling time, but a little scary too. Worrying about what other people might think, worrying how the whole dating thing was supposed to work. And then sex! Well, not that sex with Alex had caused her great angst. She'd wanted Alex so badly that the worry paled in comparison to her desire. She'd put her career on the line to love Alex, and the gamble had more than paid off because she'd never been happier in her life.

She took Corey's hand, giving it a reassuring pat. "I'm here for you, honey. And so is Alex. You know that, right?"

"Yes," Corey said. "At least I hope so."

"No, it's a given. You don't ever have to question that."

"Jane." Corey's glance darted about nervously. She took a deep breath and blurted out, "I'm bringing Julia Landen as my date."

If Jane thought this day couldn't get any worse—this whole week in fact—it just had. Exasperated, she dropped Corey's hand. "Seriously?"

"Yes, of course I'm serious."

"Why? I mean, why *her*?" She hadn't noticed anything going on between the two of them. Of course, some days a volcano could erupt in her office and she wouldn't notice. But Corey and Julia…she definitely would have noticed *that*.

Corey stiffened, looking much more resolved now and much less worried about Jane's reaction. She seemed to be growing braver by the second. "I'm attracted to her. I'd like to get to know her. Isn't that the usual reason two people date?"

"Yes, of course, but she's…she's Alex's ex!" Jane felt stupid for stating the obvious. *Goddamn it! How could she want to date that woman? The same woman who'd been such a shit to Alex?*

"I know, but—"

"No, I'm not sure that you do. This isn't some reality show or some stupid dating game. If you want to date a woman, there are plenty of good catches out there. I mean, look at Nell Andrews, the congresswoman from Illinois. She's a hottie! Or how about Shelly Constantine on the Federal Reserve Board, or...I don't know, there are tons of women I could easily hook you up with."

God! Jane thought. This was a problem she could solve with a little more time and cooperation from Corey, who didn't need to start dating the first lesbian—Julia Landen of all people—who'd given her the time of day, and who looked good in heels and a tight sweater. Yes, she'd certainly noticed how sexy Julia was, but so what?

Corey stood her ground. "I don't want to date anyone else. I like her, and I'm attracted to her. And I think she likes me too."

Damn it. Corey was being selfish, clearly not considering how she and Alex might feel about the situation, that it might be uncomfortable or even painful for them. "So I'm supposed to, what? Start inviting her to family dinners? Wouldn't that be cozy."

"Jane, I'm sorry. I know this hurts you, which is why I wanted to talk to you about it in private."

"Okay, great, you've done your duty and told me. Now you can date her with a free conscience." Jane was about to rise when Corey firmly clasped her wrist and pulled her back down.

"I'm not doing this to hurt you or Alex, okay?" Corey said. "Will you please try to understand? And give me some time to see if there's anything worth exploring with Julia?"

"But why *her*?"

Corey shrugged lightly, smiling like a love-struck teenager. "She's a beautiful woman. And she's smart and fun. I feel more alive when I'm with her than I have for a long time."

Jane was angry, her characteristic cool demeanor long ago shattered by Corey's unsettling news. "Look, if you want sex with a woman, fine, go have it. Just not with her!"

Corey's shoulders slumped but her voice remained defiant. "It's not just sex. It's about much more than that. It's about figuring out who I am and who I want to be with, and right now it feels like I want to be with her."

"You barely know her, Corey."

"I know that, but that's exactly the point. I want to get to know her better. Believe me, I wish she wasn't Alex's ex, either. But she is."

"That's exactly my point. She *is* Alex's ex, and that is a big deal to me."

"I know, and that part has given me some hesitation. I don't want anyone to be uncomfortable, but at the same time, I can't pick and choose my dates based on your prior approval. I'm sorry, but I'm going with my heart on this one."

Corey had a good point. Jane wasn't her parent, and Corey didn't need her permission. She understood how sensitive her sister could sometimes be about being the younger sibling. One way or another, Corey had spent most of her life in Jane's shadow, and it had to be difficult sometimes.

Jane remembered Corey coming home from her first day at junior high, crying because all the teachers could talk about was her older sister, the wonderful student. It'd been hard for Corey to carve out her own identity, and was the reason why she'd spent years in Britain, away from the Kincaid political dynasty.

"You're right," Jane said, softening her tone considerably. "You shouldn't have to run your dates past me first."

"Do you hate her, Jane?"

Hate was a strong word, too strong for how she felt about Julia, Jane decided. She wasn't really sure how she felt about the woman. She only knew her through Alex, so that obviously colored her perception. Her bias was strictly based on love and loyalty for Alex, and on wanting to protect Alex. And yes, if she were honest with herself, she felt a bit jealous of Julia.

"No, of course I don't hate her," she finally said. "But I'm biased against her because she hurt my wife. Treated her like crap, to tell you the truth."

"I understand Julia left Alex high and dry, and yes, it wasn't a very nice thing to do. But neither of us knows the details of their relationship, how they treated each other on a daily basis, whether they really were in love, if it was more one-sided or what. Jeez, they were only in their twenties when they were together. How many people in their twenties even know what the hell they're doing?"

"I don't know, but I know Alex loved her then, and I know when Alex loves someone, she loves them fiercely and gives everything she's got."

"No, she gives *you* everything she's got because you're the love of her life. You and I don't know the first thing about how Alex and Julia were together. I don't think we should judge their relationship."

Jane supposed Corey was right. Making comparisons wasn't fair. "You're one hell of a woman, baby sister."

"Huh?"

Corey knew exactly how to get to the point, how to find truth and balance, how to consider all sides of an argument. Her qualities were what had made Jane desperately want Corey to work for her. "Never mind. Look." Jane hesitated, gathering her thoughts. She wanted to be honest. "When I see Julia…" She sighed and shook her head unhappily. "I can't help picturing the two of them in bed together. I hate that, but I can't get the vision out of my head."

"I know. It's perfectly understandable that you'd be a little jealous."

Annoyed and defensive suddenly, Jane blurted, "Jealous? Who said I was jealous?" Julia Landen had nothing over her. She wasn't smarter, she wasn't funnier, she wasn't nearly as accomplished— but then, what woman was? Julia wasn't even better looking. *Well, okay, she* is *good looking. And she has nice tits. And a nice ass. And she's younger. But so what? I'm not exactly chopped liver.* "All right, I guess I am a little, but only a little."

Corey patted her hand and gazed out at the distant lawn, probably thinking about Julia's tits, and that nice ass, and what she might like to do with them. *Crap.* More Julia visuals she could do without.

"Are you nervous?" she asked.

Corey blinked. "Yes, a little."

"It's a big step, your first date with a woman. Just go slow, okay?"

"I will. Are you kidding? I don't even know what to do, for God's sake."

"Want to borrow my copy of *The Joy of Lesbian Sex*?"

Corey immediately perked up. "Can I?"

"No, at least not until the fifth or sixth date!"

Corey pouted. "Fine, be that way. They say experience is the best teacher anyway."

"Okay, look. I'm trying to get used to the idea of you dating Julia, but I'm definitely not ready to think about you sleeping with her."

Corey laughed. "Don't worry, I'm not there yet either."

"I'm very glad to hear that." Jane had to get to her next meeting. She rose in unison with Corey.

"Thank you for listening," Corey said softly. "And for understanding."

"Well, it isn't the best news I've heard in the world, but I love you, and I will always support you, Corey."

They hugged beneath the climbing roses. While she knew she could eventually get past the fact that her sister was dating Alex's ex, she wasn't so sure about Alex.

CHAPTER TEN

Julia's awkwardness as she walked the red carpet on Corey's arm extended only as far as her press colleagues, who watched from the sidelines with what was surely envy and bewilderment. She hadn't told anyone but Dane that she would be Corey Kincaid's date at the dinner. She hadn't wanted to put up with their questions, their criticisms, or their jokes that she would do anything to curry favor with the administration.

She avoided looking at them as she entered the Washington Hilton. Corey gave her a wink of reassurance and her spirits lifted immediately. While she didn't feel entirely comfortable being among Hollywood's and Washington's elite, it felt right to be by Corey's side.

In the limo, Corey had told her how ravishing she looked in the silver Halston dress that had cost her two weeks' salary, but she sure didn't feel like Corey's equal tonight. Looking delicious in a lavender Alexander McQueen dress that hugged her hips and thighs, her hair flowing softly over bare shoulders, and a string of fine pearls around her neck, Corey could have had her pick of women or men. She was absolutely stunning.

Julia noticed more than a few admiring glances sliding over Corey as they followed the other guests to the ballroom. She was thrilled to be Corey's date, but she felt pressure too. She didn't want to disappoint Corey because she knew this was her first date with a woman. There was additional pressure in the fact that she was also here to work.

Corey pointed to their table. They would sit with Steph Cameron, her husband, and Will Carter at the front of the room. Jane and Alex would sit with the president and his wife at the head table a few feet away, which came as a relief to Julia. She wasn't ready to sit with Alex and Jane and make small talk, and she feared they had taken the news about her coming as Corey's date badly. Jane was professional enough to be polite to her, but she would bet good money that Alex would throw some animosity in her path, probably enough to crash a bus.

A friendly waiter carrying a tray of champagne flutes stopped beside them. She and Corey each took a glass, clinking them together quietly.

Over the rim, Julia surreptitiously cast her gaze around the room, which was quickly filling with guests. The event was black tie, the men in tuxedoes, the women in gowns spilling their cleavage. Bling dripped from everyone like fat, glistening raindrops.

Corey soon began attracting a small throng of people who wanted to pay their respects and make small talk, perfect for Julia to make her escape. She apologized, promised she wouldn't be long, and slipped away. Work first, play later, she told herself.

Julia guessed most of her colleagues had begun drinking hours ago at any number of the predinner receptions. Journalists were famous for their boozing ways, particularly when the alcohol was complimentary. They should be well lubricated by now, and the more lubricated, the more talkative they would be—the perfect time for a little reconnaissance work.

She decided to ask a few of them discreetly if they knew any inside gossip about the president's personal life. She hadn't been able to get those damned photos out of her mind, the two grainy eight-by-tens stuffed in an envelope left under that recycle box at the train station for her. Two grainy photos showing President Collins hugging a slender but shapely woman, her face shadowed by a wide-brimmed, floral-printed hat.

Possibly the pictures were taken in Florida, Julia figured, because Collins was from the Miami area. He still had a home there as well as his main campaign office. While she'd never heard anything sinister or gossipy about Collins back in Miami, that didn't mean he wasn't successfully hiding something.

First, she set her sights on Sally Knoblauch, an old-time television correspondent, well past her prime, and about three hours past prime time. Sally's network had relegated her to doing soft one-on-ones for late evening specials every couple of months like her contemporary, Barbara Walters. Sally had been in D.C. longer than Lincoln's statue. If there was dirt to be had, surely she'd at least know where to find the shovels.

As soon as Julia mentioned the president, Sally gushed like a smitten teenager, prattling on about how good looking and how presidential he was, how dashing and how *nice* he seemed.

"Why," she said in her Texas drawl, "he just takes a girl's breath away, doesn't he, dear?"

No, Julia thought. *He doesn't.* There was something sleazy about Collins, and the woman he clutched in the photo sure didn't look like a daughter or a niece. In fact, he didn't have any kids. As for Sally, she was far too enamored with the man to be any help.

She moved on, sidling up to Marcus Gentry. Marcus had a reputation as a lush—he was halfway drunk now—but he also had a reputation for being competent and extremely knowledgeable. A straight shooter, he was a long-time television correspondent in Washington for Canada's top broadcaster, the CBC. If anyone knew what went on behind the scenes in this town, he did.

"Buy you a drink, sugar?" Marcus's eyes already looked slightly glassy.

"Sure, but didn't anyone here tell you the bar is free?"

"Damn, and here they've been charging me all this time." He laughed, a low boozy chuckle, and plucked another glass of champagne off a passing waiter's tray. He handed the glass to her with a chivalrous bow and a provocative wink.

"Oh, Marcus, I'm sure you know I'm here with Corey Kincaid." She didn't want him to think she was interested in him.

"Wanna tell me something I hadn't already figured out? You two set everyone's tongues wagging the minute you walked in together. Holy Mother of God, I'd be in heaven if you two—"

"Now, now," she scolded lightly. "Not into threesomes, Marcus, darling, so don't even go there."

"Don't know what you're missing," he teased.

She knew Marcus had been married three or four times, and had a reputation as a notorious womanizer. Everyone joked about it, as much to his face as behind his back.

Julia sipped her champagne slowly, deciding this would be her last drink until much later. She wanted to stay sharp. "Speaking of threesomes, I know I'm new in town, but I hear there's a lot of kinky stuff around. If you're into it, that is."

"You got that right, sister." Marcus leaned against the bar looking relaxed and confident, handsome in a slightly rebellious way. She could see why women found him attractive. "There's a whole underbelly of that kind of thing. Swingers clubs, live sex shows, you name it. Same stuff you get in every city, but here you never know who might be jerking off in the seat beside you."

Julia wasn't pleased with the image Marcus had just provided. As a cop, she'd seen plenty of stuff she didn't ever want to see again. She leaned closer to him, keeping her voice low. "Ever hear of Collins being into anything…you know…less than virtuous?"

Marcus laughed cynically. "The president prides himself on being clean as a whistle."

"Is he?" She looked unblinking at him.

He shrugged and sipped his martini, never dropping his gaze from hers. "I doubt it. Most of them aren't. I've heard rumblings, but nothing concrete. The official line, of course, is that he and his wife have been happily married for twenty-six years, so believe it or don't. Why are you asking?"

"No reason. Just curious."

Marcus narrowed his eyes, either in warning, or trying to check her truthfulness. "Well, don't be curious. I learned a long time ago it's best to stay away from that Pandora's box if you want to work in this town. Saw a lot of good journalists run out of here in the Clinton years because they got sidetracked by the sleaze. Hell, some of them are reporting on fall fairs and birthdays in places like Tulsa and Tuscon now." He shook his head forlornly. "No fucking thank you."

"Good point. I'll remember that."

"Hey, kid, just do your job. Don't go trying to be the next Pulitzer winner, okay? There's a lot of powerful people in this town. People who don't care if they ruin some pissant journalists like us. It ain't worth it."

"I know. You're right. I won't do anything stupid."

Half drunk or not, Marcus seemed smart enough to know her curiosity wasn't as innocent as she tried to pretend. He was probably right. Pursuing the lead might be dangerous for her.

The fine hairs on the back of her neck stood on end. Turning slowly, she saw Jake Ainsworth—Colby Harrison's assistant campaign manager—staring at her from across the room. Now *that* man gave her the creeps, knowing who she was before she'd introduced herself and acting so forward with her at the Hay-Adams bar. Something was up with him. Could *he* be her Deep Throat? Was he the one trying to get Collins into shit with those slimy photos, hoping she'd do some kind of exposé? The voice on the phone hadn't sounded like his, but he could have disguised it or had someone else do the dirty work.

She shifted her gaze, catching Corey's questioning eyes. Dinner was about to begin. "Later, Marcus. I enjoyed our little talk."

"Yeah. Hey, give my best to the Kincaid sisters. And tell big sis I'd love an exclusive one of these days."

***

Throughout dinner, Corey remained aware of the heat charging her skin every time her arm or thigh accidentally brushed against Julia's. There was electricity between them, she thought. More like a nuclear meltdown. She'd felt it before, but not like this, sitting in such close proximity for so long. Sure the attraction was too potent to be one-sided, she wondered if Julia felt the heat too. She hoped she did.

Before the speeches began, Ellen did a comedic routine that was razor sharp in its sarcasm toward the president. She was kinder to Jane however, teasing that *she* wanted to be her bodyguard, and pretending to challenge Alex to a duel at sunrise.

Afterward, Collins took his turn at the podium. He cut the media to shreds, calling out a couple of well-known journalists for some on-air flubs they'd made, and skewering another reporter for misspelling the Secretary of Defense's name in a front-page story. He didn't poke much fun at himself, bucking a long tradition at the annual press dinner, but he did level some caustic jokes at Jane, calling her Wonder Woman, her Jane to his Tarzan, and insinuating he was the brains and she merely the eye candy.

Corey saw Jane silently seething over Collins's words, even though she put up with it like a good sport. Her jaw was ropey, tight and immovable, her eyes cold and hard as granite. No one looked more formidable than Jane when she was angry.

She still remembered the verbal lambasting Jane had given an ice cream salesman for trying to cheat the two sisters out of a dollar when they were kids. Poor guy, he was practically crying when Jane was done with him. Just as well, she thought, that Jane wouldn't be taking a turn roasting the president, because she'd verbally murder him, and it'd be damn messy.

The formal part of the evening was coming to a close when Jane politely asked her, "You two coming to the after-party at the French ambassador's house?"

She'd kept her word tonight and treated Julia with respect, for which Corey was grateful. Alex had been distinctly cool, though not impolite. She looked at Julia for an answer to Jane's invitation. She didn't want to deprive her of the full experience of the glamour of a private after-party with international leaders and celebrities. But if it was up to her, she'd take Julia someplace far more private. She tried to sound impartial as she asked, "What do you say?"

"To be honest, I'm pretty much partied out for tonight," Julia replied. "Would you mind seeing me home, Corey?"

Corey's heart thumped miserably. She hoped Julia wasn't ready for the night to end, because she felt as though their date had hardly begun. "Sure thing. I'll alert my driver."

She and Julia said goodbye to Jane and Alex, Will, Steph and her husband, and a few others before climbing into the limo. Julia gave the driver her address, which turned out to be an apartment above a bookstore in the Adams Morgan neighborhood.

"Trendy neighborhood for young professionals," Corey noted. "There's a great coffee shop there, Sassafras. Are you familiar with it?"

"Familiar? I practically live there on weekends."

Corey sat back, easily visualizing them sitting together at a small bistro patio table outside the café, sharing a *Washington Post* and drinking espressos. She would love to spend a leisurely day with Julia that way: hanging out, drinking coffee, going for walks in the park, chatting, and maybe even holding hands. Though totally presumptuous, the vision felt surprisingly more like a memory than a fantasy. Like something she and Julia had actually done rather than something they might do in the future.

"Here we are," Julia announced, turning to Corey in the darkness made even blacker by the heavily tinted windows. "Would you like to come in? Meet Ralph?"

Corey's heart cartwheeled. "I'd love to meet Ralph."

The bookstore looked quaint, both contemporary books and collector's editions in its large picture window. Julia led Corey to a locked door beside the shop, explaining she lived on the second floor of the three-story red brick building. Each window on the upper levels was adorned with bright red shutters, giving the building an almost New England look.

"What should I tell my driver?" Corey swallowed, nervous about the answer.

"Tell him to circle the block about a hundred times."

A fist pump seemed out of the question, so Corey simply grinned and told her driver she would call him in a while. Wordlessly, she followed Julia up the stairs, watching her ass move within the confines of her gown's sleek fabric. If only she had the guts, she thought, she'd grab that ass and give it a little squeeze. No chance she was brave enough for that, at least not without a few more drinks. Or about a dozen more dates.

Ralph the tabby cat greeted them at the door, meowing loudly and curling like a noodle around their legs. Julia reached down to pet him, that tight round ass beckoning again to be squeezed. *Damn!* Corey wanted to touch it, pull it into her midsection, and rub against it. Rip that dress off while she was at it. She didn't really know what to do after that point, but she was pretty sure something would come to mind.

Julia turned, caught her looking, and grinned. "See something you like?"

"Um, y-yes! Great place you have here." *I will not admit that I want her to lead me to the bedroom. Especially since I told her I wanted us to go slow. Christ, what was I thinking?*

Julia grabbed her hand and tugged. Had she read her mind? Corey wondered. Her stomach flipped over. *Oh, God, wait! I'm not ready for the bedroom yet!*

Her worries proved unfounded as Julia towed her to the living room, where she turned on a Tiffany lamp beside the leather sofa. Muted light cast multicolored shadows. The sofa was chocolate brown and smooth as butter. It was all so romantic, with soft music the only thing missing.

Putting a hand on the small of her back, Julia gave Corey a playful shove until she tumbled onto the sofa. She gasped in surprise, but there was no time to be nervous, not when Julia hiked up her tight dress so she could straddle her lap.

Oh, God, is this really happening? Yes, it was. Julia was on her lap, her hands on her shoulders, staring sexily into her eyes.

"Are you okay?" Julia breathed.

Corey couldn't speak, just nod.

"Good, because I am dying to kiss you. I've been wanting to kiss you all evening."

"You have?" Corey squeaked.

"Oh, yes. Other things too. Like wanting to touch you."

Julia's warm breath fluttered against her neck. Corey tilted her head to give Julia better access. "Touch me where?"

Julia's lips brushed her neck. "Here," she whispered. "And here."

The soft lips moved to her throat. Corey threw her head back and closed her eyes. A soft moan deep in her throat fought to escape. She swallowed it down. *Too much. It's too much.* But apparently, it was not too much for Julia.

Julia's kisses covered her throat with warm wetness, each one electrifying and building a slow, torturous current inside her. Oh, how she wanted to give in, to be swept away in this storm that was Julia. She had not let herself be swept away by anyone before, not even Jason. Her relationships had always been methodical, incremental, discussed, analyzed and planned each step of the way. Nothing had ever been like this, pure attraction on all levels, the attraction setting the pace. Setting her on fire.

Julia's mouth found hers, softness melding with softness. Corey was shocked by the softness of their mouths coming together, like satin on satin, warmth on warmth, a gradual coming home, the rightness of fitting the perfect piece into the perfect slot, the click of perfection. Yes, she wanted this. She hungrily kissed Julia back, kissed her with the yearning and the trepidation of a woman who'd never been kissed by another woman, but had always wanted it to happen. Julia answered each kiss with more authority, more desire.

Corey opened her mouth wider. Julia's tongue touched hers. Corey's hands moved to Julia's ass, and she pulled her closer. Julia's body felt so warm against hers. She felt Julia's heart beating against her own, Julia's chest heaving with the same excitement that powered her own heartbeat.

Julia ripped her mouth away to suck on Corey's earlobe. *Oh, God!* Every part of her that Julia touched came alive as a bundle of sensitivity, so much sensory overload that she almost couldn't take it. She began to breathe harder, no longer quelling the moans deep in her throat. She pulsed inside and she was wet, wetter than any man's kisses had ever made her.

"Too much?" Julia whispered.

"A little," Corey gasped.

"We can stop."

No. If Julia stopped, she'd surely die. "I don't want you to stop."

Julia's mouth was on hers again. Her hands moved to Corey's waist, drawing tiny circles, caressing lightly.

Corey involuntarily arched her back, sending a signal that she wanted those hands on her breasts. *Oh, God, I'm being such a slut, but I can't help it!* She felt like a hormonal teenager without a care in the world, without any responsibilities, guided only by the magic of young lust.

Where was her sense of decorum? Of reasonableness? Of playing hard to get? she wondered. It was their first date, after all. Her first real date with a woman. Her first real date with anyone in a long time. She was supposed to…what? Julia's kisses drove her mad, taking her breath away. She was supposed to…to something. Stop maybe? Slow down? She couldn't think anymore. She didn't even know how long they'd been kissing, or even where they were. *Yes, okay.* They were still on the sofa, Julia still straddled her lap, but hours might have gone by since they'd started fooling around. She had no idea.

Julia's hands touched her sides. *Oh, yes.* Another wrenching away of her breath as Julia's palms suddenly found her breasts, cupping them lightly. Her eyes snapped shut. She thought of Julia's breasts, which looked so round, fuller than her own, and only inches from her face now. She imagined them both soft and firm at the same time. How would those breasts feel in her palms? How would they feel beneath her stroking fingers? Against her lips? Beneath her tongue? *Oh, God!* She squeezed her legs together in a useless effort to clamp down on the hard throbbing there.

Julia's mouth moved to Corey's throat again. Her hands lightly squeezed Corey's breasts, and then her thumbs found her nipples, lightly caressing them through the satiny fabric of her dress. Jesus, her nipples were so hard, she feared they might poke right through the fabric. If they did, they'd be right there, naked and ready for Julia's wet, warm mouth. *Oh, Jesus.* She'd come if Julia put her mouth on her nipples and sucked, she knew it. She'd never come like that before, but she knew she would now. With Julia. *Oh!* She cried out, needing much more, but Julia stopped suddenly, looking deeply into her eyes.

Julia lightly touched her forehead to Corey's. "There is so much I want to do to you, Corey. Naked, in my bedroom. Oh, God. I want to be on my knees. I want to kiss you everywhere, touch you everywhere. Lick you everywhere until you come about a hundred times."

Corey swallowed, her throat parched beyond belief. She was slowly melting, slowly coming undone in Julia's hands, totally defenseless, totally weak and helpless. Totally wrecked. She would do anything Julia wanted right now. Let Julia do anything to her. She did not care in the least that she didn't know how to make Julia come and didn't understand all the mechanics involved. Nor did she care that sex on a first date was much faster than she'd wanted things to go. She didn't care about anything right now beyond Julia continuing what she'd started.

"Please," Corey moaned softly.

"Oh, Corey, I want to. I want to make love to you so badly. But we can't right now."

"What?"

"I mean we *shouldn't* right now."

Like a drunk abruptly sobering, Corey's attention shifted into alertness. "What do you mean? Why not?" *Goddamn it*! Did she need to beg? She would if she had to.

Julia's blue-gray eyes were still smoky with lust. "Damn it, do you know how badly I want to?"

"Yes. I-I think so." *Then quit talking and do it!*

"You're so beautiful. And I can tell you're as turned on as I am," Julia whispered.

"Then why shouldn't we?"

Julia pulled back further. "I don't think it's a good idea to rush things."

"Isn't that something we should decide together?" Corey tried not to sound exasperated. Surely Julia wasn't trying to hurt her or frustrate the crap out of her.

"Yes, but right now, our libidos are doing the deciding. I don't think that's a good idea."

Julia pulled herself off Corey's lap, dropping down beside her with a heavy sigh.

The weight of her absence felt crushing. Tears lurked just beneath the surface, but Corey fought to keep them there.

"I'm sorry," Julia said. "I want to, so very much." Her hand slipped into Corey's. "I can't even believe I'm stupid enough—or smart enough—to stop like this."

"Is it because I'm…you know. Because I haven't been with a

woman before?" It hurt to think that Julia might be rejecting her because of her lack of experience. She wasn't a kid and she wasn't some flake who was experimenting, didn't Julia know that?

"Partly, but not really. I trust that you know what you're doing, that you know what you want."

"Then what is it?"

"I don't want to screw this up."

"You don't?"

Julia shook her head and smiled. "I want to do things the right way with you."

"And the right way means waiting?"

"It means going slower than…this."

Shit. Figured that just when she was ready to lose her lesbian virginity, everything came crashing to a screaming halt, but maybe Julia had a point.

"All right," she granted. "I trust you that going slow is the right thing to do. But goddamn, this is harder than organizing a rally in Republican country. Or staring down Collins and his henchmen."

"I know. Trust me, I know. I think I need to go change my underwear." Julia laughed.

Corey laughed too. Boy, she knew what wet underwear felt like right now.

Julia rose, still holding Corey's hand. "How about we make a pot of tea?"

"That sounds perfect. Well, not perfect, but it sounds like a safe alternative," Corey said.

Moments later over tea, they talked about the evening, rehashing the funny parts of the dinner and the not-so-funny parts. Without getting into specifics, they talked about Jane's barely concealed contempt for the president.

"I get the feeling he's not the nicest guy in the world," Julia said.

Corey didn't know Collins outside of his official duties as president, but she agreed with Julia. He was calculating, yes. Shrewd and unfeeling, yes. "I don't really know, but he's not my favorite person. He's sure not a guy you'd want to sit down and have a leisurely drink with."

"What about his morals?"

Corey shrugged. She really had no idea, though she didn't trust him not to stab Jane in the back.

"I mean," Julia continued, "is he the kind of guy who screws around on his wife?"

"Aren't most men? Especially in this town."

"So I take it that's a yes?"

"Jeez, I don't know. I don't want to think of the guy that way. Yuck!"

Julia frowned in concentration, clearly serious about the subject. "Have you heard anything like that about him?"

"Okay, wait. I feel like we're suddenly on the record or something, and I don't like it. I can't be making out with you in your living room, and then two minutes later you're grilling me like this is an interview or something."

"You're right, I'm sorry. I didn't mean to—"

"Go all reporter on me?"

"Exactly." Julia grinned.

"Why do you want to know, anyway?"

"No reason, just curious."

Corey wasn't so sure. In her experience, when a reporter said they were *just curious* about something, that usually meant they were already well on their way to investigating, or least they'd come to some kind of educated conclusion about the topic.

"Let's talk about us," Corey said. "Like when we're going to see each other again, and how I don't want any lines blurred between us when we're on a date, okay?"

Julia's eyes sparkled, the lust returning. "All right, I want to see you again as soon as we can manage it."

***

Clutching the stem of her champagne glass, Alex listened to Jane vent to her old friend Clara Stevens about Collins. They'd found a quiet corner of the massive patio at the French ambassador's house, which was nearly a palace, and Jane held nothing back. She could barely tolerate Collins these days, she told Clara, and the worst part was that she and Collins had to campaign together for the next six months, acting as though they liked each other.

Clara nodded in sympathy. She didn't much care for Collins either, Alex knew, and she'd made it clear four years ago that she was in Jane's corner. She'd pretty much blackmailed Collins into taking Jane as his running mate. Clara Stevens was a goddess in the Democratic party, once head of the DNC, now a doyenne with more unofficial influence than just about anyone else in the party. She'd been a close friend to Jane's father in his years as governor, so her Kincaid loyalty went back decades.

"It's like a bad marriage you're stuck with," Clara offered. "Not that I would know about such things."

Alex asked, "How is that gorgeous wife of yours? And why isn't she here?"

Clara's dark eyes softened at the mention of Sophie, her long-time partner. There had been a time, decades ago, when Clara's sexuality had kept her from running for office herself. She'd made a choice to live her life honestly, even if it meant sacrificing political office. Times were certainly a lot different now.

"She's been a little under the weather the last couple of days," Clara replied.

Jane's eyebrows rose in concern. "She okay?"

"A bad cold that won't go away, that's all."

Sophie was a good decade younger than Clara, but Alex knew that her health was a little frail.

"Promise me," Jane said, "that if she's not better soon, she'll see a doctor."

"Of course, but she's fine."

"And what about you?" Alex asked Clara. "How are you doing these days?"

"Now look, just because I have to use a cane once in a while, I am *not* falling apart."

Alex chuckled. "All right, then how about you and I find the nearest table and do a little arm wrestling."

"Now you're talking." Clara winked at Alex. "But I wouldn't want to embarrass one of the Secret Service's finest."

"You're right. We wouldn't want that. I'd never live it down."

"Jane, my dear." Clara's smile dissolved as she turned to Jane. "You're the best damned vice president this country's ever had and our party is damned lucky to have you. You'll be our next president."

Jane looked close to tears, something Alex rarely saw. Her heart constricted.

"It's so damned hard to hold onto that dream some days," Jane whispered in a trembling voice. Alex reached for her hand, squeezing it gently. Jane acknowledged the gesture by squeezing back. "Some days it doesn't seem worth it."

"I know that, and so does every man or woman who's ever had the same dream as you. It's part of what keeps you humble and makes you human. It's exactly why you're the politician of the future."

Jane laughed a little bitterly. "If this is supposed to be a pep talk, I'm not sure it's working. But I appreciate it, Clara."

"Nonsense, child. Collins is a dinosaur, the last of his kind."

"That may be, but my fate is dependent on that dinosaur right now, so I don't want him to choose this year to go extinct."

Clara's eyes narrowed. She went ominously silent for a minute or two. "His going the way of tyrannosaurus rex might not be such a bad thing, you know."

"What are you talking about?" Jane shook her head, her question purely rhetorical because Clara's suggestion was ridiculous. "Look. That would be disastrous for me. I'm counting on us to be re-elected, and then for him not to screw things up too badly over the next four years."

"Unfortunately, that last part is what I'm most worried about. The status quo is one of three options, and the one I like the least."

Alex asserted herself, not liking the direction of the conversation. "What three options? I thought staying the course was the only one."

Clara lowered her voice to a somber whisper. "There's the option of letting Collins boot Jane off the ticket, which would absolutely decimate him and he'd lose the election."

Jane gasped audibly. "That would set the party back years!"

"No. Only four years. The Republicans would win, but you'd run in four years or eight, depending on the conditions. And you'd win."

From a selfish point of view, Alex loved the idea of having Jane to herself for the next four years. But Jane looked decidedly unhappy. Clearly, she wasn't mad about the scenario.

"That's far too risky," Jane said, shaking her head. "We can't gamble on the party—or me—recovering that quickly. I can't imagine what being out of the public eye for three or four years would do to my career, Clara. It's not something I want to experiment with."

"Yes. That's why I like the remaining option best."

"What?" Alex and Jane asked in unison.

Clara's smile reminded Alex of a mafia don. "Getting him to reverse with you. Put *you* at the top of the ticket."

Alex whistled softly in astonishment while Jane rolled her eyes.

"What science fiction novel have you been reading?" Jane asked sarcastically.

"Oh, I'm not talking fantasy."

"Well, to me it is. I won't even entertain ideas like that. It's never been done before, and Collins sure isn't going to be the first to go for it."

Clara's expression was unreadable, but before she could continue, they were interrupted by the approaching *click click* of stilettos belonging to Under Secretary of State Margaret Tanner. Alex forced a smile, unsure whether she was relieved or annoyed by the interruption.

CHAPTER ELEVEN

A second envelope arrived at her apartment. Another photograph, grainy again, but clear enough to show Dennis Collins, the same woman and a toddler playing in a park, looking happy and comfortable together. The park looked empty, private. There were palm trees, but nothing else to give any indication of where the photo had been taken or when. It seemed recent because Collins appeared exactly the same. If he weren't the president, Julia considered, it might have been a photo of an anonymous couple and their child, or a grandpa with his daughter and grandchild. But it *was* the president, and whether it was true or not, the photo implied that he had a mistress and a love child.

"Damn it," Julia muttered to herself. Who the hell was playing with her? And what on earth did they want her to do with this stuff? Well, *that* she could guess. They wanted her to break the scandal. But why *her*? Was it because she was from Miami—the president's home city and perhaps where the mystery woman and child lived? Was it because she had a connection to Alex? Because she was new to D.C. and perhaps a little on the naïve side? Or was it because she hadn't yet made a name for herself in the news business and might be eager to do so? The mysterious source's motives could be all of the above, she supposed, or none.

Whatever the reasons, she had been given this little collection of potentially damaging photos, and it was up to her to figure out what to do with them and who might be behind them.

A lifetime in politics had probably produced many enemies for Collins, and it was an election year. Someone with power sure as hell didn't want to see Dennis Collins re-elected. Julia couldn't begin to guess who that might be out of thousands of suspects. Colby Harrison seemed like the obvious first choice, but she was pretty sure the answer wouldn't be that simple.

She considered her options. She could do nothing, or she could go full at it and break the scandal. She didn't have much stomach for extremes. Well, at least not since she'd taken the extreme action of pulling up stakes and walking out on Alex. She was much more cautious now. The best thing to do, she decided, was to take her time and try to figure out who was behind this dirty little deed.

She'd not had any luck with discreet inquiries about Collins's personal life. His image as a happily married man remained cemented. She could show the photos to Corey and get her involved, but she dismissed that idea quickly. She and Corey had decided to keep their professional lives as far from their dating relationship as possible, since neither of them wanted to juggle conflicts, ethical issues or accusations of favoritism. Besides, it was refreshing to spend time together and *not* talk heavy shop.

Julia checked her watch. She was supposed to meet Corey soon for a late dinner. The life of a campaign manager was extremely busy these days, and Corey was only going to get busier as summer wore on and the nomination convention drew closer.

She and Corey barely had time for a date once a week, which also meant they hadn't slept together yet. She sometimes wished she hadn't suggested they go slow because now their relationship was at a crawl thanks to their busy schedules. *Christ*. They should have gone for it on that first date three weeks ago. They'd been *this* close to enjoying one another's bodies! *Oh, well.* Going slow did have its advantages, she thought. It allowed them to get to know one another without pressure, and the gradual building of sexual tension was very sweet.

Crap, she had to get going or she'd be late. Julia put the envelope down and made a snap decision to place a call to the *Miami Herald*'s top political reporter, Chase Benson. She didn't know Chase Benson very well, but she'd had to endure some snarky remarks and killer looks from him across the newsroom when she'd been given the White House assignment.

It hardly mattered whether he liked her or not, or whether he was pissed at her. She needed his help to unravel this predicament because she did not have the resources or the skill to do it alone. That didn't mean she had to go forward and break the scandal. She simply wanted to know who and what were behind these photos, and then she could at least make an informed decision about what to do with them.

Picking up her cell phone, Julia clicked on the familiar number of the *Miami Herald* newsroom.

***

Along with most of the nation, Jane found herself shocked and upset by the deadly tornado that had swept across northern Texas and into Oklahoma days ago, slicing through the latter state's third largest city. Lawton had a population of just over ninety thousand people. At least ninety-eight of them died in the disaster, which was quickly looking like the third deadliest tornado in the nation's history. Searchers were still looking for the missing.

With Alex, Jane watched the carnage on television, wanting to do something but unsure what she could do until Alex announced that she wanted to go down to assist in an unofficial capacity. She'd love to spend a week helping people there rebuild, she said, even handing out bottles of water if that's what was needed. She'd do whatever it took, as long as she could do *something* to help.

Jane admired her partner's instinct to help others, and more than that, her desire to do something tangible. She felt exactly the same way, but as vice president, particularly during a campaign, she couldn't exactly travel down to Lawton and pound nails or hand out blankets. She could, however, pay the city a visit and try to give the people there a morale boost, especially since Collins so far gave no indication he was interested in visiting the embattled citizens of Lawton.

It was common for presidents to visit areas hit by disasters, natural or otherwise, particularly when there had been loss of life. If Collins shrugged it off, Jane thought in frustration, he'd be doing a disservice to all Americans, and most especially to himself and the office of the president. Not that she needed one, but his reluctance was another reason to despise him.

"He's not going," Corey confirmed to her on the third day of the disaster after marching into Jane's office.

"What?" Jane wasn't completely surprised, but still, it was hard to digest that Collins would be so insensitive, so out of touch. Was he losing his grip on reality?

"He's going to hold to his schedule. He'll be in Boston for the next two days, giving speeches on the economy. He says the economy is more important to most Americans right now than some tornado in Bumfuck, Oklahoma."

Anger blazed in Jane's chest. "He didn't actually say that to you, did he?"

"Yup. Word for word."

"Jesus, Corey." Of course the lagging economy was important, but it was incumbent upon leaders to show compassion, and to show leadership when peoples' lives were so drastically upended. A community in pain needed to know the nation's leaders cared, but she didn't need to explain that to Corey.

"Well, I'm going," she announced spontaneously. Alex clearly wanted to go, so why not go together? "You, Carter and Steph set it up, okay? Day after tomorrow?"

"Sure, but a word of caution. Whatever you do there, do not make it look like you're campaigning."

"Don't worry, I won't. I'm going as the vice president, seeing that our *president* doesn't feel it's worth his time. Alex will want to go. She wants to roll up her sleeves and help out." Jane had a momentary flash of Alex in a sleeveless shirt, her biceps bulging. Alex had a killer body, enough to distract her in numerous ways, and almost enough to make her forget about the deadly tornado. "You coming with us?"

"Better not," Corey replied. "I don't think your campaign manager should be seen in Lawton or it could send the wrong signals. Besides, I've got enough here to keep me busy. You'll be happy to know that I'll be going with you to the annual governors' conference next week."

"Thank God. You can keep Amy Roberts away from me."

Corey laughed. "As long as it's not at the expense of having her attach herself to me like some kind of deer fly."

"Speaking of attaching oneself, how are things going with Julia?"

With a heavy sigh, Corey slouched in the chair. "I don't really know. It feels like we're hardly dating since we've had exactly four dates."

"I'm sorry. Relationships, even deep-rooted ones, are difficult in this whirlwind. When this is all over, I want you to take at least a month off. Go somewhere warm where the drinks are served with little umbrellas." Jane winced to herself. It had been years since she'd had a vacation like that, and it would probably be several more before she did it again.

Corey cocked an eyebrow at her. "I will when you do the same, sis."

"Touché. Anyway, my point is, if she makes you happy, it'll work out. It's frustrating, but be patient."

"She does make me happy," Corey declared, sitting up straighter. "It's easy being with her. Do you know what I mean?"

"Yes, I do. Being with Alex is the easiest, purest thing I've ever done." Jane instantly regretted the direction of the conversation, not meaning to bring Alex into it. Truth was, she still had a hard time with the Alex-Julia-Corey connection. What was it about Julia that had attracted Alex, and now Corey? And if Alex had once been so attracted to Julia, could it happen again? The last thought made her gasp out loud.

"Are you okay?" Corey asked.

Jane pursed her lips, felt her heart beating faster, and reminded herself that this was about Corey, not herself or Alex. "I'm fine. Look, going slow is good, okay?"

"Yes, and so is being happy."

"Yes," Jane granted. She'd told Corey before that her happiness was all that mattered when it came to Julia, and she would not go back on that sentiment. "You're right. And I'm sorry if things between you two are going slower than you want, but if it's meant to be, it'll work out."

Jane was conflicted about Julia, and she knew she wasn't doing a very good job of hiding her mixed feelings from Corey. She wanted to be supportive, and she really did have Corey's welfare at heart, but she wasn't truly ready yet to give this arrangement her full, heartfelt blessing.

It seemed Corey recognized her hesitation, because she stood tensely and said, "I'm a big girl. And if Julia breaks my heart, then so be it. But I want to—no, I *need* to—see where this goes."

Jane nodded as Corey turned and departed. For Corey's sake, she'd need to try harder to be more accepting and to keep an open mind about Julia.

***

Alex didn't know what to expect upon arrival in Lawton, but she'd come prepared to stay for a week to help any way she could. Jane would only stay the day—a speech at the community center, an hour or so handing out food and bottled water at the temporary shelter for those left homeless by the storm, as well as a tour of some of the damaged areas.

A year ago, she and Jane had visited some flooded communities along the Mississippi, but nothing that matched the loss of life and the carnage caused by the Lawton tornado.

"Watcha thinking about?" Jane asked quietly.

Alex pulled her gaze from the window. They were on Air Force Two, somewhere over Missouri. "About how terrible this is going to be."

Jane sighed. "I know. Me too. I always feel like there should be more I can do."

"You being there will do all sorts of good."

"I hope so, but I'd rather be doing what you're going to be doing. Helping for real instead of just giving speeches and doling out hugs."

They'd had this debate before, with Jane wishing she could do more in crises than give speeches and pose for photo ops. But her job was so much bigger and so much more important than sawing wood, Alex knew.

Alex smiled at Jane, drinking her lover in. "Like I've told you about a hundred times before, my love, anyone can pound nails and paint walls, but not anyone can be vice president of the United States. Your office, your compassion, are your strengths."

"Oh, Alex, you're damned good for my ego."

"That and other things, I hope."

Jane's eyes sparkled, making Alex recall the sweet memory of last night's lovemaking. They'd gone slow, starting with full body massages, countless kisses, a good half hour of foreplay and cuddling before making their way to delicious orgasms.

"Always," Jane replied, her smile dazzling, her finger stroking Alex's wrist. "You're the best thing that's ever happened to me."

When Jane said those things to her, Alex always sucked in her breath and resisted the urge to cry. Jane knew how to say things that reached right in and grabbed hold of her heart, and knew how to make her feel well and truly loved for the first time in her life. Or at least, the first time in her life where someone actually meant it.

Alex pulled Jane's fingers to her lips, kissing them one at a time. "That makes us even then, since you're the best thing that's ever happened to me."

"Good." Jane's smile faded. "Perfect timing for me to ask you something."

Alex laughed. "Should I be scared?"

"I don't think so, but unfortunately, the question has to do with Julia. We've never talked much about your time with her."

"For good reason."

"Because she hurt you?"

"Yes, and because afterward was a very hard time for me."

"I know, sweetheart, and I understand. But since she's dating Corey, we need to talk about her."

"Now?"

"Why not? We have another thirty minutes or so before we land."

Alex wanted to banish all thoughts and discussions of Julia. She would have liked to banish the woman from her life too, just as she'd managed to forget about her the last few years, but that didn't seem likely anymore. Julia was here to stay, at least for a while.

She blew out an exasperated breath. "All right. What do you want to know?"

Jane asked the obvious. "Does it bother you that she and Corey are dating?"

"Of course it does. Doesn't it bother you?"

"Yes, but probably for different reasons. I don't want my baby sister to get hurt."

"That's the only reason it bothers you? She could get hurt by anyone she was dating."

"True." Jane frowned, looking out the tiny window for a moment. "The truth?" She turned back to Alex, her eyes hard. "I hate that you and Julia have a history together, that you lived together, had dreams together, loved each other. It bothers me that she knew you so intimately, as intimately as I do. Every time I see her, I'm reminded of those things."

"Oh, honey, no one knows me the way you do. She and I never had anything close to what you and I have," Alex replied, surprised by Jane's jealousy. "You have to believe that. There's absolutely no comparison."

"I do believe it, but…"

"But what? There is no but."

Jane took a deep breath—preparing for battle, Alex supposed—before she continued, "The sex. That bothers me. That the two of you had sex together. Lots of it, I'm sure."

"Okay, wait. Lots?"

"Alex, you were in your twenties. Are you going to tell me the two of you *didn't* have a lot of sex?"

No, Alex decided, she couldn't lie. She and Julia had had a lot of sex. Tons of it in every room and on practically every surface of their house, out on a park bench one night, in a friend's hot tub, in the restroom of their college library, in the changing room at Macy's. And there was the time they were on patrol together where they'd pulled off into a wooded area and had sex in the backseat of the police cruiser. *Yup. Lots of sex.*

"Never mind," Jane ground out. "I can see it all over your face."

"What? What'd I do?"

"You're remembering every orgasm you ever had with her, aren't you?"

"No, of course not! Look, what do you want me to say? We had a lot of sex. Big deal."

"It is a big deal. To me it is."

"Sex is a big deal to me too. With *you*. But with her, it was just...I don't know. We were young. We were hot for each other. She had a great body," Alex admitted. Damn, every word was another shovel digging her deeper and deeper. "Look," she pleaded as Jane's face darkened with anger, her eyes as black as storm clouds. "I don't want to fight."

"Who says we're fighting?"

"Well, it feels like one, but I can't do anything about my past, okay? I can't change it. I can't pretend Julia never happened."

"I know." Jane softened, or at least her mouth did, and then her eyes. A wave of resignation swept across her face. "I see her and that gorgeous body of hers, and I think about you and her, and it...it makes me jealous, which totally pisses me off."

Alex braved a chuckle. "You don't think you're allowed to be jealous?"

"No, damn it. It's beneath me."

"Apparently it isn't," Alex said, teasing.

"Maybe now that we've talked about it, it won't bother me so much. Maybe I can let it go now."

"Good, because it shouldn't bother you. The sex I had with Julia was crazy, but it wasn't from the heart, not the way it is between us. It doesn't even compare. It's like cereal versus bacon and eggs for breakfast. Johnny Walker Red versus single malt. Or black-and-white television versus high def."

Jane began to smile. "Oh, my love, you're such a poet. Damn it, I love you so much, but Emily Dickinson you are not."

"Shit, you mean you didn't pick me because of my way with words?"

Jane rose and plopped down in Alex's lap. She planted a soft kiss on her lips. "Now that we have all that stupid, jealous crap out of the way, how do you feel about Julia now? Are you still angry at her for what she did to you?"

"I'll always be pissed at her for the way she treated me. Guess that's not what I'm supposed to say, is it?"

"Being completely honest is one of the things I value most about our relationship, Alex. But anger is toxic. It sucks away your energy, and I don't want that to happen to you. Or me. Anger's not worth holding onto, tempting as it is sometimes."

"I know. You're right. It's been easy to hang onto it, that's all."

"It's almost always easier to feel like a victim than it is to forgive."

Jane knew something about being a victim, and something about survival and forgiveness too, Alex knew. Her husband, Dan, had been killed in a plane crash over a dozen years ago, shattering Jane's life as she knew it, forcing herself to remake it, to re-examine her goals and desires. Her husband's death and her ensuing freedom ultimately drove her into the world of politics.

"I forget sometimes," Alex said, contrite, "that you know a hell of a lot more about pain than I do. And yet you're not bitter."

"Oh, I was bitter at one time until I decided it's baggage I'd rather not carry around with me anymore. It wasn't easy letting it go. Do you think you can let go of your anger at Julia?"

Alex's fierce loyalty often kept her holding onto grudges far longer than she knew was wise. She pretty much saw the world in black and white, in definite terms of right and wrong. Always had. Yet that narrow view was such a poor excuse for being an unforgiving bitch. She'd learned sometimes there were curves in the road, shades of gray. She was smart enough and compassionate enough to look beneath the first layer, and to consider all the possibilities, all the reasons that lay behind peoples' actions. Fear kept her from doing so in this case, and fear was damned limiting. Jane had taught her that. Jane was the bravest person she knew.

She touched her forehead to Jane's. "You never stop amazing me, do you know that?"

"No, I didn't know that. But now that you've told me, I hope I never stop."

"I have a funny feeling you won't."

"Good. Now will you answer my question?"

Alex smiled. "Are you sure you're really a doctor and not a lawyer?"

"Oh, I'm sure. In fact, I'll play a little doctor with you right now to prove it."

"Ah, I'd love to, but I think we're already descending. I'll book an appointment with Dr. Kincaid tonight though." Alex nibbled Jane's earlobe, eliciting a squeal. "And as for your question about not being so angry anymore, I'll try to let it go."

"Really?"

"Yes, really. I'm really going to try because to be honest, being angry at Julia is starting to feel damned old." Alex chuckled bitterly. "Or maybe it's *me* who's feeling old."

"Oh, Alex, I love you so much. And as long as you're leaving that anger behind, I'm going to kick my jealousy to the curb."

"That sounds like a deal, honey."

As they began to kiss, the pilot announced over the speakers that Air Force Two was descending to four thousand feet, following the path of the tornado before landing in Lawton. She and Jane both pressed their faces to the window. What they saw left them speechless.

"Jesus," Alex muttered. It was enough to convey how she felt about what she saw below.

***

She'd covered a hurricane once in Florida's panhandle, but Julia had never seen anything this devastating before. The tornado had cut a swath a mile wide and six miles long, zigzagging right through a high density area of the city, and tearing up everything in its path. Homes lay in splinters, trees had been reduced to skeletal sticks, and debris shredded into the tiniest pieces had scattered for miles like confetti.

The scene looked like what she imagined a plane crash might resemble, the force of the winds sending scraps of toys, clothes and household items up into treetops. A football helmet lay on a rooftop. A car looked like it'd been crushed at the junkyard. A massive pile of bricks had once been a plaza. In one decimated house, she could see a closet, its door gone, but clothes still hanging intact—proof of the strange randomness of the storm. Her shock and amazement soon gave way to deep sadness and horror as she thought about how she would deal with such a disaster if it happened to her.

She resisted the urge to interview the survivors, the people who would have to rebuild. She wanted to question them on their resilience, their spirit and faith, but there were plenty of reporters in Lawton doing exactly that. She was here to cover Jane's activities.

Jane and Alex were taken on a tour through much of the damaged area, first by helicopter, and then on a golf cart, since many of the streets were not yet passable for cars, or else filled with heavy equipment working on the cleanup. Jane and Alex had chatted with some of the displaced people who'd lost everything, including loved ones. Both women looked genuinely moved, offering spontaneous hugs to people and words of encouragement. More than a few tears were shed. Afterward, they handed out food and water at a distribution center.

By early evening, thousands of city residents gathered at the baseball park to hear Jane's speech. A weary silence greeted her introduction. When she began to speak, the loosening of the crowd's emotions was slow but steady, like the gradual release of a kite to greater heights. Their disconnection to outsiders began to disappear with every word Jane uttered.

"I feel your pain, your loss, your burden," Jane told them. "Your country also feels the sting of your grief, your heartbreak, because our hearts are breaking too. Citizens of Lawton, you will not walk through this tragedy alone. Let us—all of us in this great country of ours—be here for you. Let us help you in any way we can. And let us lend you *our* strength and *our* hope when yours is weakened."

Julia marveled at the evangelical quality of Jane's oratory. The vice president spoke with a unique blend of empathy, eloquence, honesty and divinity. She stirred people, drew them to her, and they eagerly accepted her comfort and leadership.

Jane talked about the kindnesses people showed one another in the aftermath, strangers helping other strangers. "And in every catastrophe, hope and cooperation are born. Let us always remember this generosity of spirit, this sharing of humanity. We are all brothers and sisters today. Today, we are all citizens of Lawton, but you are the true heroes."

The applause and standing ovation lasted several minutes, but instead of basking in people's approval on the grandstand, Jane dove into the crowd, shaking hands, dispensing more hugs, talking to people in small groups or one at a time. In the commotion, Julia searched out Alex near the stage.

"I hear you're staying here for a week or so, helping with the cleanup and rebuild," she said.

Alex nodded coolly. "The Red Cross is letting me tag along."

"Surely it's more than that. Can I interview you about what you'll be doing, why you want to help, that sort of thing?"

"I'd rather you didn't."

Okay, so it was going to be like that, Julia thought dismally. "Look, can't we put our personal differences aside? I'm certainly willing to. This is a story, Alex."

"I don't have any differences with you. Not anymore. I just don't want to talk about what I'm doing here in an official way. I'm doing this on my own time because I want to help, not for any publicity. It's a private matter."

"All right, if that's the way you want it. But for the record, I think people should know what you're doing. And you're not a private person, Alex. Not anymore."

"Sorry, but it's the way I want it."

As much as she wished Alex would talk on the record about her visit to Lawton, she couldn't argue with Alex's innate goodness or her altruistic motives. Her ex-lover and Jane seemed like a fairytale couple, almost too good to be true. These two near-perfect souls probably did deserve each other.

"You're looking at me funny," Alex said quietly, her soft North Carolina drawl sounding achingly familiar. "You know, the look you used to give me when we were both state troopers, and I'd just handed some street person my last ten-dollar bill."

Smiling, Julia shook her head. "That's why you never had money to buy coffee."

"Yeah, but some poor sucker like you would feel sorry for me and buy me one."

Julia grew quiet, a small sob crowding her throat suddenly. "You know something?" Alex's goodness had always cast a shadow over her, had always been something she felt she could never equal. "I was never as good as you, Alex. I was never the kind of person who instinctively drops everything to help someone else, no matter what the cost. The kind of person who never puts herself first. The way you are. I could never live up to your standards."

"I never expected you to," Alex answered quietly. "I never expected you to be anyone other than yourself."

Julia wiped away an unexpected tear on her cheek. "I guess maybe a big part of me thought I was never good enough for you."

"And so you had to sabotage us. Is that what you're saying?"

"Maybe, I guess. God, I was such a failure at me and you. I can understand why you hate me. I'd probably hate me too."

"I don't hate you."

"Okay, then I can understand why you're still angry at me."

Alex looked at her for a long moment. She appeared far sadder than Julia had ever seen her these last few months.

"I'm not angry anymore," Alex finally said. "I regret that I wasted a lot of my energy being angry at you all those years. I can't do that anymore. But it doesn't mean I'm not a little bit sad. A little hurt still."

"I know. I will always be sad about us, Alex. But glad for what we had, too, and for sharing that part of our lives. And I'll always be sorry for hurting you the way I did."

With a visible effort, Alex tried to smile, but her mouth trembled a little. "I should probably thank you. If you hadn't left, I never would have found Jane."

"Well, as I've heard Jane say in her speeches, even in terrible things often something good comes out of it. I guess I was a little bit like this tornado in your life, wrecking the hell out of it, but you came out of it stronger. Better." Julia didn't know if she could say the same about herself. She'd come out of their relationship happier with her new career choice, but the brand of heart-stopping, life-changing love that Alex seemed to have with Jane had eluded her so far.

As if reading her mind, Alex said, "I hope one day you'll be as happy with someone as I am with Jane."

"Even if it's with Corey?"

"Yes, even if it's with Corey. But if you hurt her, you'll have to contend with Jane. And me."

"I know. Trust me, I know."

Alex offered a handshake. "Don't tell me we're finally getting past this. You know, *us*."

Julia shook her head and smiled, and then she stepped close to Alex and put her arms around her in a fierce hug. Alex had finally forgiven her. "Thank you," she whispered.

Moments later, Julia strayed to the fringes of the crowd, pulled out a cell phone, and called Corey. She felt lighter after her conversation with Alex. She wanted to share her mood with Corey, but she would not recite her conversation with Alex over the phone. She'd save that for next time she and Corey were together.

"Hi," Julia said after Corey answered on the third ring. "Busy?"

"Never too busy to talk to you," Corey said. Julia could tell she was smiling. "How are you doing down there?"

"Okay, but the things I'm seeing…it's terrible. I can't imagine how terrifying it must have been when it happened, and how overwhelming it must be for these people. I feel so bad for them. I mean, there's blocks and blocks of houses, buildings, that are absolutely destroyed."

"I know. I saw a lot of the images on television. I guess the human will to survive and to keep going is quite amazing, isn't it?"

"Yes, it is. I think Jane and Alex being here is really helping lift peoples' spirits. The speech went well."

"I know. I've been keeping abreast of things."

Julia smiled. "Abreast, huh?"

"Oh, don't you dare get me going." Corey's voice dropped a couple of octaves. "I miss those, um, breasts of yours."

Their last date had resulted in another heavy session of fooling around. Corey's hands had been all over her, but once again she had slowed things down. She needed to be sure Corey was ready for the next step, that they were both ready.

Julia smiled into the phone. "I'm going to be at the annual governors' conference in Denver next week. Please tell me you're going to be there too." She was anxious to get Corey out of D.C., anxious for them to spend some time together on neutral territory. A couple of nights out of town might be romantic, even if they weren't exactly going away together.

"I am, as a matter of fact. Shall we call it a date?"

"Oh, yeah! It's the only thing about the assignment I'll look forward to."

"Good, because it will keep me sane and give me something to look forward to as well."

Julia took a deep breath. Dating someone as busy and as in demand as Corey was challenging. Getting together even once a week took an effort akin to planning the invasion of another country. "I miss you, baby."

"I miss you too."

CHAPTER TWELVE

Corey could care less about going to a baseball game at Coors Field, the Rockies versus the Cubs. She hadn't a clue about the score, yet she was nearly overcome with anticipation. She laughed at herself and her situation. Jane, who would fly in right before tomorrow night's opening reception, had urged her to take some downtime and come early to the governors' conference. The ball game was on the itinerary for the early arrivals, part of the welcoming activities. While normally she would have skipped it, she'd come only because Julia had joined a gaggle of reporters at the game.

With a surge of excitement, Corey let her thoughts drift to the fantasy of her and Julia skipping the game and going straight to a romantic dinner, maybe a walk, and then another white-hot make-out session at the hotel. An intimate evening together with no demands and no schedules. As much she didn't want to be here watching players slug at a little white ball—and neither, she suspected, did Julia—the game was, unfortunately, part of their cover. Neither of them liked the fact they were hiding their relationship, but they had deliberately chosen to do so because they didn't want to become a source of gossip and a distraction for Jane right now, nor risk Julia's professional credibility. Besides, conducting a new relationship was hard enough outside the spotlight, never mind beneath the glare of public scrutiny. They would out themselves eventually, but not yet.

Attempting the covertness of a CIA-trained spy, Corey glanced sidelong at Julia, sitting down a row and over a few seats. One more out, and Julia was going to slip away from her colleagues, who looked settled in for the long haul with their fists full of beers and hot dogs. Corey would take her leave at the end of the seventh inning, feigning exhaustion. Well, she was exhausted, but not too exhausted for a drink with Julia and a little playtime.

The few make-out sessions they'd enjoyed had only whetted her appetite for more. All that kissing and plenty of over-the-clothing groping had led to incredible frustration, sexual frustration like she'd never known. But they were trying to do things right, trying to be slow and deliberate, like there was a recipe to a successful first-time lesbian relationship.

Corey would like nothing more than to throw that recipe out and wing it. She would love to see what might happen if she went braless, unbuttoned her blouse, and pulled Julia's face into her cleavage. Or if she went commando, unzipped her jeans, and jammed Julia's hand inside. How could Julia resist her then?

A delicious smile spread slowly across her face. She could think of all kinds of scenarios that sure as hell didn't involve sitting at a ball game right now.

She watched as Julia stood, flipped her baseball cap backward—the signal that she was headed back to the hotel—and jogged down the stairs. Half an inning to go, and she would do the same.

She almost cheered out loud when the first Colorado batter

struck out, and then the second one grounded out to third base. Her quiet fist pump earned her a couple of glares. The third batter walked, an agonizing wait, but the fourth batter came through for her, hitting a fly ball that was soundly caught. As soon as she heard the muffled thwack of the leather mitt snagging the ball, she jumped up and made her excuses.

Minutes later at the hotel, she knocked quietly on Julia's door. The door burst open. Julia stood before her, totally sexy in a white terrycloth bathrobe, and wearing a huge grin that said she was as happy to see Corey as Corey was to see her. Julia clutched full champagne flutes in each hand.

"You read my mind," Corey purred, accepting a glass and closing the door behind her.

Julia cocked a flirtatious eyebrow at her. "The champagne or slipping into something more comfortable?"

"Both."

"I like a woman who knows what she wants."

They settled side by side on the loveseat, which faced a large window with a view of the Rockies in the distance, the white snow on the mountain peaks bright against the dark sky. A dazzling sight, but Corey would trade it in an instant for a view of the inside of Julia's bedroom.

"Do you?" Corey asked cautiously. "Because what I want is you."

Julia set her glass down on the coffee table and took Corey's hand. "I know we've been doing a lot of flirting and a lot of fooling around, but I want you to be sure."

"I am sure."

"It's a big step. I don't want you to change your mind partway through, or worse, regret it later. I don't think I could handle that."

Corey placed a finger softly against Julia's lips to silence her. "I won't change my mind, and I won't regret it. I care about you, Julia, so much. I'm ready for this."

Julia kissed the admonishing finger before placing Corey's hand back in her lap. "Okay. But I'm not sure I am."

The admission stunned Corey. "Why not? Are you unsure of your feelings about me?"

"No, it's not that. I care about you too, and I'm incredibly attracted to you. I want to intimately know everything about you, including your body, but…"

"I don't understand," Corey pleaded, more wrecked by the second. "Is it because you don't want to sleep with someone who's never been with a woman before?"

Julia bit her bottom lip as though stifling a laugh, even though nothing about this conversation was funny. "No, Corey, I am not afraid of your inexperience. In fact, I am absolutely honored that you've chosen me to be your first."

"Is it Alex? Are you still in love with her?"

Julia did laugh this time. "No, I can assure you I am not in love with Alex, though we seem to have made some progress in clearing the air between us. Look, the truth is, I'm afraid of falling in love with you because I seem to suck at relationships. My track record doesn't fill me with great confidence. I don't want to hurt you. Or me."

Julia looked so morose, so lost, that Corey wanted to put her arms around her and hold her tight. "Don't let your fears get in the way of us, okay? If we never tried to get past our failures, we'd never get anywhere. I'm asking you, please don't give up. Give me a chance."

"I gotta hand it to you, that Kincaid charm works wonders." Julia grinned as she spoke, but it wasn't funny to Corey.

"I'm not trying to charm you," she said, "I'm serious. No one is perfect at relationships. I certainly am not. But I like you Julia, *so* much. I think about you all the time. I fantasize about making love with you. I can't even concentrate half the time at work anymore!"

"You can't?"

"Nope."

"Good. Me neither."

Corey scooted closer, boldly planting a hand on Julia's robed thigh. "You should know that I'm a quick learner." She kissed Julia's neck. "And I'm open to all suggestions." Another kiss on Julia's neck, lower this time. "I take criticism well." Her lips moved to Julia's throat. "I'm tireless, and I like to practice new things until I do them perfectly."

Julia threw her head back, inviting more kisses. "I love an eager student."

"Oh, I'm eager all right." Corey's hand slid up Julia's thigh, and then dipped beneath the terrycloth fabric to her warm skin, soft and fiery beneath her fingertips.

"Jesus, are you sure you haven't done this before?"

Corey let out a husky laugh. Turned on, she was anxious to take things further. She hoped Julia wouldn't put the brakes on like all the other times. "Please. Let me love you."

Julia visibly swallowed, lowering her head to meet Corey's gaze. "I'm not even sure how to take a chance with someone anymore. It's been a long time."

"Then trust me," Corey whispered. "We'll try this together, okay?" It was as though Julia had become the student and she the teacher, which filled her with bold confidence.

"Okay."

Julia leaned in for a kiss. Corey accepted it gently at first, and then more hungrily. She touched Julia, careful not to dance her fingers higher along her thigh yet or push her too hard. She would take this as slow as Julia wanted and wait for her signals.

The wait wasn't long. Julia's body began to come alive against her, warm and more open, moving gently, melding softly with hers, quivering slightly. Julia's thighs parted in invitation. Yes, Corey thought before her rational mind fled and her instincts took over.

Corey let her hand paint circles lightly along Julia's inner thighs until Julia began to groan softly. Her hand move closer to the center of Julia's pleasure, keeping the pressure from her fingers light. She moved her mouth down Julia's throat, nipping and sucking. No one had ever begged for her love, but Julia begged her now, urging her on, pleading with her not to stop. She didn't know what came next, but she'd figure it out. Julia would guide her.

Julia sank further down into the sofa so that Corey's hand cupped the warmth of her desire. Julia was wet, so wet. Like me, she realized. It dawned on her that she could do all the things to Julia that she wanted done to herself. Making love with a woman was really that simple.

Corey's breathing echoed Julia's as she began massaging her, first in soft, wide circles until Julia's hand came to rest on hers, pushing down. Obedient, she pressed harder. Faster too, until Julia gasped and moaned, her pelvis moving in time to the rhythm she set.

"Oh, yes, baby," Julia repeated. "Oh, Corey, yes. Just like that."

Corey thumbed Julia's hard, swollen clit. Loving Julia this way seemed so familiar to her, not at all as though she'd never done it before. Julia's pleasure mattered to her. She wanted to give even more to pleasure her. Much more. She wanted to use her mouth, wanted to taste her, roll her tongue over Julia's clit, make her scream. She began moving down Julia's body, but Julia halted her, placing a firm hand beneath Corey's chin and raising her head until their eyes met.

"No," Julia whispered.

"Why not?"

"Not this time, baby."

Corey obeyed, but she wished Julia would fully open herself up and stop trying to take things slow. She wanted to experience everything with her. It must be a trust issue, more to do with Julia's faith in herself than anything to do with her, she decided. But they'd talk about those things later. Right now, there was the matter of Julia needing to come. She slipped a finger inside Julia and moved her thumb and forefinger in tandem.

Julia responded quickly. She rocked against Corey's touch, her body stiffening. Small trembles, like the waves in a pond, swept up her legs. She shattered in a sudden explosion, crying out and grinding Corey's hand harder against her as she rocked, riding out the storm of her orgasm.

"Oh, Corey!" Julia fought for breath. "Oh!"

Corey remained pressed against Julia. She marveled at the softness, the wetness, and the lingering spasms against her finger. Making love to a woman was a beautiful thing. "Thank you, Julia. You were wonderful."

"No, you were wonderful. And you're right, you *are* a quick learner!"

Corey lay with her new lover on the cramped sofa, relaxing in her embrace. After a few moments of silence, she began stroking Julia's face soothingly. "I want you to do something for me, okay?"

"Anything. Especially if it involves doing to you what you just did to me."

"Besides that."

"Okay."

"Julia, I want you to forgive yourself."

"What?"

"Forgive yourself." Corey let her words linger, waiting for Julia to grasp their meaning.

"I'm trying to."

Corey shifted so she could look at Julia. "You have to forgive yourself for what happened between you and Alex. Until that happens, you and I can't truly have anything meaningful between us."

Tears spilled down Julia's cheeks. "I know," she answered haltingly. "And I will."

"Good, that's all I ask." Corey gave Julia a lewd grin, a new heat burning inside her. "Well, there is something else I'd like."

Julia returned the grin through her tears. "I thought there might be something."

Corey didn't know exactly what she wanted until Julia began to open her blouse, spreading the fabric aside and kissing a trail on her bare chest as she slid down her body.

She didn't need to think about what she wanted, Corey realized, because Julia would answer her desires unasked.

Julia's touch was soft but skilled, insistent but yielding too. She kissed Corey's stomach as butterfly soft fingers moved between her thighs. Those seductive actions took away most of Corey's conscious awareness, as though her body and mind had melded and entered a blissful place where nothing but her own pleasure existed.

She was numb except for the fiery nerve endings between her legs. Not until she felt the first wet stroke of Julia's tongue did she even realize her pants and underwear had been pulled down around her ankles, and Julia had moved to kneel on the floor, placing Corey's legs over her shoulders. Now Julia's hot mouth pressed against her, lips and tongue moving in a perfectly timed rhythm.

Corey tried to find her voice, but her throat was dry and tight.

Weakened by her consuming pleasure, she managed to touch a hand to Julia's head, wanting her to stop but—*Oh, God!*—not wanting her to stop. Not ever. She gasped and finally muttered, "No fair. You...you wouldn't let me do this to you."

Julia stopped only long enough to declare that love wasn't always fair and neither was sex. Helpless against that skillful mouth, Corey threw her head back and let the sensations ripple through her entire body, beginning at her toes and collecting somewhere in her throat. With no self-control left, she pressed a hand to the back of Julia's head to urge her on, matching Julia's rhythm with her own little pelvic thrusts.

With a hunger she'd never known, she demanded more from Julia, selfishly taking her oral gifts to the precipice of climax. If there was some kind of God out there, surely this was as close to belief as she'd ever been because the pleasure was far beyond anything she'd experienced in the past. *This* was heaven, and Julia Landen her guiding angel.

Her orgasm ripped through her pelvis with magnificent force. Like a stone cast into a body of water, the waves reverberated outward, sweeping everything in their path and collecting in her heart, which pounded furiously. She cried out, clutched Julia's head, and let the spasms rock her body until she was spent. At last, Julia released her, moving back on the sofa to envelop her in a fierce hug.

"Oh, Julia." It was the most Corey could manage.

"Shh, don't say anything. Just let me hold you."

Corey did. *So this is what great sex is like!* She smiled at the only thought that seemed able to form in her head right now. Not just great sex, but making love. Making wonderful love with Julia, a beautiful woman she wanted to build a much deeper relationship with. Yes, maybe even a life with. She wanted so much more of this, and so much more of Julia.

***

Jane hated attending formal receptions without Alex. Alex was her touchstone, her true north. She kept Jane grounded, sane, and patient so she could endure anything. Which in this case was a lot of glad-handing, mutual sucking up with the country's governors, useless small talk and meaningless compliments.

A roomful of professional politicians was unlike any other gathering of people, Jane mused. All of them lions in the jungle, pretending they weren't hungry, pretending they weren't mindful of territories. Everyone here wanted something, but for her it was simpler. She needed their support, not only because they were super delegates, but because of their influence in their own states.

Colorado's Governor John Kirkton gave the welcoming speech. Jane followed, speaking about health care and the environment. A dinner of homegrown beef roasted to perfection was served. At last, only pleasantries and socializing remained. Jane hoped she could steal away soon and give Alex a goodnight call.

"Missing her, aren't you?" Corey whispered in her ear.

"Am I that predictable?"

"Yes. And that in love."

Jane smiled and looked at her sister, surprised by what she saw. Corey was practically glowing. Or maybe it was buzzing. She appeared positively happy about something. "What, did you win the lottery? No wait. You got Alabama's governor to support our ticket!"

Corey gave her a puzzled look before erupting into a laugh.

"Okay, give it up," Jane ordered. "You look like you've got everyone beat in the happiness department here. Well, everyone except *her*." Jane winked in the direction of California Governor Amy Roberts, who wore a sloppy smile and held a glass of rust-colored liquor in her hand. Probably that California brandy she liked to brag about, the Germain-Robin. After a little research, she'd discovered the brandy was made by a distillery owned by Forrest Mitchell.

"Amy looks well on her way to getting hammered." Corey smiled sarcastically.

"What else is new? So you never answered my question: who died and made you the queen of the world?"

"Ha, queen of the world? That's going to be you, my dear. One of these days!"

"Well, not if Dennis Collins has anything to say about it, I'm sure. Or Colby Harrison."

"Screw those good old boys. The world is changing and they're just pissed that they're being left at the curb."

"My, aren't you cocky tonight." Yup, Corey was still glowing. In fact, she was lit up like the top of the Empire State building. Realization struck Jane. She grasped her sister's arm tightly. "Oh, my God! You slept with her, didn't you?"

Corey laughed cynically. "Amy? Not on your life!"

"Very funny, little sister. As if you don't know who I'm talking about."

Corey grinned like a fool. An oversexed fool at that, Jane thought.

"All right," Jane said. "Later, in my room over a glass of wine, I want to hear more about this." She shook her head at Corey, not admonishing her. "Congratulations on your happiness, Corey. I mean that."

"I know you do. Thank you for saying so." Corey kissed Jane's cheek lightly. "Now if you'll excuse me for a bit, I want to go chat with Arizona's lieutenant governor." She lowered her voice to a conspiratorial whisper. "I've heard she's a dyke."

Jane stifled a laugh. "You lose your virginity and suddenly you're an expert on who's gay?"

Corey shrugged. "Gotta try out this new gaydar thing."

"All right, but if you spot Amy trying to steer me off to her drunken lair, please come rescue me."

"Deal. I won't abandon you, I promise."

To Jane's chagrin, it wasn't long before Amy homed in on her.

"Where's your sidekick, Madam Vice President?" Amy asked.

"Alex is still in Lawton helping with the cleanup and the rebuild."

"How sweet." Amy looked like she'd just swallowed something distasteful. "Actually, I was talking about the president."

"I'm sure you know the president is in France meeting with the G20."

"Ah, leaving you to do all the campaign heavy lifting again, is he?"

"Not at all. In any case, I'm not here to campaign. If you were paying attention to my speech, I'm here to push my agenda on health care and the environment."

Amy took a healthy slug of her drink. "Unofficially, then, how is the campaign going?"

Jane desperately scanned the crowd in the ballroom. She noticed several people she could talk to, all of them preferable to Amy Roberts. "It's going well, thank you. Listen, maybe later we could talk about the endorsement speech the president and I would like you to give at the convention."

"The endorsement speech I'll give *you*, you mean," Amy slurred.

Jane wasn't sure she'd heard correctly. "Sorry, what did you say?"

Amy swayed a little, resting her hand on Jane's arm for support and squeezing it intimately. Her touch felt like a snake bite. "You're the one everyone wants. The one *I* want, anyway." She continued in a barely audible hiss. "Dennis Collins is nothing but a disingenuous sleazeball. You'll be lucky if you don't get caught up in his filth."

Jane was rendered speechless. Whatever Amy Roberts alluded to, she wanted no knowledge of it. At least, she wanted no knowledge from Amy. Amy was treading on dangerous territory with her backhanded accusations and drunken allusions. It was exactly this kind of talk that could throw the ticket into a quagmire of damaging and dangerous gossip. Even baseless gossip was harmful if it picked up any amount of credibility or made it into the press.

"Excuse me, Governor," she said curtly. "There's someone I need to talk to."

***

Over a continental breakfast the next morning in her hotel room, Jane told Corey about the strange discussion with Amy Roberts. Corey agreed it was weird, even for Amy.

"Is she trying to suggest she knows something odious about Collins?"

Jane shrugged. She was tired and hadn't slept well, and today's schedule was jammed with meetings. She usually slept badly when she and Alex were apart. "I don't know, but she was getting at something. I don't think it was just idle drunken gossip."

"Are you going to call her on it? Get her to spill her guts?"

"Hell, no. You think I want her believing I want any part of such garbage? I do *not* want to get down in the trenches with Amy Roberts."

"Nope. As Mom likes to say, lie down with dogs and you'll get up with fleas."

Jane chuckled. Their mother, Maria, was a walking dictionary of old sayings, but the prospect of Collins harboring a scandal was no laughing matter. She had nothing to hide in her own life, but if Collins was dirty, she'd surely be swept up as collateral damage—a possibility that made her stomach cramp.

"I need to know if there's something or someone waiting in the weeds to torpedo us," Jane said. "Amy Roberts might be a drunk, and she might even be crazy, but even a broken clock is right twice a day."

"I know exactly what you mean." Corey let out an exasperated sigh. "I can discreetly ask around, but there's not much else I can do and remain under the radar."

"I know. Any inquiries *must* stay under the radar." She prided herself and the campaign on complete honesty and transparency. If Collins was hiding anything, she'd kill the son of a bitch.

"I just remembered something," Corey said around bites of spicy sausage and scrambled eggs. "A while ago, on my date with Julia at the White House Correspondents' dinner, she asked me if Collins was the type to screw around on his wife."

"What'd you say to her?"

"I said I hadn't a clue. Then we agreed we wouldn't mix business with pleasure and we changed the subject."

"Any idea why she was asking?"

"Nope, not a clue. She said it was just idle curiosity."

"I doubt that. A good journalist is never innocently curious. I expect she's fishing around for a story."

"Meaning she might know something?"

"Maybe. She may not know anything more than I know, which is just a bunch of smoke from a drunken Amy Roberts."

Corey thought for a moment. "Even if Julia only knew vague gossip, it would be enough to stir the bloodhound in her, I suppose. I'll ask her more about it."

"Look, I don't want you to harm your relationship for the sake of prying information out of her, okay? It'll put her in a very awkward spot."

"Yes, it will. But Jane, this is your future. Our future. The country's future. It's too important." Corey looked decidedly unhappy, but her jaw was set in that Kincaid determination.

Jane would leave it in her sister's hands. It wouldn't be wise for the vice president to start poking around in the president's private business. Doing so might look as though she were trying to find evidence to help her usurp him. She'd told Amy Roberts there would be no coup d'etat, and she meant it.

***

Julia opened her hotel room door and smiled happily. "Good morning, darling. This is a nice surprise."

Corey stepped in and hugged her tightly, giving her a kiss that nearly knocked her legs out from under her. "Good morning to you too, beautiful. Damn, I wish I'd stayed here all night. Then we'd be saying good morning naked."

"You could have, you know. It wasn't *my* idea for you to sneak out of here in the middle of the night."

"I know, I know." Corey pulled away, frowning deeply. "You're proving to be a wonderful incentive to get this damn election over with."

"If it doesn't kill us before then."

"Yes, there is that. It's only going to get more grueling as time goes on, so they say."

"Want some coffee with me?" Julia asked. "There's still some left. Unfortunately, it's all we have time for." She'd like nothing better than to whisk Corey into the bedroom and continue last night's delicious activities. "I have to be at that press conference downstairs in twenty minutes."

"I think we should both quit and go live in the Caribbean together for, oh, the next five months," Corey suggested.

"Hmm, that would coincide perfectly with the end of the election."

"Exactly my point."

"Well, it's a nice thought, but somehow I don't think the Caribbean is in our future right now. Have a seat and let me get you that coffee."

Corey sat down, watching Julia pour coffee from a carafe into a cup. "Will you think about a Caribbean vacation after the election?"

Julia handed her the cup and tried to hide her surprise. "Seriously?"

"Yes."

Julia was ready to go anywhere with this woman. There wasn't a single thing she didn't like about Corey. She was sweet, intelligent, beautiful, generous, and she'd proven a wonderful lover. Besides, the election was five more months of a very long and torturous grind for both of them. There would not be much time for them as a couple, and the prospect of a long vacation together was extremely alluring.

"I would love to go away with you when all of this is over," she said.

Corey leaned toward her and kissed her again. "Good. It's a date."

"I'm going to mark the trip in my calendar, so don't even think about trying to weasel out of it."

"Are you kidding? It's the election I'd like to weasel out of."

"You're not serious, are you? I mean, are you having second thoughts about working for your sister?"

Corey settled back on the sofa, exhaustion deepening the lines around her eyes. Staying up half the night having sex certainly couldn't have helped, but Julia wouldn't have traded it for more sleep. She doubted Corey would have either.

"No," Corey answered. "I'm not having second thoughts, but I do feel terribly unprepared at times. And overwhelmed."

"I'm no expert at this, but you've got good instincts, Corey. They'll serve you well."

"I know. That's what Jane says too. She says she feels the same way herself sometimes, and says some days it's just a matter of putting your head down, rolling up your sleeves, and plodding through it, even if you feel like you don't know what you're doing."

"Sounds like good advice. For myself too."

"Listen, there's something I want to ask you about."

"Hmm, you look very serious."

"It is serious. At the correspondents' dinner, you asked me if Collins was the type to screw around on his wife. Why did you ask me that?"

A kernel of panic edged into her gut. She hadn't told anyone about the compromising photos of President Collins other than her Miami colleague, who was diligently investigating. She hadn't snooped around since that night at the correspondents' dinner either, having decided to wash her hands of the matter and let Chase Benson stick his neck out. To her, the involvement wasn't worth the risks.

"I, ah, was just curious," she replied. "I didn't know much about Collins and was trying to get a feel for him. It seems like most U.S. presidents have mistresses. I was just wondering if he was like all the others."

Corey gave her a scrutinizing look. "So was it an innocent question? Or do you know something?"

Shit. Julia really didn't want to lie to Corey, but there wasn't much to tell. The photos might be totally innocent, and Chase Benson hadn't reported any news back to her yet. She didn't want to involve Corey, at least not yet. She forced a smile. "I thought we'd agreed we weren't going to talk business when we're together."

Corey sighed loudly and rubbed her tired eyes. "I know. You're right. I'm sorry. The convention is less than three months away, and the Republicans are going to start turning up the heat any day. I don't want any surprises, that's all."

Julia wished she could help, but remaining neutral was her job. As a reporter, she wasn't supposed to *help* anyone. Besides, she told herself again, she had nothing concrete on Collins. The evidence she'd been given was completely inconclusive, and she had absolutely no idea who was behind it. Nothing she could do or say would shed any light on it.

She felt helpless. Clasping Corey's hand, she raised it to her lips. "I understand."

CHAPTER THIRTEEN

Standing in line at a famous Arlington hamburger joint to place her order didn't bother Jane, but Dennis Collins looked determinedly unhappy. She didn't know which he despised more: her company, or rubbing shoulders with the working-class patrons of the restaurant.

In her opinion, their visit here was a brilliant public relations move. It was Corey's idea to have her and Collins grab a burger together with only a couple of strategically placed photographers to keep it as real as possible—blatant campaigning without having to stump or even travel far from the White House. She and the president would be seen as a united team, two buddies out for a burger together in the presence of everyday people.

Jane ordered her burger and sweet potato fries at the counter. Collins did the same before they moved to a worn wooden booth and waited for their number to be called. They attracted plenty of looks, waves and smiles from the other patrons, which she happily returned. She was at her most comfortable doing the everyday things that others took for granted.

Collins, on the other hand, appeared awkward, almost resentful, and totally out of his element. The longer he was president, the more he wanted to stay secluded in the White House. An election year was most definitely not the time for him to play possum. Jane wished like hell he'd start realizing that.

"You could try a little harder you know," she mumbled to him, unable to help herself. Some days it felt like Amy Roberts was right—*she* was doing most of the heavy lifting in this campaign.

"I think it's a ridiculous idea," he snapped. "It's like the Queen of England sitting in a London pub hoisting a beer with the peasants. People don't want their president hanging out at a crappy burger joint."

"It's not a crappy burger joint. It's the most popular place around these parts. And I disagree. People want to see that we're everyday people. Living in a castle, untouchable and out of touch, doesn't cut it anymore. I think even the Queen would agree with that."

"Thanks for the life lesson," Collins fired back.

Jane almost felt sorry for him. He could be tremendously popular if he'd connect with people, try to relate to them, get off his high horse and down to their level. He was an enigma even to her. She had no idea what made him tick. He was very guarded about his personal life, stubbornly clinging to the image of an all-knowing, all-powerful but distant entity, the unapproachable father figure who garnered respect through fear and a little mystery. For a politician, it was an outdated, dangerous way to think.

Their number was called. Jane went to the counter to retrieve their food. She noticed that Collins looked slightly terrified at being left alone, and the sight made her chuckle to herself.

She turned to each person in line. "Hello, how are you? Nice to see you." Everyone she spoke to looked astonished to see her in their midst, but she smiled at them as though this was a common occurrence. "Thank you so much," she said to the aproned woman who handed her two full plates. "It looks wonderful! Enjoy, everyone."

She resumed her seat and began to tuck into the huge burger, knowing she'd never be able to finish it.

"What do you know, it's not half bad," Collins grumbled around a mouthful of beef.

Jane ate in silence, having little to say to him outside the confines of the West Wing. They'd never be buddies, which was fine with her. What she needed from him was reliability, steadiness, predictability, and more than halfhearted efforts on the campaign trail.

With the convention only five weeks away, Colby Harrison's attacks were becoming more frequent and more intense. They could rebuff the head-on volleys easily enough. What Jane feared most was an ambush. She had nothing to hide, no grenade about to blow up in her face, but she wasn't so sure about Collins. She'd heard nothing more about Amy Roberts's boozy insinuations, but that didn't mean there wasn't a shred of truth behind them.

"Dennis," she ventured. "I want to talk about the campaign."

"What's to talk about? We're polling well. Harrison can't touch us."

"Are you sure about that?"

"What the hell is that supposed to mean?"

Jane set down her half-eaten burger and carefully wiped mustard from the corner of her mouth. "Is there anything that could catch us unawares? Anything that could suddenly torpedo our chances?"

Collins refused to pick up on her hint. "I don't have a clue what you're talking about."

"All right. Is there anything in your past or in your current life that our opponents might use against us?"

Collins narrowed his eyes angrily, his face reddening. "*You* are asking *me* if my personal life is a liability in this campaign?"

Jane smiled so it wouldn't appear that they were arguing. Her smile was also meant to show Collins that his stinging tone had no effect on her. "Yes. I'm asking."

Dismissively, Collins returned to consuming his burger in silence. When he finished, he looked levelly at Jane and said, "You don't need to worry about me. Nothing is going to sabotage this campaign."

Something about his words didn't ring true. She was not at all reassured.

***

For days, Jane had not been her usual energetic and optimistic self, Alex noticed with concern. Now it was Sunday and a rare day off from campaigning. Tomorrow, her campaign would stop in Des Moines, Iowa, then Omaha, Nebraska, before swinging down to Kansas City, then Jefferson City, Missouri, and finally Indianapolis. Jane would need to quickly get out of her funk if she wanted her campaign appearances to make a positive impact, particularly since many of her stops weren't exactly Democratic strongholds. She'd need to be on her game.

Over breakfast at the kitchen table, Alex's impatience grew. She wanted to get to the bottom of things, and was unable to hold back any longer. "Honey, what's wrong?"

Jane threw the *Post* down on the table before resuming the halfhearted attempts at eating her French toast. "Nothing. Why do you ask?"

"Because I know something's bothering you, and I'd really like to talk about it. Are you worried about the campaign? Carter says everything's going smoothly." The latest poll showed the Collins-Kincaid ticket well ahead of Republican frontrunner, Colby Harrison.

"Yes, it's on track. But right now I'm just really looking forward to it all being over."

Jane's statement was a huge red flag. "That's not like you, sweetheart. You love campaigning. I know you're confident about the outcome. Is it the pace? Because I really think you should slow it down a bit, maybe even take a short break and—"

"No way. You know a break right now is out of the question. With the convention a month away, things are really starting to ramp up."

"I know, but a three- or four-day holiday at your mom's would give you a nice break and recharge your batteries."

"My batteries are fine."

"They're not, actually," Alex said.

She and Jane hadn't made love in almost two weeks. Jane wasn't eating much. She was too thin and getting dark circles under her eyes. However, Alex wasn't masochistic enough to point those things out at the moment.

"You've been really tired the last couple of weeks, and you've been moping around lately," she said carefully. "So either you're exhausted or something's worrying you. Which is it?"

Jane set her fork down a little too loudly. "Look, I'm fine, okay?"

"Sweetheart, I know you better than anybody, and I'm worried about you. Please tell me what's going on, okay?" Alex grinned provocatively. "Or am I going to have to subject you to my interrogation techniques?"

Jane didn't smile at the joke. She sighed instead. "I'm just... Oh, hell, everything's fine. I'm being a little paranoid, that's all."

"About what?"

Jane sipped her coffee in silence for a moment. "I'm a little worried about Collins," she said at last.

"Worried how?"

"I've got this sinking feeling in the pit of my stomach that there's something about him, either something in his past or something in his present that he's hiding. Something that's going to blow up in our faces."

Alex knew that Jane was often right about her gut feelings. "How long has this been bothering you?"

"A while. Since the governors' conference in Denver."

"That long? Why didn't you tell me?"

"I didn't want to alarm you. And I didn't want you to try to *handle* it."

Alex's spine stiffened. Jane wouldn't purposely try to insult her by insinuating she sometimes got too involved, but still, the words hurt. She would do anything for Jane, go to any wall, take any risk to help her out of a jam. Jane almost sounded as if she resented it.

"You make it sound like my help is a liability," she said.

"I'm sorry. I didn't mean it like that. Amy Roberts said something to me at the conference that touched a nerve. She was drunk, but she made some comment about Collins being a sleazeball."

"Yeah, so. I'm sure he's greased a few wheels over the years to get where he is."

"No, I don't think she meant that kind of thing. I got the feeling she was referring to his personal life."

Alex couldn't suppress a laugh. "Well, if he's JFK with call girls coming to the White House, I haven't heard a thing about it. And if he was doing that kind of thing, I *would* have heard about it. You would have too."

"No, I don't think he's that reckless. I don't know, Alex. But if he's up to something that could hurt the campaign, he's playing with my future too. That's got me very worried."

"Jane, I know you have great gut instincts, but considering the source—"

"It's not just Amy. Julia asked Corey once—a couple of months ago when they first started dating—if Collins was screwing around on his wife."

"Probably just nasty reporter gossip, you know how they are. They all think politicians screw around."

"You think that's all it is?"

"Yes. In fact, I'll ask her about it if you want."

"No!" Jane nearly leapt out of her chair before easing back down. "I don't want her thinking there's something to this. It'll just set her radar off. Besides, Corey did ask her if there was anything behind her question and she said no."

Jane was right. If she gave the least bit of credence to some suggestion, or even hinted that it had merit, reporters would take it as gospel. On the flip side, it was also important that Jane not appear to be complicit if Collins was hiding anything about his personal life. That could put her in a real bind if the public thought she knew something unethical about the president but remained silent. Dialoguing with a journalist about the matter was absolutely out of the question.

"Shit," Alex said. "I see how this could be a real problem."

"I know. I'm screwed if I'm caught by surprise and I'm screwed if I uncover anything."

"Let's hope neither scenario is going to happen."

"Alex, *hope* isn't part of my vocabulary. Something either happens or it doesn't. I don't want to sit and wait to be collateral damage, but I can't get my hands dirty digging around either. I don't know what the hell to do."

"How about we get someone who's not connected to you and not connected to your campaign, but who will keep their mouth shut, to do a little digging?"

Jane shook her head forcefully. "Too risky."

"Okay. What about getting Clara or the DNC to privately lean on him? Force him to clean up his act. Or come clean about it and resign."

Jane stared morosely into her coffee cup. "We're getting ahead of ourselves. We don't even know if he's done anything wrong. And if we get Clara or the DNC involved, he's going to say I'm a bitch gunning to get him off the ticket."

"Damn it, there's got to be something we can do."

"I don't like any of our options."

Alex disliked the grim reality of Jane being put in the position of a helpless victim waiting for the ax to fall if the media or her Republican opponents uncovered anything sinister about Collins. Exposure might even come down to a loose cannon like Amy Roberts if she decided to break the story open.

She could not sit idly by and watch Jane's political career unravel through no fault of her own. It suddenly occurred to her what she must do. She would not tell Jane. Jane would beg her not to get involved, but it was vital that Jane stay at arm's length from all of this.

Alex picked up the newspaper Jane had tossed aside earlier. "One thing I know about President Collins is that he isn't a stupid man. If he's got anything to hide, he'll keep it buried about a hundred feet deep."

"He'd better or I'll make him damned sorry."

"That's the spirit, my love. Now you're sounding like the Jane Kincaid I know and love."

"I feel so powerless against something that could affect my life so deeply."

"I know," Alex said soothingly. Jane might be powerless but *she* was not.

CHAPTER FOURTEEN

Nebraska was home to the flattest land Julia had ever seen. Flatter even than her native Michigan, which at least was broken up by lakes Michigan and Huron. She stared glumly out of the window of the press bus at the endless miles of identical cornfields, wondering how many states she'd visited in the last three months. At least sixteen, probably more, she thought. Some blurred into others. For instance, Indiana resembled much of Illinois, as did Minnesota. And Iowa and Nebraska were almost indistinguishable. Ditto for Kansas and Oklahoma. The travel sometimes wore her down to the point of exhaustion. She knew it grated on Corey too, and probably Jane, but Jane wasn't allowed to display her fatigue in public.

Julia thought about Jane's speech yesterday in Des Moines. For the first time in the campaign, she'd directly addressed the economy. Collins typically spoke about the country's number one concern, as though he were the lead actor who got all the best lines and all the best parts. Only fair since he was the president, she supposed.

Jane's foray into new territory had come as a surprise, possibly signaling that she was unafraid of the bigger issues, ready to be taken seriously as presidential material herself one day, perhaps in the not-too-distant future. Julia's more cynical side mused that Jane might even be purposely trying to steal some of the president's thunder.

In the speech, she addressed tax breaks and the need to do away with those that favored the wealthy. The tax code, she pointed out, was filled with $1.1 trillion in credits, deductions and exemptions, an average of about $8,000 per taxpayer. The wealthy, she said to loud cheers, have much better access to more lucrative tax breaks than people with lower incomes. The wealthy need to pay "so that the amount of taxes *you* pay isn't determined by what kind of accountant you can afford." The law, she said, is "packed with tax breaks that help narrow special interests. With a surgeon's precision, I'd like to keep the tax breaks that benefit everyday average Americans and slice out the ones that favor those who can most afford to pay the taxes in the first place."

Julia considered the possibility that Jane might become president, or at least a contender, much sooner than anyone expected. If the walls caved in on Dennis Collins, if he did have a mistress and a love child and the public found out, Jane might not have to wait four more years. She might suddenly find herself at the top of the Democratic heap if scandal sank Collins, or she might sink right along with him.

She was not expert enough to guess how Jane might fare, but she felt relieved the decision to break the scandal—*if* a scandal existed—was out of her hands. Yes, she'd played a role by passing the incriminating photos on to her colleague in Miami, because it wasn't her place to turn a blind eye to such potentially explosive evidence. As a journalist, it was her duty to uncover the truth, or at least to advance the truth. If there was no scandal, then Collins's enemies were shooting blanks and would eventually be exposed. If there was something sinister to the photos, it was only fair that the American people be made aware. As far as she was concerned, a president who was untruthful and kept secrets could not be trusted and did not deserve the office.

Julia didn't want to believe that her actions or inactions could change the political landscape or might alter history. She was a former cop turned journalist, not a kingmaker. Or queenmaker. It wasn't incumbent upon her to share the information with the Collins-Kincaid campaign, despite the way her loyalty to Corey and even to Jane and Alex tugged at her.

She struggled with chucking her neutrality and sending up a warning flag that something was going on. She'd lose her job if she did that, along with her credibility as a journalist. But if she didn't, she'd probably lose her girlfriend. If Corey found out about her suspicions and those photographs, she'd be mightily pissed, probably to the point of not forgiving her.

Julia cursed her dilemma. She had fallen in love with Corey. The things that mattered to Corey mattered to her too. This campaign mattered for reasons that had nothing to do with her newspaper job. She wanted to make Corey happy, but where their careers were concerned, she and Corey were individuals and professionals, each with her own set of loyalties and duties. Surely Corey would understand.

From inside her purse, Julia's cell phone rang. She dug it out, answering the call on the fourth ring. The caller was her boss, Craig Finney, an intimidating man with the demeanor of a pitbull and no patience for small talk. He got straight to the point and told her he wanted to see her in Miami this week.

"I can't," she said with a sinking feeling in her stomach that the Collins photos were at the heart of Finney's request. "This Midwest campaign swing is still in high gear. I can't possibly break free from it until next week."

Finney sighed impatiently. "I won't discuss this over the phone or by e-mail. That's why I need a meeting with you and Chase. We've got to get our ducks in a row."

"So Chase has been making progress?"

"The cake is almost ready for the oven. We still need to talk about it with legal, but I want you in on this meeting."

Shit. It was really happening. Chase Benson had obviously dug up something juicy on Collins, and the story was nearing publication. She tried to stall, both wanting to know and not wanting to know what was going on. "How about early next week?"

"Monday at 10 a.m., my office."

"I'll be there."

She hung up and sank back in her seat, closing her eyes. She'd stirred up a hornet's nest and there was no taking it back, but at least she'd find out exactly what was going on. The meeting would give her a chance to weigh in with her opinion, have some influence on the outcome. She'd take things one step at a time.

She thought of Corey, wondering how much to tell her. There wasn't much to say…yet. But after the meeting, yes, she'd have to tell Corey *something*.

***

In her nondescript Omaha hotel room, hovering on the edge of sleep, Corey held Julia close. They'd made love—extraordinary, sensual, multiorgasmic love. Exhausted after the long day of campaigning and then sex, she and Julia lay in each other's arms, both awake but barely.

Corey's thumb and fingers lightly stroked the soft skin of Julia's shoulder. How easy it was to love her, to love a woman she was so emotionally connected to. The touches fueled her emotions and set her heart soaring, as if a cage door had opened. Julia did that to her. She found it both frightening and exhilarating.

Julia held her heartstrings in her hands, a tremendous power that left Corey sometimes weak and needy. They hadn't said the words, *I love you*, but she knew they were on the verge.

Last night Corey had almost said the words. They had snuck off together in Des Moines for a twilight walk along the Center Street Bridge, the pathway romantically lit with blue lights. They stopped in the middle, gazing out at the darkened Des Moines River. She slipped her hand in Julia's. Being together felt so right, so familiar, so natural.

At times she wanted to scream from the rooftops how much

she cared for Julia. She would, someday, but not yet. Parts of their relationship would simply have to wait until after the election, when they could give each other and their relationship everything. And so she hadn't uttered the words.

Julia stirred beside her and cleared her throat in a nervous way. Corey's back involuntarily stiffened.

"I have to go to Miami to meet with my boss," Julia said.

"When?"

"Monday. I'll probably fly there Sunday, come back Monday evening."

As far as Corey knew, Julia had never been summoned back to Miami in the five months she'd been on the campaign beat. It must be serious. "Why does he want to see you? He's not reassigning you, is he?"

"No. I don't think it's anything like that."

Thank God! It was hard enough maintaining their relationship without adding geographical distance. "You're not in any sort of trouble, are you?"

Julia hesitated before laughing a little uncertainly. "Maybe he thinks I'm being too nice to you guys."

Corey smiled in the dark. "You are definitely being very nice to me!" Her stomach sank as a thought occurred. "Crap, maybe he found out about us and wants to pull you off the beat."

"No. It'd be the opposite. Craig Finney would have me pumping you for every little dark secret I could get out of you."

Corey rolled on top of Julia and began playfully nipping her neck. "I personally love the way you've embedded yourself in the campaign."

"Me too." Julia wrapped her legs around Corey. "And I don't care if you never tell me a single secret, just keep doing what you're doing, honey."

***

Alex schooled her expression and squared her shoulders, watching in satisfaction as Amy Roberts's expression changed from bemusement to concern. Sitting in her oversized leather chair behind her equally oversized glass desk, the governor eyed Alex with what was clearly suspicion.

The contemporary furnishings and the in-your-face opulence of the governor's office did not at all reflect the growing poverty of the state of California. Alex wondered why on earth Amy Roberts would want her office to look so cold, remote and ostentatious, so out of touch with the people she served. Oh, well, that was *her* concern.

Amy finally said, "Am I correct in assuming, Agent Warner, that you are not here to pay me a social call?"

"That's correct."

"That's too bad." Her smile resembled more of a smirk. "I was hoping you'd give me an update on how your wife's campaign is going. She certainly has the media seduced."

"More than the media, it seems to me."

A finely manicured eyebrow rose, but otherwise the governor's face remained inscrutable. An astute, calculating politician, Amy made up for her cool and inaccessible demeanor with successful scheming and plenty of timely, well placed ass-kissing. She was politically well connected, but Alex didn't doubt that her trail to Sacramento was littered with debts to her benefactors and the corpses of her enemies.

"What can I do for you?" Amy asked curtly, pushing aside a stack of papers with a heavy sigh, as though Alex's visit was an inconvenience of the highest order.

Alex took a seat without being invited. She didn't expect to get much out of Amy, at least not this time, but she would serve notice that she was onto her. "What do you know about the president?"

"Excuse me?"

"Look, I didn't come fourteen hundred miles out of my way to sit here and play footsie with you."

Amy laughed uncertainly and settled back in her chair. She appraised Alex cheerfully. "I can see why Jane was attracted to you. You don't play around, do you, Agent Warner?"

No, and neither does my wife. Alex simply smiled and waited.

"However, I'm afraid I don't understand your question."

"All right, let me be more explicit. You know something about President Collins that isn't common knowledge. Something personal. Something that could sink his presidency. I want to know what it is, and I want to know who else knows it."

Amy averted her eyes and crossed her arms defiantly over her chest. "I think you're mistaken, Agent Warner. I don't know any such thing about the president."

"Ah, but that's where *you're* mistaken, because I think you do. I think you're holding it like some little trump card, or someone is. And you know something, Governor? I couldn't give a rat's ass about the president, but whatever is done to him is done to Jane too. I won't see her go down the toilet with him."

"I admire your loyalty to Jane. Must be nice for her, having her own personal attack dog."

Alex leapt out of her chair to lean menacingly across Amy's desk. "I am not her attack dog, and I am not here on official business. I'm here because I intend to put a stop to whatever it is you're playing at, which I'm very happy to do on my own time."

"I'm afraid this brand of intimidation is unacceptable." Amy picked up the handset of her telephone. "I'm going to call security."

"I wouldn't do that, unless you want to raise this little debate to a whole new level." Alex unclipped her cell phone from her belt. "I have the IRS on speed dial."

Amy's face blanched. She dropped the handset back in its cradle. "I really don't know what the hell you're talking about, and I resent whatever you're trying to imply."

Alex eased back into her chair. "I understand you're friends with Forrest Mitchell."

"Acquaintances, not friends."

"Business partners too?"

Alex had done some snooping. Amy held a minority ownership in one of Mitchell's distilleries. She had money in one of his wineries as well. Alex would wager that Amy wasn't entirely upfront with the IRS about all of her business dealings.

Amy brushed the accusation away with a cool wave of her hand. "Big deal. The making of wine and brandy is a hobby to me. What is it that you want?"

"Information. Who's trying to screw Collins, and what are they planning to do?"

"Please. You think I'd be privy to some sort of conspiracy to bring down the president?"

"Probably not, but I think you know a little something about it."

She and Amy stared at each other across the desk like gunfighters at sunset. Amy blinked first. "All I know is that Dennis Collins is hiding something about his personal life. Something the public wouldn't appreciate or approve of. You and I both know the public has no appetite for anything scandalous in politicians' private lives. Or for politicians who lie."

"Aren't you afraid of being found out as a closet lesbian?" Alex asked with mock innocence.

Amy bristled. "I thought you weren't here to talk about me."

"You're right, I'm not. So what's Collins hiding? Some kind of trouble his penis has gotten him into?"

"That would be my guess, yes."

Alex shook her head in disgust. *Don't tell me the old can't-keep-it-in-his-pants is about to destroy another politician. When will these guys ever learn?* "Who knows about it, and what are they going to do with the information?"

"I don't know," Amy replied curtly. "But I presume it's some sort of powder keg that could blow at any time between now and the election."

Alex was sure Amy knew more than she was sharing. Amy might not know all the details, but she damned well knew the general plan and who was behind the scheme to bring down Dennis Collins. Among his enemies, the likeliest candidates were Colby Harrison and the power hungry Forrest Mitchell. An impatient man who wanted the Democrats to quickly advance the gay rights agenda, Mitchell was no fan of Collins.

"Fine," she said. "But I want you to pass a message on to your buddy Forrest Mitchell for me. If he takes Collins out, he takes out his golden girl Jane too, and that gives Harrison the keys to the White House. I'm sure Mitchell doesn't want that. You can also tell him that if he has anything to do with this, he'll have bigger people than me to worry about."

It infuriated her to think that someone was toying with Jane's future, throwing the dice in a gamble that could irreparably harm Jane's career and potentially set gay rights back decades. If Mitchell had his fingerprints on this, he was much more reckless than she had given him credit for.

She wanted Amy to tell Mitchell that she'd string him up

by his balls if he was planning anything to bring down Collins, but she couldn't back up the threat. She couldn't run around intimidating people on Jane's behalf or conducting a one-woman investigation. In fact, she'd taken a big risk by coming here. Most importantly, she must not let any of this lead back to Jane. If Jane was found to have any knowledge about a conspiracy against Collins, it could potentially lead to criminal charges, leaving her with more than her career to worry about.

Alex stood to go. "It's been a slice, Governor," she said sarcastically.

"I'm sure we'll cross paths at the upcoming convention."

"Count on it."

Alex found the nearest washroom and splashed cold water on her face. Something sinister was afoot—the feeling reinforced by a slow burn in her gut—but she had no idea how to stop it. She was clear about her priority, however. She had to protect Jane.

CHAPTER FIFTEEN

In what took only minutes in Craig Finney's meticulously tidy office, Julia's boss and reporter Chase Benson methodically laid out all the details of Benson's investigation.

Dennis Collins had begun an affair with one of his campaign workers four years ago. He'd fathered a child with her, a boy who was now two. He kept his mistress in a Miami condo, likely paying her a huge monthly sum to keep her happy and silent. As far as Benson could tell, Collins continued to maintain a sporadic relationship with the woman, Gina Stonehouse, and the boy, Denny. The president's wife didn't appear to know about the relationship, or if she did, she was playing dumb. Collins had shown great skill at keeping the affair and the child a secret.

Benson hadn't been able to find enough material on the record for a slam dunk, but he had the photos Julia had been given, and he'd been able to trace the condo ownership back to a third party who was on Collins's payroll.

"So we don't have enough to go on?" Julia asked hopefully. They had not much more evidence than some rag like the *Enquirer* would be happy to run.

"Oh, we have enough," Finney replied smugly. "Enough to put it out there and let people draw their own conclusions. And they will. Collins will have no choice but to answer to these allegations. The national media will hound him relentlessly and dig up every dirty scrap they can find. Not to mention the Republicans."

"It'll be fatal to his career," Benson said with a sardonic smile. "It'll throw the campaign into one hell of a shit storm. Dennis Collins is about to become a lame-duck president."

Julia looked at Finney and Benson, knowing the men sensed blood in the water. She thought they were enjoying this far too much. The story would be a boost to their careers, give them instant notoriety and fame, as well as enormous power. It wasn't often that ordinary people like them were in a position to affect politics at the highest level. She felt sick.

"Did legal give the okay to run this?" Julia asked, quietly seething. How could the newspaper publish this crap without better proof to back up their claims? The evidence was too thin, as far as she was concerned.

"Yup," Finney said. "And so did the publisher."

Julia knew her opinion wasn't worth much, but they'd asked her here and she'd damned well give it to them. "I don't like it. You've got very little proof, no one on the record to confirm the relationship, nothing on this kid other than the photos and his name being Denny, a third party owning the condo. It's yellow journalism. We'll look incompetent at best, unethical and manipulative at worst."

Finney laughed at her. "Come on, Landen. You're the one who gave us the photos. Don't go all soft on us now."

Exasperated, Julia said, "Someone targeted me with those photos. Why aren't we going after that person? Finding out who it is and why they have an ax to grind with Collins? They're using us and we're letting them."

"Who cares who gave us the pictures?" Benson cut in. "It could be anybody. Hell, it could even have been the First Lady. Or one of the president's other girlfriends, or one of his many enemies. Doesn't change anything."

"No, you're wrong," Julia said with conviction. "I think the bigger story is who's behind Collins's exposure."

"Look," Finney said crossly. "We're not the FBI. We don't have the resources or the time to run a huge investigation. Anyway, it's for the best."

"How can you say that?"

"Because it's better the American public finds out now what kind of man Collins is than after he's re-elected."

Julia was forced to agree. She'd justified passing the photos onto her newspaper with that very same argument.

"We're just about ready to run with it," Finney said.

"When?"

"Next week."

"Next week!" Julia flew out of her chair and began pacing. "But that's the convention!"

"Exactly." Finney's eyes gleamed. He looked like a hungry wolf. "Our publisher wants to break the story when it will have the biggest impact."

Julia felt her face heating in anger. "So it comes down to the almighty buck! And power. The *Herald* will stand to make a pile of money in sales and will come out looking like a major player on the national stage. It's disgusting."

Finney laughed. "My dear, you can't possibly be so naïve about the news business to think we *wouldn't* jump at a scoop any news organizations would kill for."

"Well, it makes me sick."

"Fine," Finney said, "be sick. If you can't stomach it, I'll pull you out of D.C. and put you on the local education beat."

Julia was pissed. Those were *her* photos. She should have some say in how the story played out. "I can stomach it just fine, at least until this election is over." Then she'd quit the newspaper, but not before. She'd already invested months into working the campaign beat. She wouldn't give up the assignment now, no matter how distasteful the situation had become. She felt near tears, but refused to give Finney or Benson the satisfaction of seeing her cry.

"Good. I want you to stay hot on Jane Kincaid," Finney said. "When this blows, there's going to be a lot on her shoulders. I want you reporting on her reaction. This is either going to bury her career or make her the next nominee."

Getting back on the plane for Washington, Julia's stomach was in knots. She'd known, of course, that giving those photos to her colleague would likely unleash *something*, but she hadn't considered the timing or the full ramifications of the situation. She should have insisted on going after whoever had sent the pictures to her in the first place. Benson and Finney had gotten distracted by the obvious—a secretive affair by President Collins—and played right into the hands of whoever was behind the exposé, but it was too late now. In a week, the Democratic convention would be underway, and Collins and Kincaid would be fighting for their political lives.

It'd be a fight she had a hand in making a hell of a lot worse for them.

***

Alex hadn't known she was going to greet Julia at Ronald Reagan airport until her gut instinct told her she should. Corey had mentioned something about Julia being in Miami, and Alex couldn't help but think the trip had something to do with Collins. If she was correct, she wanted to know exactly what was going on and how Julia was involved.

Startled at first, Julia quickly looked almost relieved to see Alex, who steered her into one of the airport's VIP lounges and ordered them each a glass of California white wine.

"You look exhausted," Alex said.

"Stressed out, you mean," Julia said on a long sigh.

"Okay. Stressed out. Want to tell me what took you to Miami?" Alex half expected Julia to protest or even deny a meeting with her boss, but instead she settled back in her seat, took a long sip of wine, and raised compliant eyes to meet hers.

Julia looked exhausted and red-faced, perhaps even like she'd been crying on the plane. "I know I shouldn't be telling you this, but I'm going to be telling Corey anyway, so you might as well know too. My paper is going to break a story on Collins during the convention."

Alex tensed. She had an idea what might be coming. "What kind of story?"

"That he has a mistress and an illegitimate kid."

"Aw, shit. I knew it."

"You did?"

"Sort of, but not really. I mean, I figured something was up, and it's usually these guys' dicks that get them into trouble."

Julia snorted a laugh. "Well, it seems he's as bad as the rest of them. The paper doesn't have much hard evidence, just a condo lease they can loosely trace back to him and a couple of photos that were anonymously sent to me."

"You mean you knew about this all along?"

"No!" Julia amended. "I didn't know what the photos meant. I passed them on to one of my colleagues to do some digging a couple of months ago."

"Who sent them to you?"

"I don't know. It's so damned frustrating. There's nothing to link them to anyone. The one phone call I got came up on caller ID with a blocked number."

Alex shook her head. "If you'd told me about this sooner, I might have been able to do something about it."

"I'm a reporter, Alex. I don't work for you, Jane or the administration. Besides, if I'd told you, it would have been hushed up and nothing would have come of it, and that wouldn't have been right either."

"It's not necessarily true that the story would have been swept under the carpet." Alex had to numb herself against the growing panic in her gut. Not only was Collins being set up for a fall, but Jane too. Letting her emotions get in the way right now would only make things worse. "Why did this anonymous person pick you out of all the reporters in D.C.?"

"I don't know. Maybe because I was new in town and they thought I'd be eager for a big story. Or maybe they thought I could be easily duped."

"Why are they breaking the story during the convention?" Alex already knew the answer: to cause the greatest damage to President Collins.

"It's taken all this time to work on the story. The paper's still got a couple of hoops to jump through before it's ready for print, but yeah, basically the *Herald* wants to wait for the time it will have the biggest impact."

"Fucking bastards," Alex spat.

"I agree with you, but on the other hand, if Collins was stupid enough to do what he did, he deserves to get caught."

"I know, I know, but goddamn it, Jane's going to be an innocent victim in all this."

Julia smiled enigmatically. "Or the big winner."

"Come again?"

"Who knows? Maybe she'll emerge the hero in all this. The heir apparent who stands to gain the most."

Alex felt her face warming. Incredulous, she asked, "Are you implying that she had something to do with the scandal? Or that she's happy about any of this?"

"Of course not." Julia rubbed her eyes. "I don't know what I'm saying, but we don't know yet how the chips are going to fall. I'm just saying it could end up helping Jane."

"Well, that's a hell of a long shot." Alex would be damned if she was going to sit around and do nothing over the next few days, waiting for the ax to fall at the convention. There had to be something she could do. "I want the names of your editor, your publisher and this reporter who dug up the story."

"You got it. But I need you to do one thing for me."

"Whatever you want."

"Please let me be the one to tell Corey about this, okay?"

"You really like her, don't you?"

"No." Julia shook her head. "I love her, Alex."

Alex blinked in surprise, and then raised her glass to Julia's.

***

The urgency in Julia's voice over the phone last night had been unmistakable. At first, Corey thought she was simply anxious to get together, but there'd been something distinctly ominous about her tone. Julia had pleaded to see her as soon as possible, but Corey's evening meetings on convention prep were expected to run late. Very late. Breakfast today was the best she could do, though she'd gotten little sleep wondering what was on Julia's mind.

They couldn't kiss in public, so Corey hugged Julia closely in the restaurant, an old-fashioned diner off the beaten path, complete with vinyl upholstery and checkered tiles. "I missed you, darling. How was Miami?"

Julia looked nervous, her eyes tired and red-rimmed. "Not great."

Corey's heart began to thud. Something was wrong. "You look awful. What happened?"

A waitress swung by their booth and filled their coffee cups. "Will you ladies be having breakfast?"

Simultaneously, Corey said yes, Julia no. The waitress smiled and said she'd be back.

"Honey, you need to eat," Corey ordered.

"I don't really have the stomach for food right now."

"What's wrong? You've got me scared."

Julia nervously stirred her coffee, the spoon tinking against the ceramic. "I don't quite know where to start."

"Anywhere. Just start, okay?" Corey reached over and stilled Julia's hand.

"All right, I'll start at the beginning. In April, right after the trip to New York, someone sent me an anonymous photo. And then another photo a little while later. I have no idea who—"

"A photograph of what?"

"A photo of President Collins with a woman. It wasn't sexual, but it looked intimate. And there was another photo showing him with the same woman and a toddler, the three of them in a park."

Corey had been holding her breath. Now she let it out in a soft explosion. She had a feeling where this was heading. "That's it, two photographs? Nothing else?"

"Nothing else, and no indication of who sent them."

"What did you do with these photos?"

"Nothing at first, I—"

"You could have come to me. I would have figured something out."

"I know, but I'm a reporter, Corey, I'm supposed to be neutral. I'm not supposed to run to you with information, just as you wouldn't run to me with something so volatile either."

"You're right, you're right, but someone could have been setting you up, playing you, and I could have helped. Now it's too damned late."

Julia looked tortured. She clutched her coffee cup like a lifeline, the frown between her eyes suddenly deeper. "I didn't feel like I was in a position to do my own investigation into the story. It was too risky, so I gave the photos to one of my colleagues in Miami."

Corey closed her eyes against the sudden migraine beginning to pulse in her head. The scandal was a powder keg about to blow sky-high, and it seemed Julia had been sitting on it for months. The whole time they were dating, come to think of it. *Shit*. This was a disaster, one that could have been prevented if only Julia had been up-front about it.

"That's what your meeting yesterday was about?" she asked.

"Yes."

"And what were they able to find out?" Corey figured she already knew the answer, but she needed to hear it from Julia.

Julia said softly, "Collins has a mistress, a woman who began working on his campaign four years ago. Her name is Gina Stonehouse. And they have a two-year-old son together."

The oldest scandal in politics, except these days, voters actually gave a shit, Corey said to herself. "Proof?" she asked coolly.

"Not a lot, but enough to run with the story."

"Goddamn it!" Corey burst between clenched teeth. She dropped her voice as people began looking their way. "This is lethal. Not only to Collins, but to Jane too. We have to stop this story from breaking."

"There isn't any way to stop it. I tried to talk my boss out of it but he wouldn't listen. The paper's going to break the story during the convention."

"Jesus, that's only days away."

"I know. I'm sorry."

Corey had to think, but the blood pounded in her ears, making her feel faint. The situation was catastrophic, devastating, and the timing couldn't be worse. There had to be something she could do, but what? An injunction against the paper wouldn't help. That would simply alert the rest of the media and only put off the inevitable for a few days, maybe weeks at most. There was no way they could keep this out of the campaign. Damage control was the only option, but there was also the question of how Jane should be told. And should they warn the president what was about to befall him?

"Who else knows about this?" Corey asked, her throat as dry as matchsticks.

"Just Alex. She met me at the airport last night. I think she figured something was up."

Talking to Alex was her first step. Gathering her things, Corey began to leave hastily, not wanting to waste another minute. Julia hustled to catch up to her outside.

"Wait," Julia pleaded on the front sidewalk, her eyes wide with fear. "What about us?"

Corey turned briskly away from Julia and the diner. She didn't have time right now to deal with Julia's betrayal. At least, it sure as hell felt like a betrayal to her.

***

Alex felt strange meeting covertly with Corey, Carter and Steph at One Observatory Circle. More like disingenuous. She couldn't remember a time when Jane's closest inner circle had paid a visit to the official residence of the vice president without Jane present and certainly not without her knowing.

"I know," Corey said, echoing Alex's unspoken thoughts. "It feels weird to me too, being here and talking about something Jane should be a part of. Not just a part of, but calling the shots on."

Alex and the others sat around a small patio table behind the house, drinking lemonade and acting like they were not sitting on the kind of knowledge that in all likelihood would bring down a presidency. They all spoke calmly in a silent pact to keep emotions out of the discussion. Emotions wouldn't help Jane.

No one needed to spell out that if Jane knew about the impending scandal too far in advance of the story going to print, she could be painted as a traitor to her boss, to their party, and in the eyes of the public, perhaps even complicit in perpetuating the president's secret. To protect Jane, they would have to break the news to her and the president at the same time.

"What do you think Collins will do?" Alex asked.

The political expert in the group, Steph had worked for Jane since Jane's first days in Washington. Before that, she'd worked for the mayor of Detroit.

"Depends how selfish he is," Steph said.

The group collectively rolled their eyes. Collins was selfish, all right.

"If he maintains his candidacy and tries to ignore all of this, he won't be re-elected," Steph stated confidently. "In the meantime, there'll be a massive investigation to see if he's broken any laws or breached any ethics. He'll probably face impeachment, though that process would take awhile and likely wouldn't happen before his term is up anyway."

"If he admits it and fights on?" Alex asked.

Steph shrugged. "He still won't win. There won't be enough time for him to recover from the scandal. If by some miracle he *did* win the election, he could still be impeached and lose the presidency."

"So," Carter offered, "his only option is to go quietly?"

"Yes," Steph answered. "He should admit it, tell everyone how sorry he is, and resign."

The convention started in four days and was looking more and more like it would all be for nothing. While Alex didn't voice her skepticism, she figured they might as well hand the election to the Republicans now and not even bother going through the motions. The picture was damned gloomy.

"What happens to Jane?" she asked. She felt sick with worry.

"Good question," Corey said. "There's no way of knowing if the voters will punish her too, but the first thing we need to do is get her the nomination."

Alex flinched. "You mean she now becomes the Democratic nominee for president?"

"Exactly," Steph confirmed. "What other option is there? She's the vice president. The presidency is hers to inherit, and frankly, she's the only chance the party has right now. Collins is a dead duck."

This new turn of events was too much to fathom. Jane running for president? Did she even want to? If she did and lost, she might never get the chance again. Was Jane ready? Was *she* ready? If Jane took on the fight, it was going to be one hell of an uphill battle that would probably end in a loss. But ultimately, it was Jane's decision to make.

Corey held up a cautioning hand. "Let's not talk about this aspect any further until Jane's part of the discussion. We don't want to get ahead of ourselves, and whatever we do, we don't want to look too eager right now."

"Agreed," Steph answered.

Carter looked pointedly at Alex. "What do we know about who's responsible for this?"

Alex smirked. "I'd say Collins, by not keeping it in his pants."

"Very funny," Carter said without a trace of humor. "Seriously, we need to know who's behind all of this. Can you imagine how it would look if it was some die-hard loyalist to Jane?"

"Christ, I hadn't thought of that," Corey said, instantly paling.

"I haven't been able to get very far without setting off warning bells or leaving a trail," Alex said with disappointment. Her actions would be too traceable, and because she was Jane's partner, she needed to stay at arm's length. Or at least she needed to *appear* to be at arm's length from any kind of investigation. Her little chat with Amy Roberts had been risky enough.

"The first person I'd start looking at is the *Miami Herald*'s editor, Craig Finney, and the publisher, Lloyd Frobisher," she said.

"Why them?" Carter asked. "Hell, I'd say Colby Harrison and his hacks were behind it. Or that goddamned Tea Party."

"I agree with Alex," Corey said. "The *Herald*'s intent on breaking the story on the eve of the convention. Why? It could be purely for business reasons, but there might be more to it. I mean, why not break the story today? Or last week? No. They want it to do the most damage to Collins, to embarrass the shit out of him in the biggest public forum of this campaign so far. Anyway, I agree that if we look closely enough at Finney and Frobisher, they might lead us to the real culprit."

Steph let out an impatient sigh. "As much fun as it is conjecturing about this, it's not getting us anywhere at the moment. Besides, Collins will have his private detectives on this as soon as he learns about it. The FBI will want in on it too. Whatever they uncover will be of great benefit to us, but for now, we've got to focus on Jane's response and on the convention."

"We have to prepare a statement ahead of time," Carter said. "Jane won't be able to avoid the press at the convention. She'll need to be well briefed on what she's going to say."

Corey ran her hand through her hair. "I see some all-nighters in our immediate future."

"When are you guys breaking the news to Jane and the president?" Alex asked anxiously. She wished she could forewarn Jane. She'd already spent a night tossing and turning, hating every minute she kept such an important secret from her lover.

Steph glanced at Corey. "Tomorrow?"

Corey nodded. "Let's set it up."

The meeting ended quickly. There was much to do before tomorrow, but not for Alex. The one way she could help, by investigating and using her law enforcement training, she couldn't do right now.

"Corey," she said at the front door after Carter and Steph had gone. The two of them had not shared with the others the news that it was Julia who had received the anonymous photos of Collins and passed them on. "How do you think Julia's going to fare when all this erupts?"

"It'll be hell for her if her role in it gets out," Corey said.

"If that happens, I want to know. I'll try to arrange some protection for her."

"Protection?"

"There's an army of nuts out there. She'll get death threats, harassment, who knows what."

Corey shook her head. "Julia shouldn't have kept it a secret. If she'd told us in time—"

"If she'd told us, whoever was behind it would have found

another way to get the story out. And then we'd be in shit for knowing and for trying to keep it from going public. We'd look as bad as Collins with his damned secret life."

"I suppose. But I guess I'm still too pissed off right now to hear that."

"I'm sure she didn't realize the fallout this would cause."

"Well, goddamn it, she should have. How could she not?"

"You're not thinking she's happy about the sensation this is going to cause, are you? I mean, I know she's a reporter and all, but—"

"I don't honestly know, okay? I don't know anything right now."

Alex wasn't going to defend her ex anymore. Julia and Corey would have to work it out themselves. Or not. "Well, I hope you two can figure this out. You both seemed happy. And there is life beyond this zoo we call Washington. Try not to let this color your whole world, okay?"

"Thanks Alex, but right now I've got too much in front of me to contemplate anything that might resemble dealing with my fucked-up personal life."

Alex leaned against the door, watching Corey walk briskly toward her waiting car. Everything was fucked up right now, not just Corey's personal life. There would be far more casualties in this mess than just the president. They were all affected.

CHAPTER SIXTEEN

When news of the impending scandal was announced to Jane and Collins in the Oval Office, there was an inaudible *whoosh*, as though all the air had been sucked out of the room.

Shimmering, shuddering shapes and colors floated past Jane's peripheral vision, and then a compression as heavy as a boulder settled on her chest. It hurt to breathe. She supposed Collins had to be feeling the same way because his face turned as white as chalk. He began trembling so badly that he had to clasp his hands tightly together. His ability to speak seemed to have deserted him because his chief of staff and head campaigner began asking all the questions between stammers of outrage at the preposterousness of such an accusation.

Jane's shock was so great that their words drifted past her, barely audible. When she finally identified one of the numerous feelings tumbling inside her, it was disgust. Disgust for a man who was the country's leader, its commander-in-chief, its moral compass. How could Collins have been so selfish, so ungrateful, so contemptuous of the public he served, so...so *stupid*? How could he have risked his future and the future of his entire administration? What about his marriage? His image? His legacy? His *life*? He had also lied to her when she'd asked him point-blank at the burger joint if there was anything in his private life that could hurt the campaign. He was a cheat and a liar.

No one came out and asked Collins if he was guilty. Jane didn't need to ask. She trusted Alex, Corey, Steph and Carter to the absolute max. If they were convinced, that was more than enough for her. She wouldn't sit here and waste her time listening to a bunch of denials or pathetic excuses. It wasn't productive and it did nothing to solve the crisis.

Collins, still as silent as a fence post, was showing zero leadership, so Jane took over. "We are in full crisis mode, ladies and gentlemen," she began. "We need to break off into groups and plot out how we're going to handle this, what the next step is, and the one after that. Consider every option. The convention starts in three days, so there's no time to waste." She looked at the president, trying to capture his watery gaze. He looked defeated. "Personally, I think we should cut the *Herald* off at the knees. Take it to the public before the story goes to print, just as soon as we have our battle plan drawn up. *We* should be in control of this, not the press."

Everyone looked at Collins, waiting for his approval. He finally gave it with the tiniest wave of his hand, not meeting anyone's eyes. Silently, they all rose and filed out, Jane included. She'd give Collins a couple of hours to start doing something. She understood the magnitude and gravity of the decisions he faced, but time was not a luxury she could allow him right now.

Jane needed to talk to Alex. She nodded at her staffers, mouthed Alex's name, and disappeared outside to stroll the grounds of the White House. It wasn't long before Alex materialized at her side.

"Damn it, Alex."

"I know."

They didn't speak for a while. Their strides were long, their pace brisk.

"I'm in shock," Jane finally said, shaking her head. "This ruins everything. *Everything*."

"Does it?"

Jane halted and looked frankly into Alex's eyes. "What are you saying?"

"That this is your shot. Your time, my love."

"And profit from this mess? Pick up all the crap he's left behind?"

"No." Alex shook her head firmly. "Not like that. You'd be the one to guide this country *out* of this crap. Bring politics—the entire leadership of this country—into a new era of respect, honesty and morality. Don't you see? You're the only way out of this mess. The only hope. Not just for your party, but for the country. What he did not only hurts the reputations of everyone in politics, it hurts our country's global reputation too."

"Oh, honey. I'm no savior. Please don't build me up that way." Jane was near tears, the pressure on her never more intense. She'd never heard Alex talk this way before, so sure of the road ahead and the choice she must make. Alex gave her no escape route.

"You've never shrunk from challenges before," Alex said. "Why is this any different?"

"Because—because it's entirely different," Jane spluttered, feeling completely adrift. Her confidence had abandoned her, which rarely happened. "It's everything! It's the party's future, my future, the country's! I can't fix this, Alex. It's too much, too monumental. I can't do it. I'm as dead in the water as he is, I'm—"

"No." Alex took both Jane's hands and squeezed them gently. "Take some deep breaths."

Jane obeyed, but felt no better.

"You are you, and you are exactly what your party needs, what this country needs. There has never been anyone better than you for this job, and there never will be. Hell, you should have been president four years ago. You are as ready now as you ever will be."

For reasons she couldn't understand, Jane had felt far more sure of her abilities four years ago than she did now, perhaps because Collins had never trusted her as an insider, never acknowledged her as an equal. Perhaps she'd been too long in the passenger seat. Besides, did anyone ever truly feel prepared to run for president? Four years ago she ran for the nomination and didn't get it. This time, she'd be her party's nominee for the highest office in the land. The stakes were incredible.

"I don't know. I'd like to believe you."

"Then do it," Alex said forcefully. Her expression remained calm but her handsome jaw was set. "Clara's been around the block a few times and she thinks you're ready."

"I don't know if she thinks I'm ready or she's clairvoyant about suggesting I should be at the top of the ticket."

"She's not clairvoyant. She knows you're ready, and she knows the voters want you there too. Besides, taking over from Collins is really the only option here, isn't it?"

Alex was right. Objectively, Jane knew she was the preferred choice to head the Democratic ticket now, and even if she wasn't, there was no time to anoint anyone else. "This is killing you, isn't it?"

Alex pulled Jane close and held her tightly. "Yes. I don't want to share you with everyone else for the next four years. Honestly, half of me wishes you'd throw in the towel and run away with me someplace where we can be alone and anonymous for about the next sixteen years. Sit around and read smutty lesbian novels to one another, or watch stupid reality shows on television. Anything but this rat race."

"And the other half of you?"

Alex flashed her a smile bursting with pride. Everything about Alex exuded unconditional love; her support knew no bounds. "The other half wants you to conquer the world and show everyone how wonderful you are."

"How'd I get so lucky to have you as my partner, Alex Warner?"

Alex hugged her again and kissed her cheek. "It's not luck. It's your charming, seductive, witty ways that lured me."

Jane laughed, her stress instantly diminishing. "All right. In the beginning, maybe. What's your excuse now?"

"Now my excuse is that I finally get a chance to achieve what I've always wanted."

"Oh? What's that?"

"First Lady of the United States."

Jane laughed so hard with Alex, they had to hold onto one another to keep from falling over. Being First Lady was probably the last thing Alex had ever wanted, but knowing her, she'd make the best of it and do a damned brilliant job.

"Well," Jane finally whispered with a hint of naughtiness. "You'll be the sexiest First Lady this country's ever had."

"I somehow doubt that, but *you* on the other hand will be the sexiest president this country's ever had, bar none."

"Have I told you today how much I love you?"

"Yes, but please tell me again."

"I love you."

***

The midnight oil around the White House burned as though electricity hadn't been invented yet, Corey thought.

Collins, Jane and their staffs wandered the halls like zombies, bleary-eyed and slumped with exhaustion, their tempers frayed. Makeup artists and stylists had done what they could with the president and vice president to make them look untouched by the crisis, but they weren't magicians. Everyone in the tight circle looked ready to collapse from nerves and exhaustion.

From off camera in the Green Room, Corey watched Collins solemnly speaking to the nation on live television. She noticed his hands shaking beneath the lectern. His voice sometimes quavered too. He was a man on the precipice of losing everything.

From the sidelines, Jane also watched him intently, her expression neutral, her hands clasped in her lap. Corey hadn't felt sorry for the president, not one bit, but now she did. Sure, he'd asked for it by risking an affair, and then complicating the situation by fathering a child out of wedlock. But other people had done the same and not had to pay such a high price. Collins was ruined now as a politician. So was his legacy. He would forever be tarnished by the scandal. The gravity of what he'd done was lodged in the set of his jaw and his heavy eyelids as he spoke.

His chin raised, Collins looked into the camera and told the world that he'd been unfaithful to his wife, that he'd fathered a child with a woman he didn't love but nevertheless cared about. He said his actions had defined him as a poor husband, for which he'd apologized to his wife, but that he didn't believe the affair diminished his ability to lead the nation. He couldn't seem to help remaining defiant.

Christ, is he reversing the plan? A lump of panic lodged in Corey's throat. She shared a brief look of concern with Jane across the room. According to their strategy, Collins was supposed to admit his wrongdoings, announce he was withdrawing his name from the Democratic nomination, and would be serving out the remaining four months of his term before quietly leaving politics. He would endorse Jane for the nomination and campaign for her as much or as little as she and the party deemed was wise.

"I am still the person you saw fit to elect four years ago," he said brazenly. "I am still the competent and qualified leader this nation expects. However..." His face softened, his eyes moistened, and he looked down and away for a moment. His mouth was a firm line but his jaw quivered in the most emotional display Corey had ever seen from the man.

"I do understand that many of you have lost respect for me, have lost your trust in me. For that I am very sorry." He cleared his throat, tilted his chin up at the camera, and solemnly said, "I will not seek or accept the nomination for a second term as your president. Thank you."

Corey let out the breath she had been holding. He'd gotten over the first hump. The second obstacle was the press conference in the White House press room immediately afterward.

No sad eyes or shaky hands from Collins this time as he adopted an irascible posture with the press corps. He refused to talk about his mistress, refused to give any details, and basically said nothing beyond what he'd already said on camera. The reporters shouted questions, growing intensely annoyed and impatient with the one-word answers. He was done apologizing, he stubbornly told them, and he was done answering questions for now.

Corey caught and held Julia's gaze for a moment, wondering if she would be fired for undercutting her bosses by allowing the White House to break the scandal instead of the *Herald*.

She wasn't sure if she and Julia were even talking to each other anymore. She'd brushed Julia off in the couple of attempts she'd made at contacting her. She had been so busy, she'd had no time for herself, never mind anyone else, but it was more than that. Julia's silence about the scandal all those months felt like a betrayal, and in Corey's opinion, she'd not redeemed herself by giving them a heads-up about the *Herald's* sensational plan.

Corey couldn't deny she felt heartsick about Julia. She'd begun falling in love with her, had even started thinking of them as a couple beyond this campaign, beyond politics and the White House, and beyond their jobs. She felt tears misting her eyes and had to look away from Julia. How could they possibly repair the damage between them? Too much had happened. *Damn Collins and his wandering dick for ruining my life too!*

"Mr. President," someone shouted. "What about the vice president? Will she be the nominee now?"

"That's for the delegates to decide," he grumbled.

Bastard, Corey thought. Any support from Collins would be back-ended and half-assed. *Figures*. He'd been incredibly pissed off that Jane's staff had stumbled upon the news of his affair. He acted as though they'd dug around for the information, intent on scandalizing him, on ruining him so that Jane could take all the marbles. She'd even heard him whisper to Jane that he wouldn't forgive her. If there was a way he could manage it, she was sure he'd try to prevent Jane from getting the nomination, purely out of spite. But it was in the party's hands now. There was little he could do, other than continue to be a miserable prick.

"Corey!" A *New York Times* reporter called out—she couldn't remember his name. "Is the vice president available for comment tonight?"

"No, I'm sorry, she's not." Four more reporters flocked to her, as though a hunk of meat had been tossed into shark-infested waters. Julia was not among them. "The vice president will not be made available to the press until the convention."

The reporters didn't like that one bit. They began complaining immediately, lobbing questions at her like automatic gunfire.

"I'm sorry," she repeated, and then dashed behind a curtain to make her escape.

Corey leaned against the wall in the hallway leading to the West Wing offices, relieved there would be no more press conferences for a couple of days. At the moment, Jane was up in the air in the Marine Two helicopter on her way to Andrews Air Force Base. She and Alex were secretly bound for Mackinac Island, Michigan, and the Kincaid family home there for the next thirty-six hours. After that, they'd make their way to the convention in Seattle, Washington.

As this mess was entirely focused on the president, the group had decided it would be best for Jane to disappear for a while and let things die down. Lucky her, Corey thought. She could have joined the family reunion, but preferred to hole up in her townhouse for a couple of days instead. She'd work on Jane's opening speech, maybe even get a bit of sleep, and most of all, she'd try to do something about the growing void in her heart that felt like it was about to swallow her.

An unwanted tear streaked down her cheek. For the first time in a long while, Julia had filled the loneliness in her life, made her feel loved and desired. Now she was alone again with nothing but her job and her sister to devote her time and energy to. She knew her work life would never fully satisfy her again.

CHAPTER SEVENTEEN

On the wide shaded porch of the Kincaid family home on Mackinac Island, Alex greeted her mother-in-law with a hug. Maria Kincaid felt lighter and frailer in her arms than when she'd last seen her. In her mid-seventies now, the woman still had a feisty look in her eyes, and her lithe body moved with impatient energy. Jane was clearly her mother's daughter in many ways.

"Alex, my dear, you're as strong and handsome as ever!" Maria declared.

"And you," Alex said, grinning, "are still the second most beautiful woman in the world."

Jane jokingly rolled her eyes. "Can I get in on this little lovefest?"

Maria laughed and enveloped her daughter in a hug. "Of

course you can, dear, but if you ever lose your mind and treat my favorite daughter-in-law badly, I just might have to go for her myself."

It wasn't unusual for Maria to comment on her attractiveness, which always amused Alex. Maybe the apple didn't fall far from the tree, she thought mischievously. First Jane, and then Corey... was Maria next? Not likely, but the thought provided her with an amusing, pleasant distraction.

"Come in, my dears, it's hot outside," Maria said.

Alex loved the Victorian mansion, built well over a hundred and forty years ago and perched precipitously near a cliff dropping down to the swirling, cold, freshwater straits that separated Lake Michigan and Lake Huron.

The gleaming hardwood floors, majestic marble fireplaces and polished antique furniture weren't the only things that made her nostalgic. Four years ago, she and Jane both realized their deep attraction to one another in this house when Jane had been spirited away to the island for her own protection after an escaped convict made threats against her. She and Alex grew close during the brief confinement. They kissed for the first time upstairs in Jane's old room, and might have gone further if her cell phone hadn't interrupted.

She, Jane and Maria moved to the kitchen table, where Maria poured them each a glass of lemonade.

"Do you want to talk about it, honey?" Maria asked Jane simply.

Jane shook her head. She'd talked at length with Alex and her closest staff about what she would do next. She was talked out. Alex knew she wanted time for silent reflection now. "Not now. Maybe later, okay, Mom?"

"Sure, I understand." Maria patted Jane's hand. "I wish you'd been able to talk that sister of yours into coming here with you. I could have had someone to keep me company while you two lovebirds spend some romantic time together."

"It's heavenly being here, *and* it's always romantic, whether we're alone or not." Jane gave Alex a promising wink.

Alex smiled. She and Jane had not enjoyed a quiet vacation together since they'd snuck off for a few days alone in Italy during a G20 conference a couple of years ago. "I'd love some time to just sit on the porch and watch the sunset," she said. "That's romantic enough for me."

Jane gave her a warning look. "I hope you have more romance left in you after the sunset's done, my love."

Maria laughed and concurred with Jane.

"No ganging up on the outsider," Alex said, blushing furiously.

Maria smiled at her. "My dear Alex, you are never an outsider. You're family and you have been since the first day you set foot in this house. Now if you two will excuse me, I'm going to lie down for a while before I start working on dinner."

Jane had wanted to bring a cook, Alex recalled, but Maria refused. Italian by heritage, Maria was a great hobby chef. She had insisted on preparing a roast beef dinner with all the fixings.

While Maria napped, Alex snuggled with Jane on the wide porch swing.

Jane asked her if she thought Maria looked okay. Alex considered the question. Jane and Corey worried about their mother staying on the island alone all year around despite Maria having a regular assistant who stayed with her three days a week and friends on the island who looked in on her. They'd tried persuading her to move closer to D.C., but she wouldn't hear of it.

"I think she looks great," Alex said. "A step slower maybe, but that's all."

"I wish she'd come on the campaign trail for a few days, or maybe the convention. Just so I could see her a little more," Jane said. "I worry there might not be many more years I can do that."

"I know, but you know how hard it is to get her off this island," Alex said. Maria stayed with them in Washington every Christmas, but that was it.

Jane giggled a little. "I wonder how shocked she's going to be when Corey tells her she's gay. Both daughters! So much for the fantasy that Corey was going to bear her grandchildren."

"She'll be fine with the news. She loves you two more than anything in the world."

"We're all she's got now."

Alex fell silent for a while, listening to a distant aircraft in the sky. All the quiet and peacefulness seemed almost surreal compared to the campaign trail, where someone was always phoning Jane, or asking for a minute or an hour of her time. There was always a meeting to attend, a speech to give, an appearance to make. The work was endless. Until this moment, she realized, she'd forgotten what quiet sounded like.

Staring at the horizon, Jane asked, "Do you think Corey and Julia are going to be able to work things out?"

"I have no idea, but I think Julia's head over heels for Corey."

"I think it's mutual. But I also think Corey needs to quit taking things so personally with what happened over the scandal. Sometimes I think her skin isn't thick enough for this business."

"Trust me, it takes a long time to get used to it. She'll be okay. She's tough. And smart."

"Hopefully not too tough, at least when it comes to her heart. I'm a little worried about leaving her in D.C. by herself. She's upset about Julia, and I know she's torn about what to do. Then there's the stress of this damned convention."

"Do you want to call her?"

"No!" Jane exclaimed. "I don't want to talk to anyone other than you and my mother, at least for the rest of today and tonight."

"All right. Do you want *me* to phone Corey?"

Jane thought for a moment, looked at Alex, and then grinned devilishly. "Nah, Corey's a big girl. What I *want* is for you to throw me over your shoulder and haul me off to bed."

Her lover demanding sex in plain terms made Alex hot. "Hmm, afternoon sex?" She wiggled her eyebrows. She couldn't remember the last time they'd had a little afternoon delight. "We'll have to be awfully quiet."

"Luckily, Mother's hearing isn't what it used to be." Jane stood and tugged Alex up. "And fortunately, our room is at the opposite end of the house."

***

Everything Julia touched seemed to turn to crap sooner or later—her early policing career, her relationship with Alex, and now Corey. Her newest failure was her career, or at least her career with the *Miami Herald*. Over the phone, they'd fired her this morning for leaking the Collins story to the White House.

Now she didn't know what the hell to do. Her time in Washington was finished, she knew that much. She'd have to start over at a smaller newspaper and work her way up from the bottom again, covering school board meetings and fall fairs. The idea felt so bleak, so been-there-done-that, so exhausting that she despaired. She did not want to go backward.

After an unsatisfying dinner of peanut butter on toast, she got into her car, knowing she had to get out of her apartment and go somewhere, anywhere. Without thinking, she found herself driving to Corey's house. Corey probably wasn't even home, but maybe she could slip a note in her mailbox. She couldn't leave without trying to say goodbye and apologizing one last time. She would not give up and walk away the way she'd done with Alex all those years ago. She didn't want to run anymore. She wanted to fight for Corey, even if the fight was doomed.

Corey lived in the two-story Georgetown row house that Jane still owned from her days in the Senate: a charming Colonial with an enchanting bright red door. Julia lightly rapped the antique iron door knocker, resigned to not getting an answer.

She was surprised when, a moment later, Corey tentatively opened the door.

Julia hesitated, the speech she'd practiced in the car forgotten. "Hi."

"Just happened to be in the neighborhood?" Corey asked sarcastically, frowning heavily. Her eyes were red and she looked half drunk.

"If I said yes, would you believe me?"

"No."

"Can I come in?"

Corey sighed but stepped aside. Not exactly welcoming, Julia thought, but it was better than an outright rejection.

She stood inside the foyer, waiting for Corey to lead her to the open concept living area, which featured a floor-to-ceiling stone fireplace. How romantic, she thought, regretting that they'd never spent an evening here. Their dates and overnights had always taken place on the road or at Julia's apartment, but it was easy to picture the darkened room lit only by the glow of a fire and some well-placed candles. She ached for her lover, wanting them to be happy together once again.

She sat down uninvited on the leather sofa and said simply, "I'm so sorry."

Corey slumped down beside her and picked up a nearly empty bottle of wine from the coffee table in front of them. "Like some?"

"Not right now." Julia guided the bottle back to the table before Corey could dump more into her wineglass. "Why are you sitting here alone getting hammered?"

"I'm not alone now." Corey pulled her hand from Julia's grasp and defiantly splashed more wine into her glass, emptying the bottle. "It's my first night to myself in months. Something wrong with getting hammered?"

"No, but if you're getting hammered because you're depressed or upset, it worries me."

"What do *you* think in your great analytical wisdom?"

"Look, I know you're upset with me, and you have every right to be. I don't want you drowning your sorrows in a bottle of wine, okay? Talk to me, Corey."

"What the fuck is there to talk about? You shut me out of something that you knew would annihilate this administration, something that could destroy Jane's career and mine too. You *knew* it was a fucking powder keg ready to blow! And not only did you not tell *me*, the woman you were sleeping with, but you helped break the story."

"Corey, please give me a chance to explain. I love you."

Corey's eyes, glassy from alcohol consumption, shone with anger. "Oh, that's rich. You love me. You kept secrets, destructive secrets, and yet you love me."

"Yes, I love you. I've loved you since our first date at the correspondents' dinner."

"Bullshit."

Julia had never seen Corey so angry or so miserable. It frightened her, but she would not leave without resolving things between them. "No. It's not bullshit. I wanted to tell you about those stupid photos of Collins and his mistress, but I didn't want them to be buried. If he was living a double life, I didn't think it should be covered up. And I didn't want you involved in covering up something like that. I don't agree with the way my newspaper decided to handle things, but it had to come to light, as destructive and awful as it is. Don't you see that?"

"But why did *you* have to be involved?"

"I don't know. I wish to God I hadn't been involved, but someone else involved me. I didn't go looking for it." Julia buried her head in her hands, exasperated. "I wanted to run to you. I wanted you to tell me what to do about those stupid photos, but at the same time, I was afraid to involve you. I didn't know what else to do. Don't you see that if not me, whoever sent those photos would have found someone else to give them to? Or maybe they did, for all I know."

Corey shook her head and stared at the glass clutched in her hands, looking as unconvinced as ever. "You were more loyal to your job than to me."

"No, that's not true. I love you, Corey. And I'm so sorry I had to keep it from you until the last minute. I should have told you sooner, not just a few days before the story broke. I realize that now. But I *am* loyal to you, Corey. I lost my job because of it."

The admission seemed slow to register with Corey, whose expression eventually changed from indignation to sympathetic surprise. "Oh, Christ, I'm sorry. When?"

"Today."

Corey set her wineglass down. "What are you going to do?"

"I don't know yet. I have my apartment here for at least a couple more months, and I'm subletting my condo in Miami. I could sell it, I suppose." Julia realized she was anchorless for the first time since she'd left Alex all those years ago.

In a trembling voice, Corey said, "I don't want you to go."

"You don't?" Julia's heart began to beat faster.

Corey shook her head. "Stay. Please?"

"I can't stay here without work for very long. I wouldn't be able to afford it."

"I'll support you."

Julia laughed, and then instantly regretted it when she saw the hurt in Corey's eyes. "I'm sorry, I didn't mean to laugh. I've always made my way in life, that's all. I'm not going to start being someone's mistress now."

"I didn't mean it like that. I meant I'll do whatever it takes to help you stay here."

"No. I can only stay here if there's a reason for me to stay."

"There is a reason for you to stay," Corey said, her voice full of anguish. "Damn it, don't you see I'm trying to tell you that I don't want to be without you? I love you, Julia. More than you can possibly know. I've been absolutely miserable for the past week."

Julia had longed to hear Corey's declaration of love. Now that she had, she almost didn't believe it. "But until I came here today, you weren't even talking to me."

Corey moved closer. Her shoulders slumped. She looked tortured. "I know, but seeing you here has made me realize that I've been working way too hard at staying angry at you."

Julia's heart stilled. "You have?"

"Yes, and I am so tired of feeling this way. I'm so sorry, Julia. I was an idiot. I was angry at the entire situation, and I directed my anger at you because it felt like you'd betrayed me. I was being selfish, not even giving you the time to explain things to me."

"Look, I get why you were angry with me, but it's Collins we should both be pissed at."

"I know. He's responsible for all of this." Corey sighed deeply. "But I *won't* let him be responsible for me losing you."

"That's not going to happen." Softly, Julia took Corey's hand and brought it up to her heart. She dipped her head to kiss Corey's fingertips.

"Stay with me," Corey whispered. "Tonight and always."

Julia moved with Corey to the bedroom. They fell asleep holding one another. Hours later, well into the night, she woke when Corey tenderly cupped her breast and kissed her nipple. The intensity of her touch was electrifying.

"Thank you," Corey whispered in the dark.

"For what, darling?"

"For not giving up on me. On us."

"I never will, Corey. I promise you that. Now tell me again that you love me," Julia pleaded softly.

"I love you, Julia Landen," Corey said. "I am so in love with you, do you have any idea? I want to be with you, always."

Julia arched her back, pushing her nipple harder against Corey's mouth. "I love you too baby." In that instant, she knew she was done running, done starting over alone. She would find a way to begin her life again with Corey by her side.

CHAPTER EIGHTEEN

Thousands of journalists, delegates, party insiders and political pundits swarmed the convention, forcing Jane to remain cloistered in her hotel room until it was time to make an orchestrated appearance. She couldn't risk stepping out and getting ambushed by reporters. She was allowed to do nothing spontaneous and say nothing off the cuff, which left her feeling like a prisoner in a massive suite fit for royalty.

Jane spent the opening day sequestered with her staff and with party insiders. Clara Stevens sat in on most of the discussions. She promised Jane that she had unanimous delegate support and her nomination was a foregone conclusion. While not everyone in the party's hierarchy was necessarily happy about her imminent nomination, none voiced their opposition. One of her first priorities would need to be unification of the party, Clara advised.

"No," Jane insisted. "My first priority is getting elected. I don't have time to hold the hands of prominent and aspiring Democrats. They will simply have to fall in line behind me or else this party will be extinct for the next four years and possibly beyond that. There is only one clear choice here."

Clearly dispirited, Clara said, "Some of them already think it's too late for the party."

Jane bit the inside of her cheek to keep from spewing invective about certain leaders of her party. They'd done little to help her over the years, and instead put their stock in Dennis Collins, a man who was untrustworthy and led a secret life. "The only foregone conclusion is that I'm going to have a hell of a fight on my hands getting elected, and if we don't all fight this war together, we're *all* finished politically."

"Maybe," Clara mused out loud, "the answer lies in your VP selection."

"How so?"

"You choose someone as your running mate who can unite the party. An insider who can smooth the waters for you internally. Someone well respected and highly placed who'll give your campaign immediate legitimacy with the party's stalwarts."

"Clara, you'd be perfect for the job!" Jane meant it as a joke and Clara knew it. They both laughed, the short break in tension a relief.

Truthfully, Jane barely gave a rat's ass about the party's old boys, but at some point in the campaign and beyond, she'd need them. "Can I add a few items to this miracle list of attributes? How about the fact that he or she also needs to have at least some appeal to voters on the right, as well as the moderates. My miracle worker needs to appeal to older voters, the higher socio-economic class, and needs to be seen as non-threatening, competent, personable and slightly conservative." Jesus, she thought. *This is going to be a damned tall order*.

Clara grinned wickedly. "Sounds like someone who's the opposite of a young, outspoken, left-wing lesbian."

Jane grinned back. "Well, there are lots of those around, but yes, someone to balance me and keep me in moderation. But please God, it's got to be someone I like. Or at least can tolerate. All right, since you seem willing to play magician, Clara, I'd like you to head up a small vetting committee for my future running mate, but you're going to have to be quick about it. I need someone within the next couple of weeks."

"Ouch. I'll phone my wife and tell her she'll be without me for a while."

"Good idea, though I'm sure I'll catch hell from her," Jane said, and then directed her staff to clear out. When she was alone with Clara, she said, "Clara, I have to ask you this. Did you know anything about Collins and his secret life?"

Clara's mouth opened in shock. "Of course not! I have a hard time believing his life was completely secret from everyone, but I sure didn't know about it. If I did, don't you think—"

"I know, I know. You would have kicked his butt from here to Kingdom Come. But back in the spring, you talked about how we should reverse the ticket, me at the top and Collins second. I mean, did you have some inkling something was wrong?"

Clara smiled widely. "Oh, I wish I had that kind of ESP. It would have come in very handy many, many times! But no, I had no inkling. Only a truth in my heart that *you* should be president, not Dennis Collins. I've always felt that way."

Jane nodded. Clara had been an extremely loyal supporter for years. "Tell me honestly, do you really think I can get elected?"

Clara didn't hesitate. "Absolutely."

Jane's mind raced in a dozen directions, but she tamped down any thoughts of what would happen if she actually won. She was due to hold a nationally televised news conference in a few hours. She also needed to finish writing her acceptance speech, and she wanted to plan a meeting with her staff to outline objectives and top priorities for the first month of the general campaign. They'd need to discuss how to handle Collins—how much to distance themselves from him—how to deal with the Republican and Tea Party backlash, how to handle the negative press that would follow the Collins scandal for some time, and what they could do to distract attention from the scandal and put Jane and her platform in a positive light. They also needed to discuss the endless topic of fundraising.

Before anything else, Jane had two people—three actually—that she needed a private word with. The first was Governor Amy Roberts. She ushered Clara from her suite and asked her assistant to show the governor in. Time to drop the hammer on Amy Roberts.

"Madam Vice President," the governor gushed, enthusiastically pumping Jane's hand. "I want you to know how *thrilled* I am that you are going to be the nominee of our party for president."

"I'll bet you are, but I'm sure it didn't come to you as a huge surprise," Jane said, purposely not offering Amy a seat. She wanted their meeting to stay brief and to the point.

"Sorry, but I'm not sure I follow you."

"Please, Governor, let's be straight here. At the very least, you knew the president was going down. It's what you and Mr. Mitchell wanted all along. Lucky coincidence how your wishes happened to come true, hmm?"

Amy's face darkened. "I don't know what you're talking about, Madam Vice President. Of course I've dreamed—hoped—you'd be president one day. I've always been frank with you about that. But if you think I had anything to do with—"

Jane waved her hand in dismissal. "There's really no point to this little game. We could stand here all day with me accusing you and you denying it, but I want you to know that I hold you at least partially responsible for what's happened. Yes, it was ultimately the president's own actions that led to his downfall. And yes, you could say I directly benefited from the exposure of his secret life, and that my being vaulted to the top of the ticket somehow justifies all of this, but I want to be very clear about something. I do not—*ever*—condone dirty politics. I do not respect anyone who is complicit in such machinations. I do not care what the end result is, or how commendable the goal may be, it will *not* be tolerated under my watch."

Amy quickly turned indignant. "In spite of what you might think, I did not leak that scandal. Nor was I involved in acquiring any evidence of that nature. I resent your implications."

"Resent them all you want. I know you were aware of what was happening. Mitchell's fingerprints are all over this. You condoned it and went along with it. In my book, that makes you guilty."

Jane had gone out on a limb accusing Amy Roberts that way,

but she knew all about the governor's close association with Forrest Mitchell, both business and personal. Furthermore, Amy had made no secret of a wish to see her at the top of the ticket. In fact, Amy had been acting a little like the cat that had swallowed the canary these last few months. Bottom line, she didn't respect Amy's brand of politics and wanted as little to do with her as possible.

"What makes you so sure of these accusations?" Amy asked.

"I'm not at liberty to discuss the details."

Days ago, when the scandal broke, Collins directed his close associates at the Justice Department to hurriedly seek a warrant to wiretap Mitchell and a few other likely suspects, Jane recalled. A quiet investigation had begun. She didn't entirely agree with that decision, but they'd learned that Mitchell had gotten wind of the president's supposed tightly guarded secret months ago, first through gossip, and then through an informant who worked for a close friend of Collins. Mitchell had hired a private detective to tail the Stonehouse woman. Finally, the investigation discovered that Mitchell was close friends with the *Miami Herald*'s publisher, who had been a willing partner in bringing the scandal to light. Julia was targeted to receive the incriminating photos because Mitchell knew her publisher would print the story.

Mitchell and his henchmen had taken a chance with Julia though, probably not realizing at the time that she was growing close to Corey. Perhaps they also hadn't known she was Alex's ex-lover. Julia could easily have tipped off Alex or Corey months or weeks ago, which would have thrown their plan into jeopardy.

"I can't emphasize enough," Jane continued in her most brutal tone, "how displeased these kinds of tactics make me. If I ever get wind of anything like this happening again, I will bring down every facet of the law on you like a club, whether it's the IRS, the FBI, or even if it's parking enforcement. I'll make your life miserable, Governor Roberts, for you and for Mr. Mitchell. You'd be wise to keep your distance from him in the future, because when he goes down, there will be a lot of collateral damage."

Amy's face paled considerably. She seemed contrite, her chin trembling slightly as she said, "I understand your position very clearly."

"Good. Oh, and I expect your full endorsement at the convention and beyond."

"Of course."

Jane offered her a meager smile. "Thank you, Governor."

She sighed as the door closed behind Amy. For someone who hated the hard-ass stuff, Jane knew she was good at it. She understood its necessity. In this case, she wanted no part of attaining higher office on the wings of corruption, duplicity or unlawfulness, which required her to draw a very clear line in the sand. She meant what she said. She'd come down very hard on anyone who couldn't abide by the rules and whose intentions were not honorable and transparent. Her integrity was her best asset, the one thing that differentiated her from many of her colleagues in the politics business. She would never compromise her integrity.

Forrest Mitchell was shown in next. Jane guided him to a seat across from a desk she'd been using to write her speech, wanting the seating arrangement to make it clear that their meeting was purely business and she was in charge.

He smiled, holding out his stubby, bejeweled hand to her. She shook it only long enough to be polite.

"Finally, Madam Vice President." His teeth gleamed. "This country will be yours in three months."

She resented his smug confidence. "You sound rather sure of that, Mr. Mitchell."

"Please, call me Forrest. We're friends, after all."

No, we're not, Jane thought.

"Yes, I am entirely sure of your success," he enthused. "With my backing, there will be absolutely nothing to stop you."

"First of all," Jane said tightly, "there's a party called the Republicans and an opponent named Colby Harrison who will do their damnedest to try and stop me. Secondly, I will not accept any help from you."

Mitchell smiled quizzically at her, looking like a slimy salesman who refused to take no for an answer. "I know how to stop the Republicans. Hell, they're not even a challenge. And you *will* accept my help, because you need my money, my contacts and all the volunteers I can supply. Without all of that, you can't win."

"No. I don't want a single thing from you, Mr. Mitchell. Not your money, not your contacts, not your puppets, and most certainly not your dirty little conspiracies. And I can and will win without you."

Mitchell recoiled as though he'd been slapped. Nevertheless, Jane realized, he was a man resistant to rejection. "I'm not sure I understand you correctly," he said.

"I think you do. I will win this election without any help from you. It's not welcome, and I don't condone your tactics for a single minute."

"My tactics?" he roared, angry suddenly. "If it wasn't for me, gay rights would be no further along than they were thirty years ago. Hell, you wouldn't even be where you are if not for my commitment, my...my behind-the-scenes activity. It's a war out there for us. We do whatever it takes to win."

"I disagree. I will never condone the guerilla tactics you employ." Jane detested the kind of warfare Mitchell waged from the weeds. She believed in change, not through lawlessness or dubious ethics, but through the courts, legislation and the gradual swaying of public opinion. It was the only way to make permanent changes. Mitchell tried to force change through blackmail, intimidation, bribery, threats, humiliation and any other deplorable method he could utilize.

"I get things done. You can't argue with success, Madam Vice President. And you can't argue about the cause."

"You're right. You do get things done and I can't argue about the cause, but it's the *way* you get things done that I want no part of. I know you will stop at nothing to get what you want. That's where I have a problem. You have no boundaries, Mr. Mitchell." And you're an arrogant son of a bitch, she wanted to add, but didn't.

His face flushed, his jaw tightened. "You don't seem to mind reaping the benefits of what I've sowed."

"And you don't care if you destroy people. You don't care how many bodies you pile up along the way." Jane had come across his type before. The fact that his cause was close to her own heart did not redeem him in her eyes. "You are a dangerous man. I will never allow myself or my campaign to be aligned with you in any way."

Mitchell relaxed in his seat, quickly regaining his cocky, self-righteous attitude. He lowered his voice. "You would be well advised to be my friend rather than my adversary."

"Are you threatening me, Mr. Mitchell?"

He laughed shrilly. "I'm not that stupid. I'm only stating a verifiable truth."

Jane knew better than to divulge that she knew he was behind the president's troubles. She wouldn't acknowledge to him that he had that kind of power, nor did she want to compromise any investigations.

"I will win this election," she said evenly. "Under my watch, gay rights will flourish, but so will the rights of the impoverished, the sick, the downtrodden and the hopeless. I believe in making life better for a whole hell of a lot of people in this country, not just a small group. And you know what? I will do it with honesty, respect, integrity and transparency. I am going to do it my way. That's the only way to do it."

Mitchell gave her a belittling smile. "I'll be a very old man if I wait for you to lead us all to the Promised Land."

Jane rose, signaling an end to the meeting. "Stay away from me and my campaign, Mr. Mitchell."

"Now look who's threatening."

"It's not a threat. It's a verifiable truth."

Shaking his head in disbelief and condemnation, Mitchell stalked out the room, slamming the door shut on his way out.

Jane exhaled the breath she'd been holding. She vowed to herself that when she won the election, she would bring down every government agency on his head until he was stripped of his power.

***

Julia rapped nervously on the door to Jane's suite. She had no idea why she'd been summoned to meet privately with Jane. Corey hadn't been able to enlighten her either.

Feeling a sense of trepidation, she wondered if Jane somehow blamed her for Collins having to resign. Maybe Jane was upset that she hadn't divulged what she knew, or maybe pissed off that she and Corey were back together. Whatever it was, she was sure some kind of reprimand was coming.

"Julia, welcome. Thank you for coming," Jane said when she opened the door, her smile open and friendly. She shook hands warmly.

"Any time," Julia answered with surprise. The welcome wasn't what she had expected. She followed Jane to a sofa near a large picture window with a view of Seattle and Samish Bay beyond. "You don't seem upset with me, if I may be honest."

Jane sat down beside her. "Coffee or tea? Anything to drink?"

Too nervous to drink anything, Julia declined. Perhaps there was still a fist inside the soft glove she was getting from Jane. She expected to be clobbered any minute.

Jane reached for a half-filled cup of coffee on the table beside her. "This stuff's the only thing keeping me going right now."

"It must be awfully potent coffee. I don't think anything could keep me going with as much vitality and endurance as you seem to have."

"Ah, well, there'll be time for rest someday, I hope. Now as for being upset with you, why would you think that?"

"Isn't it obvious? I didn't come to you about the compromising photos of the president sooner."

"Why should you have?"

Jane's blasé response surprised Julia. Her role in the scandal had been nearly catastrophic to her relationship with Corey, yet Jane seemed completely unconcerned. "Look at all the trouble it caused," she pointed out. "It brought down a president and it's surely handicapped your campaign."

"That's hardly your fault. Look, you're a journalist. Last time I looked, you weren't on my payroll. If you had been, then yes, I would have expected you to tell me right away."

"Point taken, but I could have destroyed those stupid photos and done nothing more with them."

"Then you wouldn't have been doing your job. Besides, if not you, someone else would have been given the photos."

Julia swallowed, hardly believing how calm and reasonable Jane was being. "Corey and Alex, they didn't take it quite this well initially."

"Their first reaction was emotional because they're extremely loyal to me. If I, on the other hand, reacted emotionally to everything in this business that upset me, I'd be taking a bucket of Prozac every day."

Julia laughed at the joke, but she understood now that Jane

was a very special breed, a consummate professional who constantly put her job ahead of herself and her own feelings. She was the ultimate politician: tough, calculating and intelligent, but caring and altruistic. It was no wonder Alex had fallen for her, and no wonder voters flocked to her in droves too. Regardless, her immense attributes might not be enough to pull out a victory in November.

"I'm so sorry if I've hurt your campaign in any way," Julia blurted, knowing and no longer caring that in her heart, she'd joined the bandwagon. She wanted Jane to win. *To hell with journalistic objectivity.*

"Thank you, but it's not necessary to apologize."

"Can you get past the Collins scandal?"

Jane sipped her coffee and looked at Julia. "Can I win in spite of the scandal? I plan to, but I won't pretend it's going to be a cakewalk," she said frankly. "It's going to be damned hard. We're going to need every engine pulling this train right up until the last ballot is counted. It's going to be the most difficult thing I've ever done."

Julia was surprised when Jane's lips curled into a smile.

"It'll make it all the more rewarding on Election Day," Jane added with a wink.

"I admire your determination."

"You can do more than that for me."

"Name it."

"I want to hire you to help me write a book about the campaign when it's over. No matter which way this thing goes, I want to write an honest, unvarnished account."

Julia's voice deserted her for a moment. A job offer was the last thing she'd expected. "Are you sure you want *me*?" she finally croaked.

Jane laughed. "One thing you'll come to see about me is that I don't do things I'm not sure about, so yes, I'm sure. You've been following my campaign for months, and you're well aware of everything anyway. I'll need you to stay on the campaign trail for the remainder of it, of course, and keep careful notes, take some photos. Is that going to be a problem?"

Julia felt gleeful. She and Corey wouldn't have to be apart.

"Well?" Jane persisted.

"Oh, yes, of course! I'd be honored! I'm sorry, I was just so... so surprised. Totally caught off guard."

Jane stood. "Excellent, Julia, I look forward to working with you. I'm sorry to rush you, but it's a full slate of appointments for me today. Do you have any other questions right now?"

"I'm sure I'll have lots of them in a day or two, but for now, just one." Julia grew nervous again, not wanting to bring up her relationship with Corey, but knowing she must. "Corey and I, our relationship...it's not a problem for you?"

"Not at all. I won't say I was over the moon about it at first, but I'm past that now. I'm always preaching about letting people love whomever they choose. It was time for me to put my money where my mouth is. I want you two to be happy. That's all that matters to me."

"Thank you for that. I appreciate you not judging me."

"Don't get too complacent about me," Jane warned, her eyes twinkling. "If you hurt my little sister, I'll kick your butt."

As fair and kind as Jane had been, Julia had no doubt she would do as promised. She smiled as she said, "Don't worry, I'll remember."

CHAPTER NINETEEN

Julia stepped next to Corey and squeezed her hand as they waited backstage at CenturyLink Field for Jane to give her acceptance speech. The boisterous crowd of more than sixty thousand people made it difficult to have a conversation.

"You sure you don't mind me tagging along on the campaign for the next three months?" Julia asked slyly.

Corey laughed in delight. "I'm thrilled to death. But I want you tagging along much longer than that."

"I wish I could kiss you right now. Instead, I'll have to settle for telling you I love you."

"Hmm, all right. That's the only thing that could come close to replacing a kiss. I love you too, darling."

The crowd grew anxious, stamping their feet, occasionally chanting Jane's name, sometimes breaking into song. The mood was celebratory, a giant exhalation of relief that Jane Kincaid would now rescue their hopes and dreams from the disgraced President Collins. Jane was their future, a bright and vibrant future.

Corey hoped they could ride the tide of enthusiasm for a while, drawing some energy and goodwill for as long as possible. Some good press too, because they'd need it heading into the general election. Colby Harrison had drawn the undecided moderates back to him and also had the conservative vote locked up. Jane and her inner circle felt her best chance to win lay in getting people to the polls who didn't normally vote. She'd need to inspire the hopeless, energize the disenfranchised, and excite the ambivalent. A tall order, but if anyone could do it, Jane could.

Jane's staff had talked about her prospects in a meeting earlier this morning. "We're going to have to sell her like cornflakes," Carter vehemently suggested. "No, scratch that. Like the latest techno gadget that everyone's got to have. She'll be everywhere. She'll be the only thing people talk about."

Jane pulled a skeptical face. "I don't want to be a fad that people get sick of."

"There's less than three months to go," Carter replied. "That's not enough time for people to get sick of you, trust me."

Corey weighed in at that point, saying Jane couldn't possibly be everywhere at once, and trying to do so would kill her. "Not to mention we don't exactly have an overflowing campaign treasure chest."

Carter grinned with confidence. They'd recruit an army of volunteers to go door to door and to blitz the Internet, he told them. They'd market the candidate with T-shirts and billboards containing slogans like See Jane Run, a logo featuring a cute stick figure running toward the White House.

Jane frowned at the idea but kept quiet.

"There's a ton of popular songs called 'Jane'," Carter enthusiastically continued, clearly on a roll. His ideas would have been laughable but for the fact that they just might work. "Barenaked Ladies, Jefferson Starship, Cowboy Junkies. Songs get inside peoples' heads. We'll couple the songs with advertisements and computer apps and play them at your personal appearances, set them as the background music to clips of you on YouTube. Phone applications that link to your itinerary, special blogs, and personalized e-mails for anyone who donates or volunteers. Tweets from you every few hours. A web page and Facebook page that's updated every hour."

As much as the selling of Jane had distasteful elements to it, they had little choice if they wanted victory. Carter's way would attract a lot of young people and first-time voters, and keep Jane hip by making her a household name.

"All right," Jane finally relented, her displeasure evident in her deep frown. "I don't want anything that makes fun of my opponent and nothing that minimizes my message. When you take away the gimmicks, it's still a platform that's the best direction for this country, the only hope for a lot of people. I don't want to lose sight of what this campaign is all about. That means we need to keep pounding out my platform."

Now, as Jane stepped onto the stage for her acceptance speech, Corey knew her sister had every intention of driving home her message of hope, of inspiration for action, of ushering in a new era of fairness, respect and honesty. She had helped her write the speech. Jane wanted to distance herself from the past administration and from the image of stuffy, arrogant and dishonest politicians who had nothing better to do than squabble with each other and let their egos get in the way of important progress.

Five minutes of wild cheering and a long standing ovation greeted Jane's appearance. She soaked up the love from the crowd, a look of peace in her smile, a glint of challenge in her eyes. Standing on stage as the nominee for president was Jane's crowning achievement in a long list of achievements: medical school, the Senate, the vice presidency. She looked truly pleased and proud.

And why not, Corey thought with pride. *She could and should be our next president.*

Julia squeezed Corey's hand again. The electricity from the atmosphere mingled with her touch.

Corey was so glad that Julia was part of the campaign's inner sanctum now. No more topics were off-limits. Nothing they discussed could cause a conflict or an ethics breach. She and Julia were on the same side, fully involved in one another's lives. She wanted to ask Julia to move in with her, or move in together somewhere new. There were many reasons she should wait until the campaign craziness ended before she asked her, but she wasn't sure she was that patient.

"I stand here before you," Jane said after finally quieting the crowd, "with the utmost humility and respect. I am your servant." The crowd erupted. Jane immediately launched into the main thrust of her speech: respect and honesty.

"Respect, humility and honesty," Jane said, "are the three most important qualities every man and woman serving in Washington should possess. They are the three qualities you can expect from me every day I work for you and in every facet of my life. Respect, humility and honesty are three things I think about every day of my life. They should be the three things you *demand* when you go to the polls on Election Day."

The crowd began chanting her name, clapping in time.

"Humility," she continued, "is not about perfection, but about serving without ego. Respect is not about blind acquiescence, but about consideration and fairness. Honesty is not only about truth, but about living my life as I am without apology and without deception."

"Yes!" the audience cried as one.

"Promises without progress are empty," Jane shouted, building to a crescendo. "Leadership without accountability is ineffective. Serving without integrity is pointless. I come to you, ladies and gentlemen, with a promise of progress under my administration. I come to you with a promise of accountability under my watch. And I come to you with a promise of integrity in the White House. Hold me to account as I hold myself to the highest standards this country deserves!"

Jane smiled and nodded as the crowd loudly agreed with her. Corey nodded too, pleased with how the speech was going. Jane had made her point that things would be different when she was president.

Jane talked next about listening and about acting on the problems the country faced. She talked about the economy, health care and education. She talked about a new era in Washington, "as fresh as a Pacific breeze and as emboldening as a cool mountain downdraft," where the people would truly have their best interests served.

"Let notice be served that there will be a new sheriff in town." Jane laughed lightly along with the audience. "Yes, Sheriff Kincaid's coming to town. Let notice be served that the infighting, the uncooperativeness and the childish clashes will come to an end in Washington! Let notice be served that we *will* start working for the people again!"

The crowd jumped to their collective feet. Jane had hit on the very theme that frustrated voters the most.

When the speech ended fifteen minutes later, Jane stood backstage, exhausted but pleased. It had been made clear that a page had been turned, that she was her own woman who planned to do things her way in Washington. The days of the egotistic, selfish, good old boys were over, as long as she had any say in the matter.

About damn time, Corey thought. She relished the idea of getting some work done—important bills passed, necessary alliances forged—without the gamesmanship. It might actually be fun going to work every day knowing their work actually resulted in positive change.

She smiled to herself.

***

With deep satisfaction and some surprise, Alex watched Jane's momentum grow in the weeks following the convention. People couldn't get enough of the Democratic nominee. Carter's marketing tactics seemed to be working since Jane was in great demand to make appearances at everything from fall fairs to college events to business luncheons.

Jane showed tremendous stamina, but at night, when the two of them were alone in an anonymous hotel room that looked every bit the same as the hotel room from the previous city, Jane's exhaustion revealed itself. She'd slump in the tub and close her eyes until Alex thought she'd fallen asleep. Just resting, she'd say in a voice made raw from speaking to massive crowds. Alex would half carry her to bed afterward and tuck her in.

People had no idea how grueling a presidential campaign was. Alex wondered in consternation how many years the effort was taking off Jane's life.

The lack of sleep, the traveling, the constant stress. There were times when Alex had to fight to get Jane to rest for a couple of hours, to get her to force some food down. But as long as Jane was prepared to pay the toll, Alex would be there for her.

Jane was set to announce her running mate this afternoon. Actually, she'd already made the announcement via text message, Twitter, and to a select group of about ninety thousand e-mail recipients. It had been Carter's stroke of brilliance to capitalize on the popularity of texting. Now Jane was ready to formally introduce former Texas Governor Jack Tomlinson to a large gathering of reporters in Hart Plaza on the shore of the Detroit River.

Alex had instantly liked Tomlinson. He was fifty-two years old, young to be a former governor, but he'd stepped down after one term to help care for his cancer-stricken teenaged daughter, who'd since died. He showed empathy in his eyes and a genuineness in his attitude and manner that couldn't be faked. He had a direct, no bullshit way about him that she respected. More than that, he seemed to respect her and Jane's relationship. He'd told them as much over dinner last night, saying that while he'd never been the grand marshal at a gay pride parade and probably never would, he believed in his heart that the love between two human beings was all that counted.

Alex was aware that Jane hoped her selection of Tomlinson would pay dividends with the moderates and undecideds. He was Southern, fiscally conservative, and he'd been an Air Force pilot during the Gulf War. On paper, he made a good counterbalance to Jane, yet privately, their views were much alike. She felt good about the union.

Jane's speech to the reporters laid out her running mate's assets and confirmed her confidence in him not only as her vice president, but as her number one counsel. Tomlinson proved almost as good a speaker as Jane, Alex thought. He said all the right things to indicate that he was a team player, he believed in Jane and her platform, and he couldn't wait to help her bring it all to fruition. Tall, trim and fit, with dark hair naturally graying at the temples, he looked somewhat like a slightly older, male version of Jane.

"What did you think?" a beaming Jane asked Alex later in their hotel room over a cup of herbal tea. She was clearly pleased with her choice.

"I think you made the right decision," Alex confirmed. "He's going to do great."

"I hear Amy's none too pleased about my selection." Jane chuckled evilly.

"What, did she think you were supposed to pick her?"

"An ego the size of hers, I'd say yes."

"She's not a stupid person, so I have to think she's delusional if she thought there was a chance you'd pick her. Think she's going to create any waves over this?"

"Nah, she knows better." Jane leaned back in the tub, her favorite place to unwind after a long day, the cup of tea clutched in her hands.

"Good, because you don't need another enemy."

"In this business, sweetheart, I'm afraid it comes with the territory."

Jane might be resigned, but Alex could never get used to it. Her priority was Jane's safety. She could never casually accept the fact that Jane had enemies.

Four years ago as a candidate, Jane had been threatened by a convicted abortion clinic bomber who'd escaped from prison. There'd been other threats over the last four years, though less serious. Alex was part of a contingent of men and women who investigated those threats and worked to protect Jane's physical safety, but political threats and manipulations fell outside her realm of knowledge and experience. To Jane, however, they were just as serious as the threats of physical harm.

The Forrest Mitchells, the Colby Harrisons and the Tea Party nevertheless gave Alex—and undoubtedly Jane—an ulcer the size of Texas. Their mandate was to either control Jane or see her fail. Some of her adversaries were prepared to go to extreme lengths to attain their goals. She had never figured out how to deal with such attacks, and it incensed her any time someone tried to cut Jane down.

"Any rumblings about Mitchell causing problems for you?" she asked.

"No. I think he's still licking his wounds. Besides, there's nothing he can do to me."

Alex chewed on her bottom lip. "I hope you're right about that."

Jane rose from the water and set her empty cup on the table beside the tub. Alex handed her a towel.

"Honey, I know you worry about me," Jane said. "We all do the best we can to avoid handing my enemies a target, literally and figuratively."

Alex watched Jane carefully dry herself off, and then wrap the fluffy white towel around herself.

Jane's body was still taut, as lithe as ever, her skin soft, her dark hair luscious. She was the most beautiful woman Alex had ever known. She never forgot it, no matter how much Jane wowed her with her intelligence, her speaking abilities, her sharp decisiveness and her generosity of spirit. If it wasn't for the worry taking root in the pit of her stomach, she'd kiss Jane in the still moist part of her neck and gently part the towel.

"I don't have a good feeling right now," Alex confessed, wrenching her thoughts from Jane's body and what she'd like to do with it.

Jane padded to the bedroom and sat down on the edge of the bed. Clasping her hands stiffly in her lap, she pursed her lips in a look Alex knew well, a look that indicated she was about to deliver unpleasant news.

Alex's stomach turned over. "Okay, what did I just hit on?"

Jane patted the bed beside her. "Come and sit down, my love."

Alex obeyed, not willing to rely on her shaky knees to hold her up any longer. "What is it?"

Jane swallowed, looked at Alex, and took her hand. "I'm going to Afghanistan. And I know you hate these war zone trips, but—"

"Wait. When?"

"Next week, I hope."

"That's pushing it to get security ready."

"I know, but after that I'm busy with those two television debates, and my campaign schedule is relentless leading into the last month. Next week is the only window."

Alex went over the details in her head. A Secret Service advance team would have to immediately depart for Afghanistan to coordinate security coverage with American and NATO forces.

War zone appearances were particularly risky since politicians were much harder to protect there than at home. It was also imperative to keep the news of Jane's overseas visit from the media until the last possible moment.

"I don't like it," she said plainly.

"It went well in Iraq two years ago. It will be fine this time too."

"This is different than Iraq. Iraq was secure when you visited there. Much of Afghanistan is still terrorized by Taliban and al-Qaida insurgents. Where in Afghanistan and for how long?"

"The Kandahar base. It's the safest place I can be over there. I want to talk to the troops, and meet with our commanding general to hear his opinion on how the war is going and how the troop withdrawal is affecting things. I need to see and hear these things on the ground."

Alex tore her thoughts from security to the political picture. Jane wasn't reckless about security. She must have good reasons for wanting to make the trip. "I agree it's a chance for voters to see that you won't make decisions about our troops without talking to them and assessing the situation for yourself."

"Precisely."

"And voters can see that you're presidential, that you're not afraid to visit a war zone, that you've got the temperament to be commander-in-chief."

"Yes, all of those things, but there's a personal element too. I want to visit the base hospital at KAF. I know the staff does tremendous work there. I want to see for myself a base hospital in a war zone."

Before she became a politician, Jane had used her medical skills with Doctors Without Borders, so it made sense that she'd want to visit the doctors and nurses in Kandahar, give them a morale boost and check out their facilities. Alex's resistance began to soften.

"I understand why you want to go. It makes me nervous, that's all."

"I know it does. It makes me a little nervous too. But I can't lead people who take risks every day of their lives without taking a few of my own. I can't sit here in my ivory tower, Alex."

Jane was right. She wouldn't be Jane if she played it safe. Alex nodded. "I'm coming with you, and I want in on all the security planning sessions."

"Good, because I want you with me, and I want you in on those meetings."

"Who else is coming from your staff?"

"Just Carter. I don't want Corey to come because this is not a campaign event. I want this to go down officially as a vice presidential visit. I don't want to send any signals that I'm campaigning over there, though Julia will be quietly joining us. She'll keep a journal, take a few photos, that sort of thing."

Alex lay down on the bed, her heart pounding. She didn't want to show fear, didn't want to throw up roadblocks when clearly Jane had made up her mind. She tugged Jane onto her back, forcing herself to smile. "Did I mention lately how glad I'll be when this campaign is over?"

Jane laughed. "Only about three hours ago."

CHAPTER TWENTY

Julia held the arms of her seat in a death grip. Jane and her entourage were on a military cargo plane since Air Force Two was too obvious and had been left back in Dubai.

She seriously questioned her sanity as the plane plummeted like a missile straight toward the desert. She never should have agreed to come, but her journalist instincts had won over. The chance to visit a war zone was hard to resist, as were Jane's reasons for wanting her to come. Jane said the trip would provide invaluable research and authenticity for the book Julia would write. In addition, she could take photographs and generally do whatever Jane, Carter or Alex needed her to do, so she had relented. But now, as her heart beat like a frantic caged bird in her chest, she wished she could change her mind.

Corey had wanted her to stay behind, had begged her to. Poor Corey, who had hated the idea of this trip from the start. She cried when the group left, the first time Julia had ever seen her cry in front of anyone but her.

Everyone important to Corey was on their way to Afghanistan, which clearly had her worried sick. She kept texting every couple of hours to make sure Julia was okay. While she hated the thought of Corey so stressed out, it actually felt nice having someone worry about her for a change, having someone to miss her.

Her stomach shot to her throat suddenly, gravity crushing her against her seat as the plane dove straight toward Kandahar Air Field. She'd been warned it would be a sharp descent, a maneuver designed to limit the chances of the plane being hit by a rocket propelled grenade. The possibility hadn't seemed real until now.

After a final shudder, the plane came to a roaring stop on the landing field. The war zone was no longer an abstract concept in Julia's mind. It was right here in the form of armed soldiers standing on the dusty tarmac, hasty commands to deplane as quickly as possible, the bulletproof vests and helmets handed to her and the rest of the group as they scrambled onto the tarmac.

The heat was oppressive, like a heavy blanket thrown over her.

"This way!" a soldier yelled. The group, which included half a dozen Secret Service agents, followed him the short distance to an old hangar.

Julia glanced at her boots, already coated with dust. The hangar floor was hard-packed, reddish brown dirt, the walls made of sheet metal dotted with jagged holes every few feet, like a giant wall of Swiss cheese. Not exactly reassuring, she thought, but the unseen planes and helicopters thundering overhead made her feel safer. There were soldiers in camouflage uniforms everywhere, and not just American soldiers. She noticed NATO troops from Canada, the Netherlands, Italy, France, Britain and even Japan. NATO was an astounding multinational organization.

"You okay?" Alex whispered beside her.

"Sure." Julia flashed Alex what she hoped was a reassuring smile. She raised her camera to take a few shots while an officer explained the rules.

They wouldn't be going outside the wire, he said. Too dangerous for such high profile VIPs, he told them, and Julia was glad for the restriction. She wasn't feeling particularly adventurous, and didn't especially want to worry about suicide attacks, roadside mines, snipers and all the rest of it. Nope, staying right here on base with all the fighter planes, attack helicopters and soldiers armed to the teeth was fine with her, thank you very much. Maybe she wasn't much of a journalist to feel so cowardly about it all, but at least she'd be safe.

The officer warned them against complacency—the part where he tried to scare them, Julia guessed. He explained about the possibility of attacks and told them about the concrete bomb shelters every hundred yards or so and how they needed to run immediately to one of them if the warning siren sounded.

She wasn't particularly worried. Jane's presence on the base was top secret, and they only had to get through twenty-four hours. What were the odds of anything happening? Low. Damned low. She'd told Corey as much.

A quick tour was next on the agenda. It struck Julia that the base looked more like a construction site, or maybe a shipping port, composed of hastily constructed buildings made of plywood and devoid of paint, galvanized steel Quonset huts, and metal shipping containers serving as offices and even living quarters. Dump trucks, fuel trucks and military vehicles rumbled around, kicking up clouds of brown dust in their wake. But she noted a bit of civilization too: a coffee shop, a couple of restaurants, a general store and a barbershop.

"Look," Alex said, pointing eagerly to a large rectangular area enclosed by three-foot-high plywood boards. "An outdoor hockey arena!"

Julia shook her head while Jane laughed. She knew Alex would not leave KAF until she played a game of ball hockey with the troops. Alex was a hockey nut. She had been a star player in college, even playing for the American national team in the 1998 Olympics. Hockey was her first serious love.

Carter nudged Alex. "Do you even know how to play hockey without skates?"

"I think I can manage somehow," Alex replied. "Luckily I brought running shoes."

Following a brief visit to the large dining facility or DFAC, Julia and the group trudged the short distance to the base hospital, the Multinational Medical Unit.

Jane perked up immediately, asking questions about their diagnostic equipment, what kind of surgeries and trauma care they performed, how many beds, how many staff members, how many patients on a given day. Mostly, her questions zeroed in on what they were lacking. The colonel conducting the tour hesitated.

"Please," Jane persisted. "I'm extremely impressed with your facility, but is there anything you need here? I might be able to help."

Finally, the colonel shrugged and gave her a reluctant smile. "We could use more overhead surgical lights and another portable ultrasound machine."

Jane nodded at Carter, who scribbled in his notebook.

"What happens in here when there's an attack?" Alex asked.

"We move the patients who are mobile," the colonel answered. "The ones who are too sick to move, we cover them up as much as we can and hope for the best. We've never lost anyone that way yet." He made a show of crossing his fingers.

Jane continued to quiz the colonel on the hospital, marveling out loud at how much modern medicine they could perform so close to the battlefields. In fact, right in the middle of the war zone, the doctors could perform full surgeries, and even had the luxury of a modern blood lab, X-rays and a CT scanner.

In the First World War, the colonel explained, injured soldiers might not receive medical attention for two or three days, by which time most of them died. By comparison, injured soldiers now could be evacuated in minutes and on an operating table inside of an hour.

Alex's attention had clearly drifted, because next she quietly asked the colonel if there was any chance she could join a pickup hockey game in the afternoon.

The colonel grinned. "I believe there's a game starting in about an hour. I'm sure they'd be delighted to have you join them, Ms. Warner. Hell, maybe you can show them a move or two."

Alex nearly bounced on her toes with excitement. Perfect, Julia thought. She'd take pictures of the future First Lady playing ball hockey with war zone soldiers.

With Jane and Alex potentially in the White House in a couple of months, it occurred to Julia that there would be many firsts. Being part of this new frontier was the thrill of a lifetime. She couldn't remember a time when there'd been so much excitement in her life, so much promise for the future. For the first time in a long time, she felt truly happy and perfectly fulfilled.

Glancing at Alex and seeing her excitement over playing hockey, their early years in college came rushing back to her. They'd been new lovers then, full of innocent and abstract plans for their future, excited to be on the edge of something grand. She and Alex were much different people now, yet here they were, again on the edge of something grand. *Whoever would have thought we'd end up in the middle of a presidential campaign? And in a war zone!*

Alex's timing for joining the ball hockey game worked out well with Jane's schedule. Jane was meeting privately with General Steven Neal, which meant Julia and Carter were free to watch Alex strut her athletic skills.

In the rink, Julia raised her camera to take a few shots of Alex warming up. She had always been in awe of Alex's athletic prowess, even more so now that they were middle-aged. Alex was trim but muscular and moved with grace, speed and efficient precision. Her slap shot was as hard as the guys' and her wrist shot wickedly accurate and deceptive. She'd not lost her touch.

Sudden regret hit Julia hard, like a sucker punch to the gut. She'd been stupid to leave Alex, stupid to desert such a good woman. If she'd stayed, maybe their relationship wouldn't have worked out in the long run anyway, but she couldn't help feeling she'd given up far too soon. She loved Corey now, wanted a future only with Corey, but that didn't mean she couldn't wonder what might have happened had she stayed with Alex.

She swallowed a dry sob. It had all worked out for the best. She knew that. Alex was happy now, and *she* was finally happy too. She had Corey. She had a new career as a journalist and now biographer. Life had happened to them. They'd survived and thrived with new avenues of happiness. They'd even come full circle, becoming friends again. Yes, that was worth something, and it was something to celebrate. She needed to remember the good things, not the regrets. She needed to be thankful for what she had.

She cleared her throat, telling Carter she was heading to the other side of the rink to take more photos. "I'll be back in a few minutes."

"Don't hurry," he teased, lowering his voice. "With any luck, one of these hunky soldiers will take me to the shower with him."

Julia laughed. "You wish!"

"Yes, sadly, it's just a wish that will never be fulfilled. At least not as long as I'm part of this fish bowl called politics. Oh, poor me."

Julia laughed as she walked away. *Poor Carter*. He didn't have much of a life because his life entirely revolved around Jane. But he'd made his choice. When it was time for him to move on, she supposed he'd have his pick of jobs on Wall Street, at Ivy League universities or a big bank somewhere. And what a ride he was on in the meantime, she thought. He'd told her just days ago that he was right where he wanted to be and had absolutely no regrets. He seemed excited for the future.

Raising the camera to her eyes again and focusing on the subject of her only regret, she decided that no matter how good everything had turned out in the end, she'd always feel remorse over the way she'd dumped Alex.

Out of nowhere, a strange whistling noise, high-pitched and ragged, screamed past Julia. Her camera flew from her hands as a massive explosion rocked the ground where she'd been standing moments before. She felt a flash of fire too, the force of the blast convulsing through her chest like a tiny earthquake. Her face landed in the dirt, hard, as though someone had body slammed her from behind. Pain shot through her nose, her eyes and her ears. Her whole head hurt. All she could think was, *I don't hear the warning siren.*

A heavy silence fell. She sensed the thick, acrid smell of things burning. This, she realized, was the smell, the sound and the sight of a bomb exploding. They'd been hit.

Carefully, Julia pulled herself to a sitting position. She was bleeding, the front of her shirt splotched with red. Her nose. The blood came from her nose. Her ears were ringing, her boots missing. Thoughts came in fleeting fragments. She'd been hurt. She remembered the explosion as deafening, though it was silent now. Smoke, dirt, dust and debris littered the ground everywhere she looked.

All hell broke loose again. The warning siren began screeching— *too late, goddamn it!*—boots thudded on the earth, voices yelled, there were more sirens. A low-flying attack helicopter screamed overhead. The war had just landed at her feet and dumped her on her ass. *Holy Christ!*

Julia tried to stand, wobbled, and fell back on her butt again. A uniformed soldier with the symbol of a medic on the shoulder of his uniform squatted beside her, breathless and dripping sweat. "Are you all right, ma'am?"

"Yes. No. I don't know. What happened?" There was dust in her throat. Blood too. She choked for a moment.

"There's been an explosion," he said. "A rocket fired from somewhere along the perimeter of the base. You'll need some medical attention, ma'am."

Julia shook her head. "Are there others hurt?"

He nodded grimly. She looked past him. Alex and the soldiers who'd been playing ball hockey were sitting or lying down. A couple of them stumbled around, bloody and disheveled. She thought Alex was one of the ones stumbling around, but she couldn't be sure.

Carter, she thought with sudden desperation. Where was Carter? The bleachers he'd been sitting on, the place she had been sitting just moments ago, were gone. A blackened crater yawned bleakly in its place. Bits of wood and metal lay splintered around it.

"Oh God," she rasped. "No. Please, no."

***

At the sound of the explosion, Jane and General Neal rushed from their seats inside the Quonset hut. Just outside the door, two Secret Service agents attempted to stop her.

"We need to get you to a shelter immediately, Madam Vice President," an agent announced.

"No. I need to find Alex," she countered.

"The base appears to be under attack," he said forcefully.

"I don't care. I will not cower in a shelter."

A soldier jogged up to them, clutching his rifle. "I'll escort you to the shelter, ma'am."

"Not until I know what's happened."

"There's been a missile strike," the soldier said calmly. "Just one, but it was a fairly significant hit, ma'am. We've got air support now and some armored vehicles tracking down the insurgents. They'll destroy the enemy targets in no time."

Jane's heart throbbed in her throat. The base had been attacked. Was it her fault? Had the enemy somehow found out she was here? Had the attack been directed at her? She swallowed down her fear, trying to slow the adrenaline surging through her body. "Are there casualties?"

"Afraid so, ma'am. I don't know the extent."

She dreaded the answer to her next question. "Where did the missile strike? What part of the base?"

"Beside the hockey pad, ma'am."

Oh, God. Alex. If anything has happened to her, I'll never forgive myself. It took every ounce of her strength to remain calm. "Take me there, sergeant."

"I don't have authorization to do that, ma'am. All civilians are to move immediately to the nearest bomb shelter until the all-clear."

The Secret Service agents agreed, each grabbing an elbow to steer her in the right direction, but Jane dug in her heels. She couldn't stand the thought of being kept in the dark and hiding out until the danger was over. She needed to know what was going on. She needed to know if Alex, Carter and Julia were safe. She needed to *do* something, to help, to be in the middle of things. She was a leader, not a follower.

"I'm a doctor," she said firmly, wrenching herself away. "I can help."

***

Pain shot through Alex's right arm like an electrical current. She had to hold the useless limb with her good arm. As she quickly took stock of herself, she was relieved to discover that a broken arm seemed to be the worst of her injuries.

Some sort of debris had hit her hard and left her bruised, but luckily the deadly shrapnel had missed anything vital. She was covered in dust. Her head throbbed from the bomb's concussion, but she was okay. More okay than most of the people around her.

Stumbling around the arena, Alex surveyed the shocking damage. Several of her fellow hockey players—all of them men she'd been introduced to only minutes before but whose names she couldn't remember now—lay on the ground, some groaning, some bleeding, some unconscious. Some were dead. She knew she was in shock, but her training kicked in.

She couldn't help the dead, so she went to the first seriously injured but living person she came across. A soldier lay on his back, gasping for breath, bloody spittle dribbling down his chin. He tried to sit up. Using her good arm, she gently pushed him back down. His T-shirt was bloody. Shrapnel, a collapsed lung, she guessed.

"Alex!" Jane rushed to her side, an armed soldier and two Secret Service agents on her heels. "Sweetheart, are you hurt?"

Alex stood and pressed herself to Jane. Her knees went suddenly weak. She wanted to collapse into Jane's arms, to be soothed and reassured, but she needed to hold it together and remain strong for at least a little longer. "I'm okay. A broken arm, I think."

"Oh, God, let me see."

"No." Alex pulled away despite the pain shooting through her arm. "These guys need more help than I do."

Jane dropped to her knees, commanding the soldier who'd accompanied her to find a litter to transport the prone man to the hospital a few hundred yards away.

The air still smelled of smoke, flame, blood and death, Alex thought dizzily.

Jane took the injured man's pulse and respiration breaths— there was little else she could do without the proper equipment— and then moved to the next victim a few feet away. The lower part of his left arm was shredded from shrapnel and bleeding heavily. Bone and tissue were visible. Alex wondered if his arm could be saved.

"Give me your necktie," Jane commanded the agent beside her.

He obeyed. Jane quickly fashioned the necktie into a tourniquet before moving along to triage and give basic first aid to more of the injured. She worked efficiently and purposefully. Alex noticed none of the soldiers commented on Jane's identity. Perhaps they were in too much shock to notice that the woman attending them was the vice president of the United States.

Medics and able-bodied soldiers arrived in throngs to begin collecting and transporting the injured. Jane finally stopped. She was covered in grime, sweat and smeared with the blood of the casualties. Her eyes looked tired but her jaw was set in grim determination.

"Alex, you need to go to the hospital and get that arm set," she said sternly.

"Not until they're done treating everyone else."

Jane let out an unhappy sigh. "All right, then. Let's go find Julia and Carter."

"There," Alex said, pointing to Julia some distance away. She was holding a bloodied rag or shirt to her nose. "Julia!"

Julia stumbled uncertainly toward Alex and Jane. "Thank God you're both okay."

"Looks like you've got a broken nose," Jane advised. "You need to get it looked at. How are you doing otherwise?"

Julia shook her head. Tears began spilling down her cheeks. "Carter. I-I don't know what happened to him. I can't find him."

"Okay, take it slow," Alex said. "Where did you last see him?"

"Over there." She pointed to the blackened, smoking and splintered mess that had once been the bleachers. "We were sitting there, watching you play hockey, then I moved to the other side of the rink to take more photos. That's w-when it happened."

Alex felt her stomach fall to her shoes. She looked again toward the spot where Julia had pointed, seeing nothing left of the small grandstands but charred bits of wood, debris and a crater the size of a small swimming pool. *Oh, God.* "Are you sure?"

Julia began to sob. "Yes, I'm sure. I haven't seen him since."

Alex put her good arm around Julia's shoulders. "It's going to be okay. We're going to get through this, no matter what." If she said it enough times, maybe it would come true.

Smoke hung heavily in the air like an exclamation mark to

Alex's words. Jane slowly sank to her knees, weeping openly, her shoulders shaking. Alex knew—they all knew—that Carter was gone.

CHAPTER TWENTY-ONE

Corey wrapped her arms around her chest as she stood on the White House lawn, waiting for Marine Two to bring her loved ones home. It wasn't just the October chill in the air, but the chill in her heart that made her shiver. Will Carter was dead, killed instantly in the insurgent strike on the base at Kandahar—the only civilian killed in the attack. Her lover had been injured. Alex too. And Jane, while she wasn't physically hurt, still had a month left of a grueling campaign. Would she be up for it now? Would she be shaken, distracted by trauma and grief? Disillusioned? How were they all going to get through this final month now?

It was ironic that in the two days since the deadly attack, Jane's heroism under fire had gone viral across news outlets and on the

Internet. She was the candidate who rose above despair, chaos and danger to emerge a brilliant and fearless leader. But Corey knew Jane better than almost anyone on this earth. She knew Jane opposed this kind of worshipful attention.

Jane had told Corey over the phone that she did not want the event in Kandahar to become the defining moment of her campaign or a political feather in her cap. It was a terrible tragedy, she'd tearfully said, a heartbreaking nightmare where she, Alex, Julia and Carter had simply been in the wrong place at the wrong time. It'd been a coincidence that insurgents had attacked the base during her visit. A fluke. She'd done what anyone in her position would have done. None of it had anything to do with the campaign.

"I do *not* want this to become part of the campaign. That's not what this is about, Corey. It's a tragedy and should be treated as such," Jane had repeated.

Yet the attack *was* part of the campaign now. It had suddenly become the driving force, which clearly showed how little control they actually had over the campaign and over Jane's image, Corey thought.

Colby Harrison was being relentlessly skewered by the media for sitting at home watching the baseball playoffs while Jane saved lives in a war zone. Poor bastard, Corey thought, recalling the cartoon in the *Washington Post* this morning depicting Harrison in a La-Z-Boy, drinking a beer and watching a ball game while a news ticker reporting on Jane's war feats flashed on his television. He was constantly pestered by reporters and repeatedly questioned and berated over his lack of bravery and his commitment to the troops.

He wasn't handling it well. He'd gone off over a condemning question on CNN, shouting that he didn't have a chest full of medals, couldn't save people's lives with a medical degree, but that didn't mean he was a useless human being or unfit to serve as president.

The attack in Afghanistan was pivotal to the campaign, whether Jane and Harrison wanted it or not. With election day coming quickly, voters would remember the images of Jane, bloodied and bedraggled, tending to the injured on the base, and they'd remember Harrison angrily trying to justify himself while he'd done nothing.

Corey trembled again when the helicopter came into view, its rotor blades thundering in the sky. She felt frightened for all of them. What was Jane's state of mind? How badly had Julia's beautiful face been injured? Was her lover going to be okay or would she be traumatized? How were they going to handle the crush of press attention over the coming days? And how were they going to handle the grueling demands of the campaign in its last weeks, especially without the brilliant Will Carter. *Oh, God, poor Carter...*

Corey wiped tears from her face as the helicopter landed. One by one, the people she loved slowly descended the metal steps as a uniformed Marine stood by saluting.

Alex descended first. Corey ran to her and hugged her fiercely, careful to avoid the plaster casted arm in its sling. She reached for Jane next, holding her for a long and poignant moment, just two sisters clutching one another in a way they hadn't done in years. Both dissolved into tears. Jane whispered she was okay, but that things would never be the same again because they'd lost one of their own.

"I know sweetie, I know," Corey muttered before pulling away and moving to Julia.

"Oh, my sweet love," she whispered between broken sobs. She hugged Julia close, pressing her face into her neck. "I'm so glad you're alive. So glad you're in my arms again. Oh, God, I was so scared. I could have lost you."

"You didn't lose me, I'm right here," Julia replied in a voice made raw by emotion. "But there was a moment when—"

"I know, sweetheart, I know. How are you feeling? How is your nose?" Corey pulled back to study Julia's face, noting the black and blue bruises. Her nose was bandaged and her eyes were like a raccoon mask.

"It's okay, but my modeling days..."

Buoyed by Julia's attempt at a joke, Corey hugged her fiercely again. "You're here with me, and I'm never letting you out of my sight!" She meant it. She wouldn't risk Julia that way ever again. If anything happened, she wanted them to be together.

She knew she could do little except hover around her sister, sister-in-law and lover the rest of the day and evening, offering physical and verbal support.

The three had been treated at a U.S. military hospital in Landstuhl, Germany, after leaving Afghanistan. Now that they had returned home, they'd be re-examined at Walter Reed hospital in the next day or two, Corey had been told, just to double-check that they were okay.

Jane announced wearily that they would all meet with Steph tomorrow and talk about what to do next, making it clear that tonight was not a night for talking politics.

For one of the few times in their lives, Corey couldn't get a read on Jane. Sadness curtained her sister's eyes although her expression remained neutral. Jane kept her emotions in check, giving nothing away with her words or her body language. She had retreated into herself.

Corey wanted to know what she was thinking, what she was feeling, whether she was going to be okay. The three had suffered a terrible trauma, but she knew Jane well enough to know when to circle the wagons and give her some space. Now was one of those times. The campaign would wait for as long as Jane needed, and there would be no answers to Corey's questions right now.

***

A day later, Jane still found it impossible to focus on anything for more than a minute or two at a time. She opened the strategy meeting with her team by talking about Will Carter, remembering him, swapping stories, all of them laughing and crying. Steph and Corey agreed it would be a good idea for her and Alex to go to his funeral in Philadelphia later in the week.

The minute they started speaking about the campaign, however, Jane disengaged into numbness. A morass of meaningless words spilled across the room. Debate. Speech. Fort Bragg. Television. Poll. She grasped nothing, the words quicksand in her mind. She was grieving and in shock, she knew that much, finding it a chore just to put one foot in front of the other. In fact, Alex, with just her good arm, had helped her dress this morning.

It took her a moment to register that the conversation had halted. Both Steph and Corey stared at her, worry crinkling their foreheads.

"What?" she lashed out defensively.

"Are you okay?" Steph asked.

"No, I'm not okay! Jesus Christ, what do you think?"

Their expressions sharpened in surprise. Such eruptions from her were rare, almost unheard of, but what the hell did they expect? Jane seethed. Her brilliant, beautiful Carter was gone. Did they *really* think she was supposed to shed a few tears, and then carry on as though nothing had happened? Simply take a couple of days off, and get back on the campaign trail like Carter's death was a minor obstacle or delay? A temporary setback? No. As far as she was concerned, the campaign was over. She was done busting her ass and giving up months of her life when not only could all her efforts be for nothing, but life itself could end in a tragedy, just as it had for Carter. At the moment of that awful explosion, her motivation had dissolved, she realized now.

"I'm done," she said simply and with a quiet finality.

Corey and Steph stared at her in stunned disbelief.

***

Alex had never seen her partner so dispirited, so listless. They were all distraught over Will Carter's death, but days had passed and still Jane sat numbly staring out the window or sitting in the darkness for hours, speaking only when spoken to, barely eating, barely aware of the whirlwind going on around her. She was present but absent, having lost not only her friend and colleague, but her drive for the campaign.

At a complete loss, Alex finally consulted the White House physician, who suggested that the incident in Afghanistan might have triggered Jane's grief over her husband's death in a plane crash more than a dozen years ago. True or not, his diagnosis changed nothing. She had one last hope—Jane's mother.

At the end of the week, Alex and Jane boarded the train from Washington to Philadelphia, for Will Carter's funeral. Two private cars were reserved for their entourage, which included a phalanx of Secret Service agents.

The group boarded after the other passengers. The mood was somber. No one spoke. Reporters and photographers had been asked to stay away from the funeral, and so far at least, they were following orders, but Alex felt downright strange being out in public with Jane and having no cameras trained on them.

Jane took a window seat, immediately turning her face to stare drearily out at the dull, rainy skies. The weather seemed to perfectly match everyone's mood.

With silent shakes of her head, Jane rebuffed offers of something to eat or drink. Alex sighed and gave Corey a slight nod. A moment later, Maria Kincaid strolled into the private car, just as the train lurched into motion.

"Mother, what are you doing here?" Jane asked, sounding both annoyed and relieved.

Maria bent to hug her daughter. "Alex told me you needed me, and by one look at you, I see that she was right."

Jane's flash of irritation headed straight for Alex, two black daggers boring into her.

"I'm fine, Mother, other than being sad as hell about Will Carter."

Maria sat down in the seat opposite Jane. "I'm so sorry, dear. He was a lovely young man. I'm so sorry I didn't join you sooner. You do know you look like hell, don't you?"

"Thanks for the vote of confidence."

"Oh, Jane, darling, you know how much I hate to see you hurting." Maria leaned closer and lowered her voice. "We've both been through so much loss, so much pain. I do know how you feel, dear."

Jane turned her face to the rain-streaked window again as the other people in the car quietly melted away until only Jane, Alex and Maria remained.

"I only want to protect you," Maria added, emotion quaking her voice. "To help you in any way I can."

"You can't protect me, Mother. You couldn't protect me from Joe Junior's death, from Daddy's death, from Dan's death. You can't protect me from any of this. No one can, it seems."

"I know that, dear. But we can help each other heal, help each other go on. You, me, Alex, Corey, we're all we've got. We've got to help each other, don't you know that? We're family."

"Yes, I know all that. But tell me something: what the hell is all this for, anyway?"

"What?" Maria asked patiently. "What is all *what* for?"

"Killing myself to become president. Killing a dear friend in the process too."

"Now wait," Maria said, pointing a finger at Jane. "*You* did not kill your friend. But yes, you are killing yourself by not eating, not sleeping, not taking care of yourself right now."

Jane made no reply.

Maria waited awhile before she continued. "You know your father went through the very same process when Joey died? The doubts, the futility. Wanting to give up."

Alex knew that Jane had lost her older brother to leukemia when he was in college. The apple of their father's eye, Joey had been destined to follow in his political footsteps. Jane, in college herself when her brother died, had wanted nothing to do with politics until much later in life. When she finally did, it was entirely her own decision and on her own terms.

Jane turned haunted eyes back to her mother. "He did?"

"Yes. Wanted to quit politics. Blamed himself. Thought that pushing Joey too hard had made him get sick. He grieved for two years, totally unsure what to do."

"What made him change his mind about quitting politics?" It was the first hint of interest Alex had detected in Jane's voice all week.

Maria smiled faintly. "He didn't want to leave an unfinished legacy. He knew he would have been too dissatisfied in the end, too haunted by all the things he'd left undone. There came a point when he told me he would not be able to look at himself in the mirror if he gave up, that he would forever be disappointed in himself. And he felt he would be letting Joey down by not moving forward."

Jane considered for a long time before she answered in a whisper, "Damn it, Mother." She turned narrowed eyes on Alex. "And damn you too, Alex."

"What?" Alex and Maria asked in unison.

"For knowing exactly what buttons to push."

Alex shared a secret smile with her mother-in-law. Jane would get over the hump now. She would fight to finish her quest and she would fight to continue Carter's legacy as well.

As if on cue, Corey and Steph barged into the train car, Steph clutching a newspaper to her chest.

"All right," Jane said on a long sigh. "What is it you want me to see in that paper?"

Corey blinked a question at Alex. Alex nodded ever so slightly.

"It's this morning's *Post*," Corey replied. "Colby Harrison said in a press scrum last night that your disappearance from the public eye over the past week shows your disinterest in being president. He says you'd serve the country better by going back to doctoring, just like you did in Kandahar."

Alex watched Jane's features harden. Her face turned a deep angry red. Her eyes became coal black. Alex silently celebrated. *Yes!* Jane was back.

Jane leapt up from her seat in a swift, brisk motion. "Let me see that damned paper."

As Jane began earnestly scanning the newspaper, Alex noticed Maria sidle up to Corey and put an arm around her waist. "Now you, my other sweet daughter, need to come with me and have a little one-on-one chat."

"Me?" Corey looked like she feared she was in some kind of trouble.

"Yes, you, my dear. Tell me what's going on in your life."

Corey cast a helpless look in Alex's direction as her mother steered her away. Alex smiled to herself. About time Maria started focusing some attention on Corey, she thought with amusement. *Time for the old coming out talk.*

CHAPTER TWENTY-TWO

"Aren't you worried that by popping champagne, we'll jinx your sister?" Julia asked teasingly.

Corey laughed and topped up their glasses. "Not a chance. The fire is back in Jane's belly, which means she's going to absolutely *destroy* Colby Harrison tonight. In fact, I give her about six minutes before she delivers a knockout blow."

The election only a week away, it was the candidates' final televised debate. Jane had easily won the first debate. The second had been deemed a draw by the pundits, though Jane and her staff strongly disagreed. The final debate was the one everyone would remember. On the defensive since Jane's heroic Kandahar exploits, Harrison had most recently struck an adversarial pose, questioning Jane's motivations for wanting to be president and publicly doubting her emotional fitness for the office in a last-ditch effort to salvage what he could before Election Day.

Jane stayed well ahead in every poll. She could pretty much phone in tonight's debate and still kick Harrison's butt, Julia knew. But that wasn't Jane's style. She would stand over him during the ten count and make sure he didn't get up off the mat again.

Julia sipped her champagne, galvanized by Jane's positive prospects and by the question Corey had posed earlier over a home-cooked dinner of beef burgundy. The question had taken her breath away but she had not yet answered, preferring to slowly and deliciously torture her lover awhile longer.

"I still can't believe Jane let you off the hook tonight," she said. "Aren't you her good luck charm at these things?"

"She doesn't need luck, not when she's so clearly superior to Harrison." Corey nestled back on the pillow with a satisfied sigh, letting the satiny white sheet drop down to her waist. She rested the sweating glass of champagne against her naked breast. "She's also prepped to her eyeballs. She can't lose."

Although flattered that Corey had chosen to spend the evening with her instead of backstage at the debate, Julia remained skeptical. Normally, Corey would have been with Jane right up until the time to go onstage, and then she would have hung back in the shadows, giving hand signals or certain key looks to coach Jane, all the while making furious notes.

"You didn't have a disagreement with her, did you?"

Corey laughed dismissively. "A disagreement would never keep me from doing my job."

"Then what did tonight?"

"Come here."

Julia leaned against Corey, tiny, pleasurable needles of warmth and electricity prickling her skin.

"I told her I had something more important to do tonight."

"Like watch the debate in bed with me?" Julia supplied.

"Among other things, yes." Corey's lips slid over Julia's neck, the warmth and silkiness of the kisses igniting new heat.

"Hmm, will you tell me what those other things are?"

"No, but I'll show you."

Julia laughed low in her throat. "Won't we miss the debate?"

"Hell, it doesn't start for another ten minutes."

"Ten minutes is only a taste, my love."

"Then a taste is all I need," Corey said, lust thickening her voice.

Clumsily, Julia set her champagne glass on the nightstand, and then took Corey's glass and put it next to hers. She slipped into the soft, creamy confines of the bed. Quick as a cougar, Corey pounced on her breasts and began sucking ravenously, almost painfully.

"Aren't you going to kiss me first?" Julia asked, but she was only teasing. She loved it when Corey played with her breasts and had come that way more than once.

"Oh, I'm going to kiss you, darling, but not on the mouth."

Corey swiftly moved down the length of Julia's body. Instantly, Corey's expert and hungry mouth was on her, sucking and licking, her strokes bold, demanding and confident.

It occurred to Julia that they knew each other's bodies, each other's wants, so perfectly now. "Jesus," she muttered breathlessly. "You weren't kidding about the ten minutes."

Corey's fingers slipped inside her and thrust in rhythm to the furious pace of her tongue, a combination that squeezed the very center of Julia's being into a molten, quaking, breathless, groaning, writhing mass of need. Every muscle in her body went rigid. Her thoughts flattened out. She existed only on the very tip of her lover's tongue.

"Oh, God, Corey," she mumbled over and over as an orgasm violently ripped through her. She didn't want Corey to stop, but knew she could not take much more pleasure. Her energy sapped, she pulled Corey up and held her tightly as she continued to tremble. "I love when you do that to me, baby."

"Not as much as I love doing it to you."

"Oh, yeah?" Julia asked, still breathless from her orgasm. "Wanna bet?"

"Let's face it. I have to keep you satisfied at least until you answer my question."

"In that case, I may never answer."

Corey laughed sweetly. Julia knew her lover completely understood the little game they played.

"Oh, you'll answer. Trust me. I have ways of getting it out of you." She reached across Julia to hit the volume button on the television remote.

"Shit. Are those ten minutes up already?"

"Sorry, darling. But as soon as this debate is over, your body is mine again."

"Good. Let's hope you're right about Jane's knockout punch in six minutes!" Julia settled down to watch.

Jane didn't wait for her opponent to criticize her or to lob false accusations at her. In her opening remarks, she cut to the heart of Harrison's recent attacks, calling his comments, "...deplorable, weak and desperate. It is you, Mr. Harrison, who lacks the sensitivity, the compassion and the courage to lead this country. It is you who has failed to show the mettle to be president of the United States."

He flinched at the words *courage* and *mettle* as if she'd struck him a blow. Even some of the audience gasped. A smile played at Corey's lips while she watched.

"Your idea to come out of the gate like that?" Julia asked.

Corey's smile widened. "Oh, this is going to be so much fun."

***

Jane didn't let up on Harrison, Corey noted proudly. She pounded at his political record and his missteps in the campaign, using examples to illustrate his lack of vision, his narrow conservative views on social issues, and his poor skills at relating to everyday people.

"You represent everything about this country that is arrogant, insensitive, selfish and destructive. You want to tear things down, take things away, separate and divide instead of construct, facilitate and cooperate," Jane said, looking straight at Harrison and ignoring the cameras. "You want to take this country back to the 1950s, when life in America was wonderful if you were a straight, white, well-off middle-aged man. I am not going to let that happen, Mr. Harrison. I am not going to let you do that to this country!"

The audience at the debate erupted into spontaneous cheers.

Corey pumped her fist in the air before pulling Julia close for a hug. Jane was at her best one-on-one. As she had predicted, Jane was killing Harrison, delivering verbal blow after blow.

She was so proud of her sister. Without a doubt, Jane was going to be the next president. Though she hadn't let herself think too far ahead, she knew that starting tomorrow, they'd have to amass a much bigger team and start planning how Jane was going to run the country—what people did she need, what issues should she focus on first, what did she want to accomplish in her first term. A daunting task, but she couldn't wait to get started.

"You're happy, aren't you?" Julia asked, nestling against her.

"Yes. Mostly."

"Mostly?"

"Well, there is one thing I'm not quite happy about yet," Corey said.

Julia turned, her face still a little bruised from her injury. "The question?"

"The question. Or more precisely, your answer."

Julia smiled and blinked innocently. Corey knew the answer she would give, and knew she was only teasing by dragging it out this way. Neither of them wanted to lose each other or spend any more time apart than absolutely necessary. Carter's death had taught her and Julia the fragility of life, the specialness of every moment. She'd almost lost her lover once. She would not let it happen again.

"Maybe I just want more sex out of you before I answer," Julia said.

"Oh, you'll get plenty of sex out of me. Especially if you say yes and move in with me."

"Well, since you put it like that..."

Corey kissed her passionately. "You're being naughty."

"Oh, sweetheart, of course I want to move in with you. I want to go to bed with you every night and wake up with you every morning, and everything else in between."

"Even though the next four years are going to be crazy?"

"*Especially* because the next four years are going to be crazy!"

"Come here, baby." Corey grabbed Julia's ass—her hard, tight ass—and pulled her closer. Softly, she and Julia ground against one another until Julia's hand crept between them. Her fingers began to dance over Corey.

Moving onto her back, Corey shifted Julia on top of her and let her lover's hand elicit the most exquisite pleasure she'd ever known.

***

Jane refused to celebrate her resounding victory over Colby Harrison in the final debate, just as she refused to get prematurely caught up in what was sure to be a historic win in just a few days. Harrison seemed undoubtedly down for the count, but she wanted to be a gentlewoman about it. She was a leader—president material—and that meant showing magnanimity and pragmatism, not arrogance and smugness. She had never rubbed an opponent's face in his or her failure, and she would not start now.

Steph rushed into her office, dashing for the television remote control.

"Wanna tell me what disaster has just happened?" Jane asked.

Steph bubbled with elation. "Not a disaster, boss. A gift."

Jane stepped closer to the television screen as CNN sprang to life. A still photo of Harrison took up the screen, followed by campaign footage of him. From the voice-over, she heard the words, "tax evasion."

"What the hell is going on, Steph?"

"A story just broke. Harrison is supposedly a minor stakeholder in a large produce supply company that's been trading with North Korea, a little fact he seems to have kept from the IRS and from the Departments of State and Commerce."

Jane felt her stomach tighten. "This company wouldn't happen to be from California, would it?"

"Yes, as a matter of fact."

"And I suppose the news came from an anonymous tip?"

Steph made a face. "I see where you're going with this. Want me to look into it?"

"No! This has absolutely nothing to do with us, and I will not be drawn into it for one bloody second." Jane grabbed for the remote and clicked off the power button.

She would bet good money she knew who was behind this little political *gift*. It seemed Forrest Mitchell hadn't taken to heart her message to stop meddling in the campaign.

***

A final swing through California two days before the election was hardly necessary, but Jane had insisted on thanking her supporters there in person. Alex knew all polls indicated the state was hers. In fact, all polls showed she was on the verge of a decisive victory, yet Jane could not quite end the campaigning yet. It was part superstition, part loyalty to her team and to her supporters that made her continue to go through the motions. It wasn't in Jane to put her feet up and bask in her glory, not when there was *something* she could be doing.

"You know, sweetheart, you could actually take a day off," Alex recalled teasing over breakfast earlier. "The voters would forgive you."

"Yes, but there's no sense in starting bad habits now."

"Taking a day off is hardly a bad habit."

"No, but taking voters for granted is."

Alex knew when an argument was lost. She would have her work cut out for her for the next several years—*hell, for the rest of my life*—getting Jane to take time off.

She watched Jane move around the reception hall, shaking hands, whispering a few words, sharing a few laughs, swapping campaign stories. Alex followed her, joining in the conversations. They kept moving. Hundreds of people were here and Jane would not stop until she'd spoken with each one of them.

Amy Roberts stepped into their path, her smile brimming with ego and pretension. Alex felt Jane stiffen beside her.

"Governor," Jane said without smiling.

"Madam Vice President. Or should I say, Madam *President*." Amy beamed triumphantly, as though she'd had a direct stake in Jane's success. The thought turned Alex's stomach. "That title has a gorgeous ring to it, don't you think?"

Jane leaned close to the overcoiffed, overperfumed governor, her voice a gritty notch above a whisper. "You and Forrest Mitchell do not own me and will *never* own me. My fate, my political successes or failures, are in my hands and my hands only. Do I make myself clear, Governor?"

"Actually, I haven't a clue what you're talking about."

"Oh, I think you have more than a clue. I'm watching you. And I'm watching Mitchell. If either of you come anywhere near me or my people, I'll see that you can't get elected dog catcher and that Mitchell owns nothing more than a warm seat in jail." Jane's voice held more ice than the cocktail in Amy's hand. "Now get out of my way."

Alex bit back a smile, and for good measure leveled a ferocious look at the stunned-looking Amy Roberts. *Take that, Governor Asshole.*

"You okay?" Alex asked Jane moments later.

Jane broke into a cat-like grin. "I love a good ass-kicking when it's well deserved, don't you?"

"Nah. I just love it when the good guy wins. Now come here." She kissed Jane on the mouth, not caring who watched, who snickered, who smiled or who shuffled uncomfortably. She was kissing the next president of the United States. If anyone didn't like it, they could kiss her First Ass!

EPILOGUE

Election Day

Alex looked out their hotel window at the growing crowd of people filling Detroit's Hart Plaza. While it was tradition for candidates to spend election day in their home state, she wished instead she and Jane had joined the jubilant and excited crowds in San Francisco's Castro community or New York City's Greenwich Village.

In Alex's heart, tonight's victory would be a historic and unique victory for all gays and lesbians everywhere. Jane would dispute that, though. Jane would remind her that her victory, although not yet confirmed, was a victory for women, for all Democrats, for Michiganders, for the disenfranchised and for everyone who hoped for a better America.

"Penny for your thoughts," Jane said, sneaking up behind her and slipping an arm around her waist.

"It's *our* victory," Alex whispered, her eyes riveted on the crowd below. "Yours and mine, isn't it?"

"Of course it is, darling. You and I gave this fight everything we had. But it's a victory for a hell of a lot of people, including Will Carter."

Carter would always be a reminder of the terrible sacrifice made for this campaign, Alex knew. The mention of his name sapped some of the joy from the moment, but she didn't want to be sad, today least of all.

"But let's not jinx anything," Jane added. "We're only at 268 Electoral College votes."

Alex turned to her partner, studying her beautiful face. Jane looked happy, relieved, and yet somewhat disbelieving, as if a massive stroke of unexpected good luck had graced their lives. "You're going to be the best damned president this country's ever had. Do you have any idea of the footprint on history you're about to leave?"

Jane sucked in a long, slow breath. "Now you're starting to scare me."

"Don't be. All you have to do is be you. Nothing more."

"Oh, yes, there is something more. Something huge. I can't do this without you, baby."

"You won't have to."

"Is that a promise?"

Alex bit her tongue. Maybe now was as good a time as any to ask Jane. She'd warred with herself over the timing. Tonight was the biggest night of Jane's life. Did she really need to add to it? Or divide Jane's attention?

"Jane," Corey yelled from across the room, impatiently covering the mouthpiece of a telephone. "It's Colby Harrison. Would you like to take the call in the bedroom?"

Alex shared a look with Jane. "He'll be conceding."

Jane winked. "I'll be right back."

***

The crowd was large, eighty thousand at the last estimate, and filled with barely contained energy. Bodies swayed in the cool night breeze off the river. Signs stabbed the air and voices chanted Jane's name. Large speakers sprayed music in every direction, Lady Gaga's "Born This Way" inspiring people to dance where they stood. Jane smiled. Carter loved Lady Gaga. He would love all of this. Somewhere, somehow, Jane knew he had to be watching.

She waited in the small holding area beneath the impromptu stage. Harrison had conceded, the final votes had been tallied, and the announcement was about to be made. The crowd already counted her a winner, but she still felt a silent rush of air, as though a collective sigh was emitted when the PA system clicked on. It was the moment they'd all been waiting for.

When the announcer's booming voice broadcast that the required number of Electoral College votes had been achieved fifteen minutes ago to make Jane president, the crowd erupted in a roar that cut through the night and beyond. Woodward Avenue would hear them, Jane thought. So would the Canadians across the river.

Her heart pounded. She'd done it. *They'd* done it, this thing that had seemed such a distant and unobtainable dream for more than four years. Nothing would ever be the same again—not her life, not Alex's and Corey's, not her mother's life. Hell, the White House, the *country*, would never be the same again. Holy shit, she thought with a mix of pride and fear.

As thrilled as she was, she knew there was a flip side. Nervous energy made her hands shake. Awe tightened her throat and worry churned her insides. *Christ, I'm only one person. I'm just me.* For a moment, she was a little girl again, skipping through her father's office in the governor's mansion, asking him if she could play that game on the big antique globe near his desk, the game where they'd spin it, and she'd close her eyes and point to a spot, and he'd laugh and tell her those were all the places in the world she was going to visit one day.

She felt Alex squeeze her hand. "Sweetheart? You okay?"

Jane squeezed back. "I'm okay."

"Good. But before you make your big acceptance speech, there's a smaller acceptance speech I hope you'll make."

"Honey, the crowd—"

"They can wait." Alex beamed with secret knowledge. "'Cause I've been waiting all day for this. Actually, I've been waiting almost four years for this."

Her thoughts on the election, Jane mumbled, "Me too."

"You mean you've known for four years that I wanted to ask you to marry me?" Alex asked, chuckling.

"What?" Her question was rhetorical. Jane's stomach fluttered with pleasure and surprise. She knew exactly what Alex had just asked but she selfishly wanted to hear her say it again.

Alex dropped to her knees, her eyes glistening with joy and unshed tears. "Will you marry me, Jane Kincaid?"

Jane began to speak, only to trip over her tongue, as though it had suddenly been placed there to slow her down and make her stumble. For the first time in her life, she was tongue-tied.

To make matters worse, Alex began laughing at her. "I've made you speechless for once in your life, haven't I?"

Busted! Jane smiled, collected herself, and pulled Alex to her feet. "No, as a matter of fact, I'm not at a total loss for words. Alex Warner, nothing would make me happier and prouder than to be your wife."

"Does that mean I can book a wedding date in New York City?"

"Yes! But please don't make it on inauguration day."

"Deal."

Jane took Alex's face gently in her hands and softly kissed the lips she looked forward to kissing for the next forty years or so. "I love you, Alex. You've made me the happiest woman in the world."

"Good. I love you too. Now go give that crowd out there something to really cheer about."

"All right, but I want you right up there on that stage with me. After all, you're about to become the First Lady."

Alex shook her head. "Oh, no. I am not the First Lady until you make an honest woman out of me."

Jane laughed. "Okay, good point. In that case, book that New York date as soon as you can!"

Alex kissed her, this time slipping her a little tongue, and then whispered a promise of what she wanted to do to her later tonight.

"Oh, Jesus, Alex. This is not the time to make me wet," Jane protested halfheartedly.

Alex laughed and took Jane's hand again. "We'll both be wet. And besides, it'll keep us from being nervous, right?"

Fireworks erupted over the river—red, white and blue. The explosive charges made Jane flinch, but Alex reassured her with another squeeze of her hand.

The noise drowned out her response to Alex and the words, *let's begin our destiny*. Together, hand in hand, she and Alex marched up the steps to the stage.

Publications from
Bella Books, Inc.
Women. Books. Even Better Together.
P.O. Box 10543
Tallahassee, FL 32302
Phone: 800-729-4992
www.bellabooks.com

THE STRANGE PATH by D Jordan Redhawk.
Hardened by the brutal streets, Whiskey knows nothing
is free. More than ever she clings to her motto: Take
more than you give. But when you have nothing,
anything can be tempting. It all could be a dream come
true, except for the nightmares that await her if Whiskey
chooses to walk the Strange Path. First in Series.
978-1-59493-275-5

FRAGMENTARY BLUE by Erica Abbott. C.J. St.
Clair's success as a police officer has brought her a new
job and a fresh start with Internal Affairs in Colfax,
Colorado. It's a long way from her hometown of Savannah,
and among the many welcome sights on her new
horizons is Alex Ryan, the head of the Detective Unit.
978-1-59493-274-8

HIDDEN HEARTS by Ann Roberts. With staggering
student loans to repay, CC Carlson is determined
to please her new employers. The first assignment
as a real estate lawyer is easy: deliver an eviction
notice and make it clear that it will be enforced.
978-1-59493-287-8

DEERHAVEN PINES by Diana McRae. The foothills of California hold many beauties—and many secrets. The walls of Deerhaven Forest Hall protect the cherished secrets of its residents, and all that they believe and have guarded for more years than they can count.
978-1-59493-288-5

EVERYTHING PALES IN COMPARISON by Rebecca Swartz. For the reserved Emma, life with a self-absorbed musician whom she is expected to protect is the last thing she needs. Daina Buchanan, she soon finds, is used to getting what she wants.
978-1-59493-289-2

TATS TOO by Layce Gardner. It seems that there are a few details about her past that Vivian has neglected to share with Lee, and the men with the big guns are back. They want what Vivian took from them: the thirty million dollar Devil's Diamond.
978-1-59493-291-5

WRITING ON THE WALL by Jenna Rae. It doesn't take San Francisco detective Del Mason long to realize that her new neighbor, Lola Bannon, has more baggage than a cruise ship. She's seen too many victims of domestic violence not to recognize all the signs. Their mutual spark of attraction is compelling, but she knows that for now Lola needs friends, not lovers.
978-1-59493-290-8

SPRING TIDE by Robbi McCoy. The waterways of the Delta tangle and weave for hundreds of miles, hiding secret coves, serene vistas and fragile depths. But they are no match for the tides of a woman's heart.
978-1-59493-292-2

RHAPSODY by KG MacGregor. Never before Ashley she felt so contented in the company of other women. Even so, there's always the whisper from the past. Would any of them, especially Julia Whitethorn, the charismatic, appealing owner of Rhapsody, care about her if they knew the terrible secret she's kept for twenty years?
978-1-59493-293-9

IN THE UNLIKELY EVENT... by Saxon Bennett. When Chase and her BFF Lacey butt heads over the Institute, she decides it's high time she prove once and for all that she is a changed woman. Her daughter, Bud, is an eight-year-old filmmaker who will document her mother's fearlessness—once she figures out how to focus past knee caps. Chase proves she can visit Urgent Care and not wash her hands afterward. She can skateboard, teach people how to drive and—to the surprise of many, including herself—she can gift wrap anything. All these changes can only lead to one thing: the Gift Wrapping National Finals.
978-1-59493-297-7

BEING EMILY by Rachel Gold. Emily desperately wants high school in her small Minnesota town to get better. She wants to be the woman she knows is inside, but it's not until a substitute therapist and a girl named Natalie come into her life that she believes she has a chance of actually Being Emily. A story for anyone who has ever felt that the inside and outside don't match and no one else will understand...
978-1-59493-283-0